REPENTANCE

REPENTANCE

ELOÍSA DÍAZ

Copyright © 2021 by Eloísa Díaz
by agreement with Pontas Literary & Film Agency
Cover and jacket design by 2Faced Design
Interior designed and formatted by
emtippettsbookdesigns.com

ISBN 978-1-951709-46-4
Library of Congress Control Number:
Available Upon Request

First published in February 2021 by W&N
First North American edition October 2021 by Agora Books
An imprint of Polis Books, LLC
44 Brookview Lane
Aberdeen, NJ 07747
www.PolisBooks.com

To Frau Holz,

who knew I was a writer before I did

'Ni el pasado ha muerto,
no está el mañana – ni el ayer – escrito.'
ANTONIO MACHADO, *Campos de Castilla*

'The past is not dead,
neither is tomorrow – or yesterday – written.'
ANTONIO MACHADO, *Fields of Castile*

'He's asleep,' she says when she steps into the room.

From his spot on the couch he nods towards the ice-cold beer set out for her. Before she can sit and grab it, the roar of a motor. A car approaches. Tires screech. It sounds near. He darts to the window. An artichoke-green car. In the middle of the street, engine running, the Ford Falcon of his nightmares.

From each of the doors emerges a man. The four doors slam. Thud. Thud. Thud. Thud. He turns around. There's nothing to say. He looks down.

Maybe they've come for someone else.

They walk towards his block.

Fuck fuck fuck fuck fuck.

One man looks up. They lock eyes.

1

(2001)

Wednesday, December 19th; 08:30

In any other country, there would have been a war.

But this was not any other country. This was Argentina. Inspector Alzada raced down Avenida Belgrano, his right foot heavy on the gas, his vision growing dim. When was the last time he had eaten? Or really slept, for that matter? *You're not the young man you once were, Joaquín.* He could hear Paula's voice as clearly as if she were sitting beside him in the car. He readjusted the aviators on the bridge of his nose, and sighed.

It was true. He needed a break. Only last week he had kindly been summoned to HR, where he'd been made aware of the 'situation'. The inspector had understood perfectly well what the lady with the cat-eye glasses – polite to a fault – had meant when she had given him a complicit look. And yet, he'd made her say it nonetheless:

although he was eligible for retirement, the police force pension fund was not currently in a position to follow through. What he had been dreaming about for decades would have to wait. 'Just a little while longer,' the woman had said without real conviction. He was, of course, free to surrender his post at any time, she had added, but that was not something she would recommend, considering the current climate. *Interesting choice of words, 'climate'; what you mean is shitstorm.*

Alzada leaned forward against the wheel. This time of summer, the sky should have shown itself irreverently lapis-lazuli blue; instead, a dust-laden haze coated Buenos Aires in a clammy mood and colored the atmosphere a homogenous, dull grey. *Definitely not your normal climate.* A polished, slick metal lid on a pressure cooker. On the horizon, against the turbulent waters of the Río de la Plata – once described by conquistadors as 'the river the color of lions' – all green lights. Alzada shifted into third.

He had woken up on the wrong side of the bed. He had tossed and turned through the night, then overslept and consequently been forced to make an executive decision between using the precious time he had left to have breakfast or to shower. He had ended up doing neither, but instead had walked right into a difficult conversation with his wife. At that point, he had attempted to mitigate his apparent bad luck by choosing to wear his favorite shirt, the light-blue one with the white collar, but had been denied even that small pleasure: the shirt hadn't been ironed. Now he wore a grey one, an impulse buy he had regretted almost immediately and Alzada could swear to God – if the devout Catholic buried inside him would ever dare do such a thing – that in the scorching atmosphere the shirt glistened.

4

And then, the call from the coroner. Alzada had instantly recognized Dr. Petacchi on the phone when it had rung earlier – how could he ever forget that man's voice – and he had then tried his best to avoid a visit to the morgue, suggesting the coroner give him details over the phone. The doctor had cleared his throat. 'I don't know, Inspector. It's not the same as getting a visual.' Alzada had remained silent, which had prompted the coroner to add: 'Of course, I'm here to help *you*. If it's too much of an inconvenience, I'll have the report sent to the station.'

Fine.

So now, instead of sipping coffee in his backyard, he was en route to his least favorite place in all of Buenos Aires. Well, second least.

Alzada turned left and admired the breadth of Avenida 9 de Julio. *A battlefield.* The slim veneer of normalcy had been rinsed off the pavements, which now brimmed with the nervous energy of an incumbent war. People. Everywhere he looked, people. One could tell which ones were in a rush to take a side street and escape: they walked closer to the buildings, past the stores' shutters that framed empty shelves. They walked at a brisk pace, their heads down.

Aside from the perennial weekly protest by the Madres, lately the city had lived through countless demonstrations: Buenos Aires' streets were constantly filled with rage. And yet, there was definitely something different about today. Alzada just couldn't quite put his finger on what it was.

He switched on the radio. The government was holding another emergency meeting to impose further economic measures. *That's the reason for the city police restricting traffic. They're expecting a revolution.* Past the swarm of cars, Alzada observed the rivers of people converging. He knew any attempt to contain the masses would be futile: the blockades wouldn't be able to prevent the viscous mob from slowly but insistently percolating towards the Casa Rosada. The protesters were counteracting the authorities' strategy with one of their own: they were walking into traffic, where controlling them was more difficult and catching them almost impossible – especially if they were savvy enough not to wear a shirt. It was essentially urban warfare: the protesters were obstructing the city's key arteries, robbing the police of the space they needed to maneuver, eliminating their advantage. *This isn't by accident.*

Alzada scratched the patches of facial hair he was attempting to quilt into a beard. At what moment did tragedy become inevitable? He took his glasses off and held the bridge of his nose between his fingers. *Not even the siren will save me.* He was going to be late.

Why *hadn't* there been a revolution? Since President de la Rúa had decided to confidently steer the economy into the abyss, Argentinians had suffered his particular brand of incompetence in agonizing stages: first they'd been barred access to their savings accounts; then they'd been forced to watch as the frenetic inflation made life several times more expensive almost overnight; now they lived with ever-increasing restrictions on their checking accounts – in a country where people dealt almost exclusively in cash. And people had done so stoically. Sure, there had been lootings in grocery stores and petrol stations. Isolated incidents peppered conservatively throughout the poorer provinces, far from the capital. When they had seen the images on the evening news,

Paula had declared: 'God presses but doesn't suffocate.' How indeed had they survived, slowly choking over such an extended period of time? 'We've been through worse,' was a common consolation, surely brought on by the collective memory of successive military coups. *Is that why people aren't revolting? Because they don't want to give the army an excuse to take over again?*

ALZADA STOPPED AT A RED light. There was no good reason to rush: the body was already cold. The inspector noticed two boys standing at the light, just to the left of his car, the only ones not to cross the street. The older boy was in his mid-teens, the younger hadn't completely shed his baby fat yet – eight, perhaps? Two carbon copies. *Brothers.* Dreamers in Maradona jerseys. Alzada knew the type: they thought no one had ever tried to change the world before they came along. They thought they had invented outrage, they thought they wanted to start a fight. *They think they'll be able to win.* They had been lied to by grey-haired, respectable men who preached about what could have been, men who then leaned back in their leather chairs and let starry-eyed boys do their dirty work. Hungry boys who were paid in rice and bread and beans, and sometimes in chocolate bars and cigarettes.

The young ones were particularly valuable: they weren't tainted with a police record; more importantly, they weren't yet sniffing glue, which rendered them loyal only to the highest bidder. They were sent on errands of varying importance 'for the cause' – *what fucking cause* – from carrying messages to distributing weapons. Before that – and to prove their potential – an initiation in the shape of a street corner: keep an ear out and report anything unusual. And on days like this, an even clearer mission: find out which streets are barricaded and by whom, and how many cops are being deployed.

These two are clearly new to it. They hadn't yet learned to look without looking and were devoting too much attention to a riot squad stepping out of a police van across the street. The inspector could see the older one moving his lips – he was counting them. *Ten. There's ten of them.* Alzada resisted the urge to yell. In his lifetime, he had learned to count a lot of things: the number of fights he'd had with Paula; the number of dollars they could rely on until the end of the month; the number of dead bodies he'd seen at the morgue, and on the street; the number of days, then weeks, then months, then years his nephew lived without a father. Unlike other Argentinians, he had never had to count policemen. That said more about him than Alzada was ready to admit.

He looked to his right. The police van parked on the corner was built to hold four rows of bloodthirsty animals; with six squeezed into every row, that made twenty-four. Then again, if one believed the Radio Nacional updates, clusters of demonstrators were simultaneously forming in many parts of the city. Police units would be spread thin, thinner than any commissioner might feel comfortable with. The most basic of crowd control formations took ten men, so ten it was.

With riot police, knowing how many there were wouldn't make a difference anyway, once they lowered their Viking visors and roared 'charge'. Not even the golden Boca Juniors stripe across the boys' chests would save them.

Alzada rolled down his window. It was stuck. He fought against the handle to bring it halfway down.

'¡Hijo!' He motioned for the older of the kids to approach the car.

The teenager didn't move. *Smart boy.*

'Son,' he called again.

The boy turned only his head towards Alzada. He looked at the inspector as if to memorize his face, the same defiant spark that Jorge had displayed whenever confronted. Any attempt to dissuade him would be pointless.

'Why don't you take your brother home?'

The younger one was having ice cream. A luxury in these times. *This corner must be important to them.* Alzada assessed the crossing. Indeed, the particularly long red light allowed them to position their troops while hiding in the crowd. Pawns in a human chess game.

Without blinking, the older boy said: 'Go fuck yourself, old man.'

One way to catch someone's undivided attention. He certainly now had Alzada's. Around sixteen, the intensity of his feisty gaze was a poor match for a lanky physique that had doubtlessly been mocked by his peers. *He should be in school. That's how you know you're getting old: revolutionaries inspire tenderness in you.* To compensate, the boy inflated his chest like a pigeon. His left arm around his brother's shoulder, two otters making sure they didn't drift apart during high tide; his right, lax by his side, his hand white, vindictive, firm, gripping a cobble. *Let not thy left hand know what thy right hand doeth.* Alzada smiled at his own musing.

Wait – a cobble? It was obviously intended to distract from . . . *There it is.* A not-so-well-concealed bulge at the waistline of his

9

oversized jeans. *You tuck it into the back, boludo.* He'd probably seen it in a movie. *That's why you don't want to move: you're afraid you'll drop it.*

Twenty years ago, Alzada wouldn't have hesitated. He would have got out of his car – smugly left the keys in the ignition, broken the teen's head open against the lamp post, confiscated the gun, and driven away. There would have been ice cream on the pavement.

The light turned green.

2

(2001)

'If it isn't the illustrious Inspector Alzada!' the coroner announced with the grandiloquent arm gestures of a circus ringmaster. But instead of a scarlet morning coat studded with golden buttons, he wore lab whites with worn-out sleeves and 'Dr. E.M. Petacchi' embroidered on the chest pocket. *Probably by his mother.* Underneath, a business suit and black tie.

Alzada shook Petacchi's hand and walked past him up the steps into the building, but Petacchi held him firmly by the shoulder, surprising the inspector with both the energy and the affection emanating from him. Alzada removed his aviators and smiled.

'What are *you* doing here? Petacchi asked.

'I'll try not to take offense, Elías,' Alzada replied. He stepped back down to level with Petacchi's height and stood on the pavement, which over the years had become ridiculously cramped due to inconsiderate urban planning and exuberant foot traffic. 'And weren't *you* the one who called *me*?'

'I mean I was surprised when I called the station and they told me to contact you. It's been a long time since your last visit to the morgue, no?'

'Yes, since I got moved to robbery.'

'So . . . twenty years?'

Alzada took a moment to answer. *As if I didn't know it to the day.* 'Something like that. But apparently today it's all hands on deck. Imagine that: it's taken a revolution to tear me away from my desk. How about you? A lot of work these days?'

'The calm before the storm. Things will be different when night falls . . .'

Alzada cleared his throat. *Even small talk with this man is grim.*

A chopping noise overhead made the inspector look up. The old School of Medicine building. In spite of its considerable height, it lacked a suitable air of grandeur: someone had decided to mix Italian Renaissance style with sober, clean-cut materials of Germanic tradition. The result was a lesser cousin of the Haussmannian family. *It wouldn't have looked out of place on a side street in Paris.* The jacaranda blooming by the entrance, on the other hand, would have.

'How's that nephew of yours, Inspector?'

'Sorolla?' The mention of his family came as a surprise. 'Good, good,' he said, distracted.

'He's a fan of chess, isn't he? Has he beaten you yet?'

Alzada eyed Petacchi. *Harmless.* The inspector relaxed his shoulders: 'Ah, in his dreams.'

12

What *were* they waiting for? The sooner they went in, the sooner this would be over.

That's when Deputy Estrático turned the corner to answer his question, walking towards them with a spring in his step. *Great. Of course they've called him, too. What the fuck is he so happy about?* Apparently Commissioner Galante thought he couldn't even handle a simple morgue visit by himself. *I might be insubordinate, but I'm a damn good cop.*

'Good morning. I'm Orestes Estrático,' he said, extending an eager hand to the coroner, who shook it cordially. *You have to say your rank when you introduce yourself.*

'Right,' was the only reply he got from Alzada.

'Good. We're all here. You know the way,' Petacchi offered. 'I have something to show you.'

'Someone, Elías. Someone.'

'Of course. That's what I said.'

DOWN THE HALL, TILES FROM ceiling to floor. Whoever had been in charge of designing the building had forgotten that civilians visited the morgue too. The place looked like a veterinary clinic. It smelled clean in a toxic sort of way. *Hot water and bleach.* The odor sank into their brains as they followed the clacking of Petacchi's heels in the dim light of the corridor. They turned left, then right, then right again. Minutes seemed to go by. Alzada had the impression that if they stayed submerged in that stink for much longer, they would never be able to discern another smell ever again.

Meat on the grill. A ripe melon. The nape of Paula's neck.

Petacchi pushed open two swinging doors with portholes and they found themselves in the coroner's dominion.

13

'Come closer, Inspector. You don't want to miss the details,' he offered, his voice echoing against the sea of tiles. Petacchi was in his element, almost having fun. A man of about forty-five, he had deep black hair and wore more brilliantine in it than necessary. He had the eyes of an inquisitive bird, never fixing on any object or person for more than a couple of seconds. When he did, he blinked behind his thick glasses, head tilted to one side. *Weird how this man seems to light up the moment we enter the realm of the dead.*

The thought of what he was going to see was enough to turn Inspector Alzada's stomach. He scoped out the room in search of a container of some sort. Tile, tile, tile, more tile, and in the center, like a shiny throne – *a sacrificial altar* – a working table the size of a twin bed bathed in floodlights. Next to it, a metallic cart on which the coroner had scrupulously aligned the utensils required for his line of work; Alzada vaguely recognized a pair of wide scissors, a speculum, a chisel, a clamp, a macabre compass, an assortment of scalpels and a needle, indicating through its immaculate presence that Petacchi had either had enough time and courtesy to sew the dead up and clean it afterwards or was about to, in which case the body in front of them possessed a gigantic gash. *Somewhere.*

In the corner, Alzada detected a metal bin. That would do. That would *have* to do. His eyes wandered back to the table. On it, the body was covered by a white sheet. *Your life must have gone terribly wrong at some point if you end up buried in the dumpster behind the municipal morgue.* He was trying not to judge – and failing. Petacchi peeled back the sheet, folding it neatly over the torso, and revealed the victim's head and slender collarbones. Alzada's nausea rose instantly.

'As you can see, she was a looker,' was the coroner's first comment. *What the fuck is wrong with you?*

Alzada grabbed on to the silk handkerchief in his pocket. At least he hadn't had time to indulge in his habitual breakfast, a croissant with dulce de leche: it would have looked like the stew he had been forced to eat in his middle school cafeteria, there would have been chunks, like the ones Paquita had lovingly scooped onto his plate fifty years ago. Thankfully, today all he had to regret was bile.

Petacchi's abrasive voice brought him back to the present. He was reciting his conclusions with the diligent fervor of a child conjugating his Latin verbs. 'We have a female. White. Late twenties to early thirties. One point six five meters. Sixty-eight kilograms. No identification or personal belongings on her.' *Not even clothes?* The coroner veered into a more casual tone: 'As I told you over the phone, Inspector, this is the one who was found this morning.'

'How *did* they find her?' Estrático asked. He was wearing the one cheap suit he seemed to own, creased over a wrinkled shirt. He had clearly made an effort to tame his hair with gel, but by this point in the morning his unruly blond curls had managed to escape and framed his face – handsomely, Alzada had to admit.

'It's funny you should ask that because—'

'Elías.' Inspector Alzada did not like to speculate about the living, much less about the dead. He thought it the most pernicious of habits. His voice unintentionally thundered through the autopsy room: 'Is your comment about the spectacle of this unfortunate soul being fished out of a dumpster going to be of *any* relevance to the case?'

'No, but . . . It's just so unusual. It might be the first time in my career I have ever encountered a dumpster as a dumpsite . . .' *We've seen worse.* 'And what's more, right by the morgue. . .' Petacchi was gaining momentum: 'If you ask me—'

'I'd rather not,' Alzada spoke calmly. '*I* am the inspector. *You* are the coroner. We are both reasonably good at what we do, wouldn't you agree?' Petacchi nodded dutifully. 'And as the inspector, I'd recommend not starting with speculations and conspiracies. At least not yet. Now, please tell us what you found.'

Petacchi cleared his throat and returned to his notes: 'The victim shows multiple signs of violence. Nasal bone is broken. Haematomas on face, neck, arms, torso. Several broken ribs, on both sides. Twisted left ankle. No signs of sexual violence.'

'What does that tell us about the attacker, Estrático?' Alzada turned to the deputy, who was enthralled: 'Are you going to take notes, or do I need to do that, too?'

'I am now, sir.' Estrático scrambled a notepad out of his suit pocket. 'And in reply to your question, sir. That they were in a rush?'

'Oh, no,' the inspector waved the idea off. 'It would have taken quite some time to do all of this. Wouldn't you agree, Elías?'

The coroner nodded again.

'No. What we can gather from what Dr. Petacchi just said is that there's some kind of contradiction. You see, on the one hand, we have evidence that says they had a clear intention to kill her, but at the same time, in some fucked-up way – excuse the language, Elías – they decided to show her some level of respect. Why would they do that?' *Orders. They were acting on orders.*

Estrático scribbled fervently.

'It's definitely a lot to inflict on one person.' Alzada considered the woman for the first time. *And such a small one, too.* Lying there, she looked well rested, without a worry. She had a very pale, very gentle face. She must have been pretty. *She must have put up one hell of a fight.*

'She also shows a series of contusions, all post-mortem,' Petacchi continued.

'Post-mortem? Someone hit her after she was dead?' Estrático asked.

'No, no,' the coroner vigorously shook his head. 'Not that. It was most likely the consequence of leaving her in the dumpster. Once she was dead.'

'How can you tell?' This might just as well have been Estrático's first trip to the morgue: a nerd on a visit to the natural history museum. *If you're going to shackle me with a babysitter, at least make it someone who's going to be of help.*

Petacchi searched Alzada's gaze for permission to digress. *We might as well.*

'When a person is still alive, blood circulates persistently through the body. That's obvious. Now. There are two types of trauma. First, there are incisive wounds: slashes, or stabs – cuts, basically – of different sizes. When a cut is deep enough to penetrate to the subcutaneous tissues, it causes a person to bleed, towards the *outside*. Secondly, we have "blunt trauma". You might call it "hitting a mammal with an object that isn't sharp": it will cause broken vessels, but the blood will have no way out of the body. That *interior* leakage of blood is how bruises are formed; in this case, there were a couple of instances – upper thighs, elbows, lower back – where I found rips of the skin with no bleeding to accompany them. That reveals to me – to us – that when they were inflicted, the blood was no longer flowing. Ergo, she was already dead. The placement of those lesions is what tells us that she was handled without care, because let me tell you, it's very, very, very difficult to bruise a dead person.'

'Okay,' Alzada swallowed. 'So, to sum up: first, she's killed. They do that somewhere quiet, where they can take their time, where they can be thorough. But then they dump her in a way that suggests they were suddenly in a rush.'

'Two separate sets of people?' ventured Estrático. *Seriously? He can't be this stupid. Patience, Joaquín.*

'It seems to me more like something happened. Something that forced them to change their plans and made them get rid of her as fast as possible. This isn't a ritual burial ground: they chose the first spot they could find.' Alzada looked around the room. This dungeon was impervious to the outside world. *Like sitting in a silent fish tank.* But on the streets, a storm was coming. 'They thought they'd be alone. In this neighborhood, it's mostly government buildings.'

'It's not infrequent for me to be the only one on the street when I leave here,' Petacchi confirmed.

'See?' Alzada gestured at Estrático. 'They weren't expecting the protesters to stay overnight. Not even the government had foreseen that. So, they're doing what they came to do. Professionally. Methodically. That's how the first part happens. And suddenly, they have an audience. They get nervous. Change of plan. They see the dumpster. Drop her. Because how long has she been . . .?'

'Let's see.' Petacchi consulted his wristwatch. 'It's 9.20 now. Lividity has yet to fully kick in, but she's already at room temperature.' Alzada retched. 'I'd say, sometime before midnight? Definitely after dinner—' *Please don't explain how you know that.*

'Cause of death?' Alzada intervened. He was not going to make it without vomiting if they kept at this line of conversation. And he was certainly not going to do it in front of the rookie. He motioned Petacchi to cover the body.

'A perforating injury to the occipital bone.'

'Translate,' Alzada gestured to Estrático, who looked up from his notes.

'No need. I know what it means,' the deputy said. 'A blow to the head, right?'

'A contact wound,' Petacchi specified, a slight note of irritation in his tone. Still, he elaborated: 'She was shot in the back of her head.' *Definitely a job.*

'Only once?' Estrático asked.

'Three times in total. And at a very close range, too: not more than twenty centimeters away. But we say "injury", singular, because the second and third ones she wouldn't have noticed.'

'An execution?' Estrático ventured.

'Possibly . . .' Petacchi answered with caution.

'Caliber?' Alzada interrupted them again.

'I recovered the bullets. All three from the same weapon. Nine millimeter. Standard.'

'Great,' Estrático sighed. 'Half of the city is a suspect.'

'Well, you can rule out anyone who didn't know her,' Petacchi mumbled.

'What was that, Elías?' Alzada was interested.

'We can safely assume this was no accident, no robbery gone awry, no kids playing with a handgun. Someone really, *really* wanted her gone. I've taken tissue samples, of course, but my guess would be they weren't in a rush, as you previously indicated,' Petacchi said. 'On the contrary: if you go to all this trouble, then you take the time to "clean her". Hence, I expect that examination will most likely yield no results, and neither will we find anything on the dumpster. She does have a distinctive mark . . .'

'A mark?' Estrático asked.

'. . . Or should I say two: tattoos. Twin swallows, one on each hip, facing inwards. Black ink. The fading indicates it's four years old, approximately. If that is of any help in identifying her?'

'Why is the head whole?' Estrático blurted.

Alzada cringed. *It's true.* There were no signs of the firearm wounds themselves, or of Petacchi's later incursion to retrieve the bullets. *Is that what the compass was for?*

The coroner turned to Alzada and smiled. 'I see we've got ourselves a curious one, Inspector.'

'What can I say, Elías?' He faked resignation: 'The youth of today.'

Alzada caught Estrático's eyes going back and forth following their friendly banter. *Surprised that we know each other this well, are we?* 'We know each other from a past life,' was the only answer either ever provided. As if they had agreed on it. No one dared ask further. To elaborate would have been painful on Alzada's part, and, he imagined, embarrassing on the coroner's.

Still, Alzada could always tell that their reticence only prompted further questions, especially with younger people. To be fair, even he had, long ago, wondered how the world might have looked before his time. Not the ancient one, filled with artefacts from cavemen to conquistadors – no, ironically, that one was easier to grasp: it had gotten a closed casket ceremony in history books. No, people struggled to visualize a version of the past that was closer to them, one in which Alzada and Petacchi had been young, had met and somehow become friends. *That* they had trouble understanding. *That* they were less comfortable with. Because it lived on within those who were still around. Because it bled dangerously into the present.

'Well, contrary to what we see in movies, which if I may add is nonsense most of the time,' the coroner said, shaking his head in disapproval, 'the head is not always "blown open", to use a terminology you'd understand. It largely depends on the width of the projectile, the distance from the target, the angle of entry, etcetera.' Petacchi held the woman's head with both hands with surprising tenderness and rotated it slightly to show a clean wound no bigger than a shirt button. 'It's not uncommon for the bullet to pass through tissue, and even bone, without causing any major damage to the structure.' He used the same finesse to reposition her.

'Thank you for this, Elías. Impeccable work.' *Meticulous as always.*

'My pleasure. I'll give you a call at the station when the tox report comes back and send you the complete set of photos and the fingerprint analysis of the dumpster for your files.'

Inspector Alzada shook hands with him and rushed out. He barely heard Petacchi's afterthought: 'Have a good day, Inspector.'

BEHIND HIM, ESTRÁTICO STRUGGLED TO keep up with his pace. This street was quiet, but they could hear the sound of the crowd swelling a couple of streets over. *West. Towards the Casa Rosada.* How was anyone expected to take this country seriously when the seat of government was a pink building called 'the Pink House'?

'Estrático.'

'Yes, sir.'

Alzada heard the deputy's strained voice but didn't turn around. 'I need to run some errands.' *To begin with, coffee. It's not like this case is a priority.* 'Can you get to the station on your own?'

'Very well, sir.'

Estrático disappeared as furtively as he had materialized earlier. Alzada looked for a place to go. *Damn.* His new shoes in a dark puddle. *Not rain.* Then again, if all he had to worry about was dirty water.

3

(2001)

By the time Alzada got to the police station, it had begun to rain. More than rain, it was txirimiri: the relentless, almost imperceptible mist that ended up soaking your bones. The inspector stepped into the open-plan area. Originally a reception room with a sleek mahogany desk and a beautiful secretary who styled her hair like Evita, the recession had impelled the Policía Federal Argentina to make abundant cuts. The precinct had been forced to rent out the uppermost floors to a dashing foreign advertising agency and the reception had consequently morphed into an actual office where younger deputies such as Estrático sat. It was a cramped space painted a dubious mustard color and packed like a Tetris grid with plywood desks, uncomfortable, rickety chairs, a temperamental coffee machine and the jewel of the police station's furniture: a green couch familiar to every troublemaker in the Monserrat precinct. Its faux velvet didn't discriminate between police officers in civilian clothes and perps waiting to be booked, and greeted its occupants with the memory of stale cigarettes and coffee. Thirty years after its purchase it had lost most of its color and showed yellowish patches, like grass at the end of a dry summer.

Perched on it this morning – like almost every other morning – was la Dolores, who had yet again disturbed the peace of this respectable neighborhood. Dolores was thirty-seven, looked forty-seven, and showed a recurring difficulty in understanding why the same clients who promised her unconditional love during their private encounters then went on to act as though they didn't know her, especially when they took the occasional Sunday stroll with their families. Their 'other families', as she insisted on calling them.

'Good morning, Dolores.'

Her modus operandi amused Inspector Alzada.

'Good morning, Inspector.' It seemed as if she had spent the night on the couch and she was wrapped in a blanket, her eyeliner and mascara smudged.

'I look forward to the morning when I don't see you here,' Alzada said as he walked by.

'I look forward to that morning too, Inspector.'

'Let me know if the boys take more time than they need to process your paperwork. I know they like having you around, but you should have gotten home by now. Especially with what's going on today.'

'Thank you, Inspector.' She never uttered one sentence without including his title: a perfect blend of reverence and gentle mockery.

'Estrático!' he yelled.

A blond head popped out of a side door. The deputy had, much to Alzada's dismay, taken off his jacket – *the nerve* – revealing, to make things worse, a short-sleeved, button-down shirt underneath.

'You can call me Orestes, sir. Since we're going to be partners. . .'

'Estrático, I've had one partner in my life and I sure as hell don't plan on having another.' Alzada looked around, suddenly concerned. *It looks like a Sunday afternoon in here.* 'Has everyone been sent out?'

'Reinforcements,' Estrático confirmed. 'Seventy-five thousand armed forces and police personnel are on standby. An unprecedented measure.'

There is *a precedent, and that didn't end well.* The last time the military had taken to the streets the death toll had risen to thousands.

'And not us?' Alzada chuckled. 'I know what *I* did not to be considered for this heroic task, but *you*? Isn't it a little early in your career to be shunned?'

Estrático smiled uncomfortably.

'Good.' Alzada found a small pleasure in rattling his subordinate, but enough was enough. 'I guess there'll be no roll call today . . . Any news from the morgue?'

'Not yet, sir. Aside from the Jane Doe, the morning has been quiet so far.'

'So far,' Alzada grunted.

'I mean, there is a couple here to see you.'

'Me?' Alzada dropped his hands in disappointment. 'Did they mention my name specifically? Are you sure they want *me*?'

'They didn't ask for you personally.' *That's more like it.* 'They said they wanted to talk to the highest-ranking official at the station. And as you know,' the deputy paused to fake a cough, 'it's only 10 o'clock. . . . so that means you.'

'And what do they want?' Alzada chose to ignore Estrático's mention of the commissioner's famously lax work ethic.

'They wouldn't say. I took them to your office.'

He'd wasted enough time this morning between the morgue business and finding a parking spot for his grizzled Clio. Not that he had that much to do, really: without an ID, without a tox report, without a crime scene, all there was left to do was hope someone would call in a missing woman who matched the description. *The instructions for today are clear.* The commissioner liked to call it 'the protocol of minimum effort': any matter that could be postponed, would be postponed. But even if he had time to deal with them, these people had to be out of their minds: to choose today of all days to spend the morning at a police station?

'Sit in with me on this one.'

'Good morning,' Alzada announced upon entering his office.

The couple muttered a reply the inspector didn't hear.

From his office in the back the inspector could deal with these two blemishes on his otherwise 'flawless' day and simultaneously dominate the open-plan office outside: a large panel of amber glass allowed him to oversee all activity, while his door remained closed. This way, he was spared from the subordinates' clunky typing, the random gossip about things he didn't give a shit about and the coarse jokes. *The last concession from Galante. Otherwise I'd be sitting in the secretary pool.*

In a corner of Alzada's office stood a round, wobbly table, burdened with minarets of pending files, often assigned to one of the underlings who took turns working for him. The inspector was well aware that the young officers' presence wasn't a courtesy: their real mission was not to function as a personal aide to him – as he had been assured by Commissioner Galante – but rather to report anything irresponsible the wild card of the precinct might be up to, ideally *before* it happened. Recently, the commissioner had chosen Estrático as his latest minion. *He probably thinks I can't turn such a brown-noser.*

Alzada blamed the general chaos for inopportunely clogging his desk – both literally and figuratively – with ugly cases that otherwise would never have found their way to him. He wished he could find a better word – something elegant, perhaps with a touch of Latin. But in this case, it was fitting. Ugly. That's what it was: to have to devote his day to finding a reasonable explanation for a body abandoned in a dumpster behind the morgue. Ugly. If things had run normally at the station, someone in robbery would never have had to take care of a Jane Doe. But then again, when had things last been 'normal' in the precinct? In Buenos Aires?

Alzada was about to hang his umbrella on the coat stand when he paused.

'Whose coat is this?' he asked.

The two civilians before him emitted no sound.

'Mine, sir,' Estrático mumbled.

'This is not the way to hang a coat. Don't you see?' Alzada grabbed a grey suit jacket. 'You have to hang it by the sleeve. Like this,' he demonstrated. 'Otherwise you'll have yourself a jacket with a hump in no time.'

'Yes, sir.'

Inspector Alzada maneuvered around his desk, careful not to accelerate the peeling of the wall paint behind him, dropped into his chair, and rubbed his hands. 'Okay, let's get to work.'

The inspector stared at the couple, motionless as if cast in lead, and was suddenly thankful for the whirr of the table fan.

'I'm Inspector Alzada. And this is Deputy Estrático.' He motioned to the secondary table, where the young police officer had taken his place. 'He will be assisting me. You should know he's one of the most promising police officers in the force.'

Out of the corner of his eye, he saw Estrático swell with pride. *Imbecile, of course he thinks this is all about him. Civilians – even those who pay us voluntary visits – need to be eased in.* Alzada had observed this on countless occasions: people entered the station eager to help, only to become mute, as if at some point between getting a welcome nod from Basilio the security guard and sitting in front of an officer, they realized where they were. *Confused, like they'd been bitten by a yarará snake.*

'What can I do for you today?'

The man looked like an engineer – the way people look like engineers even if they're not: he wore high-prescription tortoiseshell glasses and, in spite of Buenos Aires' summer heat, his burgundy bow tie matched both his checkered shirt and his sweater. The woman was immaculately attuned to her husband – the cream-colored cardigan on her shoulders rested over a striped burgundy dress. *Schoolteacher.* Together, they looked like money.

'My sister has disappeared,' she said. Flat out. Matter-of-factly. Most people needed forty leading questions to get there. *Straight to the point. I like her.* Her lower lip trembled a bit now she was silent.

Alzada opened a drawer and pushed his flask aside in search of pen and paper. *How times have changed.* Not twenty years ago, this would have been unthinkable. The idea that someone could walk into a police station, ask to speak to the highest-ranking police officer and report a missing person? When the relationship between the police and the military, responsible for disappearing people, was one of collusion at the very least? *No, not unthinkable: reckless, dangerous, deadly.* And now here they were, these two – reporting the missing sister openly, without fear. On the same block where Coordinación Federal had stood. Where people were disappeared. People used to be so afraid they would make a detour just to avoid walking by the building.

'When is the last time you saw her?' *What would our lives have been like, if we had been able to file a complaint? If we had been tended to by a diligent policeman who had asked the right questions?* Alzada wondered if his lip was trembling, too.

'This past weekend. Saturday?'

It took all the inspector's efforts not to roll his eyes in response. He didn't want to seem dismissive. He didn't want to scare her. But he also didn't want to tell this woman the window of opportunity for finding her sister alive had come and gone. *In this chaos, and after five days . . .* Alzada looked past the couple onto the common area. *Is there really no one I can hand this off to?* The office looked dismal: a lonely Christmas tree by the entrance and two officers at their desks. *Constables – not high-enough rank for this.*

As good as Alzada thought he was at feigning interest, she must have perceived something, because she immediately tried to regain his attention: 'But I talked to her on the phone after that.'

'When?'

'Yesterday evening.'

Alzada raised his eyebrows as he set his pen down. 'You must understand, madam, that this puts us in a singular position. If indeed you had verified contact with her last night, our protocol dictates it is too early for us to establish that she has, in fact, disappeared. We can't—'

'I am well aware, Inspector,' she interrupted.

He pretended to look at his watch; he didn't need to know what time it was to make the calculation. 'It's been less than twenty-four hours. In the case of adults, we normally wait for at least one full day since the person was last accounted for—'

'Unless there are grounds to believe . . .' she interrupted. *Again.* The woman inflexed her voice, 'it could have been a forced disappearance.'

'You know, we prefer to use the term involuntary.'

'Of course you do.' *Great. An entitled one.* 'I've done my research.'

'I'm glad, madam.' He was not. Still, he offered: 'Then you probably know that our method regards a person being "missing" as merely an indicator of something wider, not as an isolated matter in itself. A symptom of a deeper issue, so to speak. People disappear – involuntarily or not,' he conceded. 'But always, *always* for a reason. In our extensive experience, we have found that the search is most effective when we prioritize focusing on that reason. Because once we have that, we can retrace her steps and get her home as soon as possible. So, what in particular makes you think the disappearance might be . . .'

'Involuntary.' *Good girl.* 'Well, when we talked on the phone yesterday, she sounded anxious.'

'I don't mean to be . . . How shall I put this?' *Yes, how shall you put this, Joaquín?* 'We're going to need something more.'

The woman lowered her gaze, folded her hands in her lap and seemed to rummage through her memory. Alzada used the brief pause to examine her. He could picture her fifteen years earlier, a superb student, front row, prim posture, irreproachable record. *Someone you would want to stand next to in a crisis.* Why then was she struggling to present a clear, coherent narrative? Something was wrong with the picture, and Alzada couldn't tell what it was.

'Just . . .' Alzada humored her, 'just tell us about your sister.'

'She's wonderful.'

'I mean. Let's start with her name.'

'Norma. Norma Eleonora Echegaray.'

Alzada saw Estrático look up from his notes.

'Echegaray like . . .' the inspector hesitated. *Like one of the most prominent landowners in the country?*

'Yes. Like that.' *Fuck. I can't possibly hand this down to Estrático. They'll be expecting top brass.* Immediately she added: 'And no, we don't live in that building anymore.'

The mention of her family's wealth had brought out a tinge of coolness in her tone that hadn't been there a moment before.

'It's been empty for a while, no?' He found himself indulging her.

31

As if reading his mind, she said: 'I'm sorry. Habit. Every single person asks me about it. You were saying . . . About my sister.'

'Yes. Norma. Has she ever done this kind of thing before? Maybe left for a couple of days and forgotten to say where she was going?'

The woman shook her head. Her husband seemed bored with the interaction; he also looked like he wanted to speak, if only for the sake of putting an end to it. *He's the one who's going to tell me.*

'Never?' Alzada pressed. 'So, it's fair to say that this disappearance of hers is completely out of character.'

'My sister-in-law has always been . . .' The husband stirred in his chair, the leather under him squeaked. *There you go.* '. . . complicated.'

'"Complicated"?' Mrs. Echegaray was indignant. 'What do you mean by that, "complicated"?'

The husband motioned for her to quiet. Alzada's pupils dilated. If he had ever tried anything like that with Paula, he would have had to sleep on a deck chair in the garden for a week – and then beg to be allowed back in. Instead, the woman obeyed.

'In the time I've known her – I've been married to my wife for six years now – Norma has systematically found herself in situations where she's inevitably needed our help. Only last month we had to bail her out after she was caught with a huge supply of liquid soap: apparently she wanted to fill the fountain in the Plaza de la Independencia with foam.' He chuckled unexpectedly. Until then, Alzada would have never thought him capable of smiling, let alone laughing. 'It was funny,' he added, as if he had to explain his sudden giddiness. 'She's a very fun girl. What can we do? That doesn't necessarily mean she's currently in danger.'

'Facundo, please.'

The engineer had a point. Still, there was something about this man: he had one of those faces – in another time, Alzada would have relished finding a reason to punch him. Instead, he asked Mrs. Echegaray: 'Do you have a picture of her?'

'Of course.' She promptly produced a passport-sized photograph from her purse. In it, Norma Echegaray was wearing a cap and gown. 'That was two or three years ago, but she looks the same.' The woman justified her choice.

And a very good one at that. As unfair as he knew it to be, the police would always be more willing to set aside homicides, robberies, rapes and assaults to devote their attention to a studious graduate of the Universidad de Buenos Aires, than they would a millionaire party girl. The blue band on her shoulder indicated she had studied economics. Alzada leaned in closer.

It's her.

The same serenity, like the faces in old portraits done in sepia. Her smile was explicit, somewhat expectant.

Is it her?

Was it the woman from the morgue? She was certainly as pale and dark and beautiful as the corpse had been. But so was half of Buenos Aires. *You're a better cop than that, Joaquín. This* woman had a different destiny waiting for her. *This* woman probably disappeared by her own means – which were considerable – and would emerge in a couple of days without a scratch. It would then all be an anecdote, something she would tell at parties, much to the dismay of her sister.

Was this his wishful thinking or his professional opinion? Alzada felt suddenly dizzy.

'Inspector?'

'Yes, madam.'

'Is everything all right?'

'Yes, yes.' Alzada regained his composure. 'I was going to say . . . Your husband does make a compelling argument, madam.' *Focus.* 'Why should we worry? Or why should we worry *so soon*? If, as per your suggestion, we rule out this being a prank or a foolish escapade, do you suspect an financial motive?' *Unlikely.* If that was the case, and they had taken her yesterday evening, the Echegarays would already have received a note. *A good kidnapping is over in less than a day.* Alzada couldn't help but remember his criminal law professor explaining it was the most difficult crime to execute correctly. He'd been shocked by the matter-of-factness with which Iraola had described its downsides: the risk of creating a bond with the kidnapped person and not being able to make clear-headed decisions, the constant surveillance one had to undertake and, most incriminatingly, once it was over, there was an eyewitness.

Mrs. Echegaray raised her left eyebrow. 'Not everything is about money, inspector. Not even for people like *us*.'

She was right: there was an 'us', and Alzada was certainly not included. These were people with their own private security and their own investigators. *Why turn to the police?* Regardless, Alzada's several decades on the force had taught him when to push and when to hold back. He had learned the lesson reluctantly, but he had learned it well. He tried again: 'Can I assume she had security?'

'Assume away,' Mrs. Echegaray said, still tense.

'Where were they?'

'She evaded them for sport, especially when—'

'I told you, a fun girl,' the husband interrupted.

Alzada chose to ignore him: 'When . . .'

'You know, when she wanted to meet up with a boyfriend or something. They're incompetent.' *That answers one question: she doesn't trust them to take care of this.*

'Is she seeing anyone?'

'No.' As if she had heard his skepticism, Mrs. Echegaray added: 'She would have told me.' *Unlikely.*

'Does she have any distinctive marks?' Estrático blurted out. He had approached the desk – surreptitious as ever – and was holding the photograph. 'A birthmark, perhaps a tattoo?' *How dare you.*

'No. *That* is definitely a no,' she turned to answer as the deputy returned to his seat. *So we're not so sure about the boyfriend.*

'In conclusion,' Alzada said, hoping to stop the situation from turning into a soap opera episode. 'I'm inclined to open a case, but to do that I need at least a shred of evidence of foul play. Is there anything you can give me?'

'She said "I'll call you back".'

The subtlety of her claim. As late as 1982, four men breaking down her door and ripping her from an apartment in the middle of the night wouldn't have been deemed enough to start an inquiry. It would have been considered an 'incident', and shelved.

The man rolled his eyes.

'I know my husband is rolling his eyes,' she said without looking at him, 'but we were talking on the phone, and she cut me off. Someone was at the door. She said she'd call me back. And she might be many things, but when she says "te llamo de vuelta", she does.' Mrs. Echegaray paused for a moment. 'She never did.'

From her frown, Alzada could tell her mind was churning out thoughts faster than she knew how to deal with them. *Ah, the mind, that powerful tool. That most dangerous weapon.* Mrs. Echegaray was asking herself: what could have I done differently? Could I have asked her who it was? Could I have stayed on the line while she opened the door? Could I have called back sooner? Could I have gone to check up on her last night instead of this morning? *No matter what transpires, she's done for.* He knew that thought process well. *Regret never leaves you.*

'It's hard to explain.' In her voice, none of the previous sassiness. She leaned forward and set her hands on Alzada's desk. French manicure, diamond engagement ring, gold wedding band adjacent. 'But Inspector – I don't know if you have siblings – if you do, do you know that feeling? The feeling of worrying about them? That feeling of . . . when you just *know*?'

Alzada knew.

4

(1981)

Friday, December 4th; 17:30

They had drunk so much wine that it was mid-afternoon and they still hadn't had lunch.

The grill stood on the edge of Jorge's terrace, opposite a small wooden garden table at which Joaquín, Paula and Adela sat comfortably, beers and olives within reach, waiting for the parrilla to reach its ideal temperature to cook the meat. Master of ceremonies Jorge tended to the grill in a flamenco-inspired apron, swaying its ruffles from side to side.

'See?' He rested one hand on his left hip and waved the other emphatically with the grill tongs, droplets of grease on the terrace tile. 'The dictatorship isn't *that* bad.'

Joaquín had promised Paula on their way there that he wouldn't make a scene or bring up any subject that could dampen the mood –

it was Friday and almost summer and they hadn't seen each other in a while, but in Jorge's presence keeping the peace meant eluding a lot of topics. Joaquín looked over to Paula, who held her glass of red wine a little tighter than necessary but didn't say a word.

'Remember when we thought we would have to go into exile?' Jorge continued.

That had been five years ago, and most of the Argentinian left had already gone by then, either abroad or underground. Jorge and Adela had mused about Rio de Janeiro and Paris. Joaquín had a clear recollection of the moment: it had given him chills, like feeling cold at sunset after a long day at the beach. In the end, his brother had decided to stay and fight – whatever that meant.

'And look at us now,' to say Jorge was inebriated would have been an understatement, 'contributing to the cause, bringing into the world a new generation of godforsaken Argentinians. What kind of world are we leaving Sorolla?'

Adela shushed him.

Joaquín knew she wasn't doing it for the baby: 'Has the neighbor given up?'

'Well, she still co-ordinates her exits with ours,' Adela said.

'Must think we're dangerous intellectuals who need to be surveilled,' Jorge added.

Joaquín heard a sliver of fear underneath the playful remark.

'Don't start, Joaco . . .'

'What? I haven't said anything!'

'You gave me a look.' Jorge knew him too well.

'I think . . .' Adela decided to intercede, 'Paula, will you help me bring out the vegetables? At this rate, we won't have eaten by Christmas. Joaquín, another Quilmes?'

'Yes, thank you.'

ONCE JOAQUÍN FOUND HIMSELF ALONE with his brother on the terrace, he stood and joined Jorge by the grill.

'You always end up overcooking the entraña,' he teased him, trying to grab the tongs from him.

'And you insist on serving it raw!' his brother retorted.

Joaquín let go of him. 'So, how have you been, hermanito?'

He knew exactly how Jorge had been: not that long ago, Joaquín had been able to pull some strings and prevent his arrest, hoping the scare would be enough to make him come to his senses. But then, last week, his brother's name had been dropped in the type of conversation in which no one would ever wish to be mentioned. People ended up in a ditch for much less.

'Good, good. We've been doing good work lately.'

'At the union?'

'Yes, Joaquín, at the union.' Jorge prodded at a steak that didn't need prodding.

'Are you being careful?' He knew stopping him altogether was impossible. Every time, Jorge gave his word, kept quiet for a week, and then started over.

'Just keep away from malas compañías, will you?' Joaquín insisted. 'Lay low for a while? Just so there are no misunderstandings. You've made it so far.'

'"Bad company", Joaco? "Misunderstandings"?' Jorge laughed. 'You're talking like them.'

'I'm not one of them,' Joaquín replied, resentful.

'You're right, you're right. I'm sorry,' Jorge apologized. 'But neither are we. We're not part of the military faction of Montoneros. We don't patrol the street in jeeps, machine guns in hand, looking for some random soldier to kill. We don't plant bombs. We're university professors, not terrorists. We might agree with them politically. But the end doesn't justify the means. And that goes for your side, too.'

'*My* side?'

'You must admit, sometimes it sounds like you've bought into it.'

'I just wanted order,' Joaquín protested.

Jorge scoffed.

'What?'

'Order? Is that what you call what is happening?'

'Look, I'm not saying I agree with everything they're doing. But we knew we would have to make some concessions . . .'

In 1976, the front page of every newspaper had celebrated the arrival of the self-styled National Reorganization Process and proclaimed the end of all subversion, corruption and anarchy. After all, the main reason for the military coup had been to stop the covert civil war that had been tearing the country apart. So, sure, a little firmness was to be expected to put a halt to the kidnappings and robberies and murders and shootings. If that meant Joaquín could stop worrying about a bomb going off every time Paula announced she was spending the afternoon downtown, all the better.

'Concessions? Joaquín, I don't recognize you anymore! Where is the Joaquín who encouraged me to read Marx and Galeano? The

Joaquín who introduced me to Carlos Mugica and lent me his books about the revolution? The man who was part of that movement *himself*? There was a time where you believed in something.'

'I grew up. And I got a job.' Joaquín was determined not to fight with Jorge. At least not until dessert. 'And it's a job like any other.'

'Is it, though?'

Silence.

'I mean. Joaco. Maybe in the beginning, but now? Knowing what we know?'

Joaquín hated when he was put in a position where someone expected him to justify a regime he did not even agree with. He also didn't feel like explaining his life choices to Jorge: he had cleaned up his act and found a respectable job away from any trouble, for the most part. He finally said: 'I'm not a part of it.'

'So you keep repeating. Then why doesn't that make me worry less?'

'And here I was coming to tell you I was worried about *you*!' Joaquín half joked. 'In any case, I'm glad to hear the proletarian revolution leaves you time to think about me,' he added sarcastically. 'And apart from strategizing how to free us from the yoke of capitalist exploiters – and worrying about your police inspector brother – do you ever find time to think about your son?'

'Yes.' Joaquín had started to notice a shift in his brother's face lately, his trademark lightness dimmed. 'I worry about him all the time. I pray he doesn't become a fascist like his uncle.'

'So now I'm a fascist?' Joaquín faked outrage. 'At least I've been promoted. What was I before? Oh, yes: an apathetic bystander. You even gave me the book last Christmas, the one about the banality of evil. Who was the author again? Hold on. Did I hear you right? Did you say you *pray*? You?'

Jorge smiled. 'This is serious, Joaco. We're at war.'

At war. Joaquín could barely remember a time when their conversations hadn't been this polarized. *This is precisely why I've been avoiding him.* At some point, it had become useless to discuss politics with Jorge. Or any subject for that matter: he had a strange talent for always bringing the conversation around to his territory.

The younger Alzada might be many things, but stupid was not one of them. Why then was he so insistent on the matter? The Montoneros' military capability was now practically non-existent: their members had been obliterated, their weapons had been confiscated, their financial support had dried up. And Jorge was probably facing pressures from within the organization, too. The fact that he was one of the few that hadn't been disappeared must have raised suspicions within his own ranks. What if it got into their heads that he was a collaborator? He wouldn't be the first montonero to have been summarily judged for treason and shot by his own comrades. *Is this what being a true believer feels like?* Joaquín had never been as deeply convinced by anything as Jorge was of his cause.

'And if we surrender – if I surrender – *they're* going to win,' Jorge continued.

Right there. Joaquín saw it right there. Of course, the trite rhetoric and the eternally defensive tone, fueled by the exhaustion of having to constantly explain himself to his 'responsible' brother. But then, the possibility of finding relief from an impossible burden. He *wanted* to tell him more. Jorge Rodolfo opened his mouth silently, like a fish gasping for air. Then, more quietly: 'This isn't the moment to abandon the fight. I feel that more than ever, we can make a difference. And for that I need to be close to the action.'

'You mean you need to be close to trouble,' Joaquín said.

Jorge's face went somber, but then he smirked. 'Yes, that too.'

All Joaquín wanted for Jorge was to survive this fucking dictatorship. He felt like screaming. *I'm running out of favors, Jorge!* He took a deep breath, then said: 'Look, I just want you to be safe. Or at least smart.'

Jorge patted his hands clean of grease on his apron and hugged him. 'I am.'

'Take care of yourself, please,' Joaquín said into his ear. It felt like begging.

'You know,' his brother whispered, 'I say it out of love.'

'You do?' Joaquín mocked him, leaning back to look him in the eye.

'Always,' Jorge confirmed, tightening his grip. Not a hint of sarcasm. 'And don't worry about me. I'm safe.' Joaquín wanted to believe him. Badly. 'Do you know why I'm safe?'

'Tell me.'

'Because I've picked sides.'

Joaquín looked puzzled.

'There's sides to everything, Joaco. Remember that. There's always sides.'

'I don't—' Joaquín was having trouble following his brother's logic.

'Some people play both. That's one risky game. Do you know that phrase, "if you don't like my principles, I have others". Marx said it.'

'Karl?'

'Groucho,' Jorge said, raising his eyebrows and smiling, the exact gesture that always got him out of trouble. 'Well. He was very, very wrong: we only have the one set of principles. And we must stand by them. And that, hermano, is how we remain safe.'

5

(2001)

The inspector decided not to walk them to the exit: he didn't have time to play the perfect host. If they couldn't find it themselves, someone else would guide them through the maze of bad taste and smelly carpets that was the police station. Still, as Mrs. Echegaray stood up, the three sitting men immediately rose to their feet. Estrático hesitated to make a gallant gesture to accompany them, but Alzada motioned him not to, and he stayed put until they were alone again.

'Okay. Let's say – if only for argument's sake – that she was . . .' Alzada cleared his throat, 'gone. Where could she be?'

'Mrs. Echegaray said her sister had hung up to get the door. That was around 9 o'clock last night,' Estrático consulted his notes.

'When she went to the apartment this morning, she was gone. That gives her a head start of . . . fifteen hours now. So, to answer your question, sir: anywhere. She could be in Paris.'

'And we can safely assume Mrs. Echegaray inspected the apartment thoroughly.' A woman like her would have walked into her sister's without hesitation, though it was certainly an uncommon reaction: most people didn't have the nerve to enter a crime scene. Fear of what they would encounter wasn't even the primary concern: no one thought of that. What most people dreaded was leaving prints, being falsely accused by the police, and consequently spending quality time within the legal system. The damage American television had done to his job. 'If she had found anything, she would have mentioned it. So, all we know is that at some point between yesterday and this morning, of her own volition or not, she left the apartment. Do we have an address?'

'Castex 2640.' A glamorous, albeit discreet block. *Good choice for a wealthy, single woman in a city where the slightest show of wealth makes you a target.*

'And the sister?'

'Also.'

'Do they own the whole building?' Alzada joked.

'They own the whole block, sir. Most of it is probably empty at this time of the year. Everyone who is anyone is in Punta by now.' Estrático inflexed his voice.

Punta, huh? No need to fake it, Estrático. He had most likely spent a couple of summers in Punta himself, maybe played rugby against the Echegaray boys at some point. *Unbelievable.* For three weeks now, no one had been allowed to withdraw more than 250 pesos a week from their checking accounts and with each passing day one could buy less and less with those 250 pesos. In the meantime, a few lucky ones had been able to not only finish their Christmas shopping but also exchange the city heat for sandy paradises. In the back of Alzada's mind remained, indelible, the footage of a news reporter being shoved aside by a group of housewives who had victoriously ransacked their local supermarket for rice, flour, and beans. '¡Queremos comer!' had been their war cry. We want to eat! A crime of desperation.

'I want to know how many entrances the building has. And if anyone might have seen her. You're right about the summer season, but maybe some neighbor is still in the city? Also, in that part of town, the building must have security cameras. And a doorman. I want to talk to him.'

'I'm on it, sir.' Estrático started making his way to the door. 'So, about the Jane Doe from this morning . . .'

'That can wait,' Alzada said.

Estrático paused.

'You look surprised.'

'Are we not going to do anything about that?' *Careful, Estrático.*

'First of all, I think you meant to say "her", no?' Alzada took a deep breath. He was not going to start a fight; the commissioner would hang him by his thumbs. 'It's a common mistake to make, especially when you so obviously lack experience. I know what you're insinuating and you will never hear me say that some cases matter more than others. But you need to bear in mind that some families are going to call the station every hour on the dot to check on our progress, and those are normally the same ones who have friends in high places. Others are not going to call because they might not even know something is wrong. I'm not going to apologize for wanting to get *this* out of the way.'

'Do you think there's something there?' *Nice pivot.* Estrático was a pain in the ass. The only thing that redeemed him in Alzada's eyes was his genuine interest in the profession.

'I hope not. A woman like that—' Paula would kill him if she heard him use those words. *The problem with stereotypes, Joaquín, is not that they aren't the truth. It's that they're not the whole truth.* But in his field, the truth was a pure numbers game. 'A woman like that has a wild night out, disturbs the peace, maybe gets charged with possession, which after a caution is filed as this week's boyfriend's fault. Maybe – *maybe* – if she *really* falls off the wagon, she has an abortion. She might choose to go on vacation on a whim and disappear without leaving a message. But without telling the sister she knows will be worried? Now *that* sounds improbable to me. Do you have siblings, Estrático?'

'No, sir.' Estrático immediately veered off subject: 'When she showed us the picture, didn't you get the impression you'd seen her before?' *Someone is not on good terms with his family.*

'Estrático?'

'Yes, sir?'

'Don't think I don't know what you're trying to do here.'

'Sir?'

'How many people live in Buenos Aires?'

'Three million?' Estrático guessed.

'Two million eight hundred thousand. But yes, three million. Now, how many of them are women between the ages of twenty-five and thirty-five?'

'Two hundred thousand?'

'Very impressive! I'm going to call that a very informed guess. So, two hundred thousand. And of those two hundred thousand, how many of them are dark-haired, and could be considered "pretty"?'

'I see what you mean, Inspector.'

'I don't think you do.'

'I only wanted to know—'

'Of course, your comment was totally innocent. As innocent as your question about a distinctive mark, no? A little more of this,' Alzada pointed at his temple, 'before you run off with some crazy theory. Especially to anyone who might listen. An Echegaray in a dumpster. Just what we needed. No. Until we can establish something that at least *resembles* a fact'. He found himself echoing an expression Commissioner Galante would use: 'I want this treated with utmost discretion. Do we understand each other?'

'Yes, sir,' Estrático said. 'I just thought it would be perfect if the woman we saw this morning was actually the same one these people are looking for.'

'Perfect? *Perfect?*' Alzada in crescendo. 'Perfect would be a morning that didn't start with a dead woman thrown out in the trash. In the trash! Perfect, you say!'

Estrático stood still, petrified.

'Leave for Castex,' Alzada barked. 'I don't want to see you until you find me the doorman. And take a look at the apartment. Interview the neighbors, all that.'

'By myself?' Equal parts of terror and pride in the deputy's voice.

'Yes, Estrático, by yourself. I'm sure you can manage without me: it's an empty apartment. And when you get back, I want you to pull up a list of all the Jane Doe open cases in the city – no, make that Greater Buenos Aires—'

'But sir, that's a lot of people—' *Someone must put this boy in his place.*

'It is. And you're going to go through them one by one to check that none of them are a match with Norma—'

'Echegaray,' Estrático offered.

'What was that?'

'Of course, sir.'

That's more like it.

'And process la Dolores, will you? She should have gone home by now.' A thought tugged at Alzada. 'And while you're at it, tell her to skip "work" tonight.'

6
(1981)

Saturday, December 5th; 00:05

In the stillness of the night, Paula Aranguren's beige bedside telephone cut through the silence of suburban spring like a butcher's blade. Paula let it ring twice while she pulled her pillow from under Joaquín and raised herself up. She couldn't see his face in the darkness, but she knew he was there, under the jungle of black curls that he refused to cut to indulge his wife. She ceremoniously cleared her throat. The phone rang a third time. Paula picked it up and spoke a serene '¿Dígame?' into the mouthpiece.

'Who the fuck calls in the middle of the—' a half-asleep Joaquín clamored, trying to discern the time in the dark.

Paula shushed him, suddenly alert.

He turned away from her to check the little Casio on his nightstand and found the alarm clock smiling insolently back at

51

him, a Cheshire-cat grin of fluorescent hands. Five past twelve. *Nothing good ever happens after midnight.* The echo of his father's explanation for the Alzada boys' curfew.

'I think you better take this,' Paula said sternly, her hand covering the mouthpiece.

That was the moment he knew.

Joaquín caught a glimpse of her wedding band. Still horizontal, he reached a tan arm over his wife and grabbed the phone, the cord tense in an unnatural curl against his white knuckles.

It was his brother's neighbor. Even in this peculiar circumstance, her voice was familiar enough that she didn't need to identify herself. From the moment Jorge Rodolfo and his wife Adela had moved across the hall from her, she had systematically spied on them. Joaquín remembered his brother's impression, imitating her shuffling motion out in the hallway, to their front door, then back to hers.

Joaquín remembered Jorge Rodolfo describing her voice as vain. Now, in a much graver tone, she said to Joaquín: 'They have come for your brother.'

He was not the first to receive such a call. Before him, many had already suffered the same uncertainty, the same fear, the same anger, the same impuissance. After him, many would make the same inquiries, yell the same insults, hold back the same tears. Years later, the ripples of those conversations would consolidate themselves as the mantra of a forsaken generation. There would be protests, there would be trials and tribulations. There would be essays and long speeches about what could and couldn't have been done. For the moment, Joaquín hung up the phone and announced: 'I'm going.'

'No,' was the only word Paula felt capable of saying, partly to deter him, partly to prevent the new reality from settling in. She repeated it when Joaquín sprung out of the bed, hoping that the accumulation of noeswould amount to the desired effect. She repeated it – to herself – when Joaquín ran to the kitchen; she was still saying it, softly, when he came back with his shoes.

He seemed to be immersed in the rhythm of his own, not-so-internal monologue. '¡Bastardos!' and '¡Hijos de puta!' made appearances in regular intervals. Joaquín, now half dressed, darted back out into the hallway. 'Where's my blazer?'

'Your blazer? It's the middle of summer, Joaquín.'

'I need it to hide my weapon.'

Paula paused. She took a deep breath before she answered. 'I think you left it on the chair by the entrance.'

She could hear his restless footsteps pacing in the hallway, slowing down then coming to a halt: finding things was having a soothing effect on him. It was not working for her.

'Come back here!' she called.

Joaquín promptly stood in the frame of their bedroom door. Paula couldn't help but remember the first time she had laid eyes on him: he had been leaning against the door to her university auditorium, just like he was now. The lecture had ended minutes before. He had probably been waiting for another girl, he had never said. Nineteen years old, and already tired of being an adult, his wiry frame concealed down to his shins in a camel-colored raincoat, his long fingers perpetually reaching for the cigarettes in his pocket, the smile of someone who always gets what he wants. He had since shed the thin beard and in return added kilos to bring

53

gravitas to the appearance of the youngest inspector in the city of Buenos Aires. Joaquín did not blink twice at the sight of Paula in her nightgown.

Silence.

He went straight for the drawer where he kept his Walther.

'Wait.' She gripped his arm.

It had been a steep learning curve for Paula, the cohabitation in such close quarters with Joaquín's service weapon. Brought up in a family of upper-class nouveaux riches by way of the metallurgical industry, her beliefs had originally oscillated between a vague trust in the rule of law and a firm disdain for anyone who was part of law enforcement themselves. Only slowly had she come to terms with the idea that somebody had to put that rule of law into practice, and that that somebody could be her husband.

Somewhat to her surprise, accepting the presence of that lethal piece of metal within her home hadn't been as difficult as she had expected. Routine had played its part: she had gotten used to Joaquín solemnly strapping it into its holster as he got dressed for work, to feeling its weight on his hip when she kissed him goodbye, to sighing in relief when he locked it back into its sarcophagus every night.

'Joaquín, let's think this through,' she tried again.

No, the hardest adjustment had been trying to cope with the various possible versions of the future the gun embodied. That one day, he might have to use it. Or worse: that one day, someone might use one just like it on Joaquín. Now, watching him standing in the doorway, she realized there would be no words powerful enough to dissuade him. He would not go over to his brother's apartment as the calm, careful, level-headed inspector she knew him to be. He would destroy anything in his path if it meant getting Jorge back.

'You get to Jorge Rodolfo's apartment. And then what? They're not going to be waiting for you. They'll be gone.'

'I don't have time for this,' he said dismissively.

'And we were there today!'

Joaquín didn't need a reminder: his head still hummed from the beer and wine.

'What if they were already there, staking out the apartment?' Paula continued. 'Are we going to be on some list now, too?'

Joaquín stopped in his tracks. *I hadn't even thought of that. They wouldn't touch a cop, would they?* He felt cold. 'Don't worry.'

'Don't worry? What do you mean, "don't worry"? All I do is worry! I worried about Jorge and now I have to worry about you too! What if they're still there?'

'All the better. I want to see them. I want to look into their eyes when they answer to me. Because they *will* answer to me. Let me tell you. If anything – *anything* – happens to Jorge . . .'

'Joaco, please.'

He stopped, suddenly aware of his own fear. What *would* he do if he ran into a well-trained military squad? His ancient Walther burned like a hot-water bottle against his hip. *What is the plan here, Joaquín?* 'Call Galante. Don't explain anything over the phone. Just tell him to join me at Jorge's.'

'He won't ask?'

'He won't ask. Then, call the neighbor. The one who just called. Her number is somewhere in the leather address book. She'll be awake.' *Nobody in that building is asleep right now.* 'Tell her to turn on a light as soon as those bastards have left.'

'Okay.'

'What apartment does she live in?'

'It's the third floor. Your brother is apartment C, so she must be A.'

'Are you sure?'

'I'm the inspector's wife, Joaquín. Not the inspector.'

Joaquín sat down next to her on the bed and took her hands in his.

'In any case, have her turn on a light in the living room once everyone's gone.'

As he spoke the words out loud, he became aware of their leaden weight. *Once everyone is gone.* They worked fast. He was going to arrive at his brother's apartment and that was precisely what he would find. Everybody gone. His brother would be gone. Adela would be gone. And the boy would be gone. The boy. Joaquín felt a sharp pain in his left side.

'What about me?' Paula asked.

'You stay here,' he said. As if to prevent an argument, he added: 'I need you to make those phone calls. And be here in case anyone tries to contact us. I'll let you know as soon as I get there. Everything will be fine.' Joaquín wondered whether he was as convincing a liar to others as he was to himself.

'Fine.'

Joaquín distractedly kissed her on the cheek and walked out. He grabbed the keys to the car from a terracotta bowl by the kitchen entrance, a souvenir from Galante's honeymoon in Mexico. Their friendship, albeit momentarily strained, was well known in the force. *Maybe it's not such a good idea to get him involved in this.* Galante might currently be in the milicos' good graces, but an incident like this could very quickly spell trouble for him. If the army were to ask questions, it was best if his former partner could answer honestly. *No. The less people know about this, the better.*

Joaquín went back into the bedroom. Paula was sitting in the exact same spot where he had left her. 'Now that I think about it,' he said as casually as he could, 'don't call Galante. I don't want to bring him into this if it's not absolutely necessary.'

Paula nodded absently.

'And lock the door behind me.'

He stormed out of the house before his wife could see him cry.

7

(2001)

Making the most out of the two signal bars his phone displayed in the interrogation basement, Alzada called Paula. It rang until her voicemail kicked in. She was probably busy working around the house. He left her a message. 'Querida, it's me. I completely forgot to tell you, I was in such a hurry this morning. I didn't want to bother you, but I found the neighbor's cat on my way out and,' Alzada turned his face towards the wall and lowered his voice, 'I put him inside the grill in their garden to make sure he doesn't cross paths with Sorolla.' He looked left and right. No sign of Estrático. 'I know, I know what you're going to say. You can call me later and yell at me if you want. But you know how Sorolla gets when he sees the cat. And I checked. He had air. Can you free him before Teresita starts missing him? Okay. Thanks. Love you. Bye.'

The deputy appeared down the hall.

'Where is he?' Alzada asked.

'Interrogation room three.'

'He didn't make you run, no?' Estrático looked like he could outrun most of the population without losing his breath.

'He was still in the building: his shift hadn't ended. Sir, I do need to talk to you about something before you—'

'It can wait.' Alzada was about to open the door marked tres in chalk when he stopped. 'What kind of mood is he in?'

'When I picked him up at Castex he was calm. Last time I checked, he was sweaty, but still silent,' Estrático reported.

'Good,' Alzada motioned towards the door. An innocent man held for interrogation would have been screaming at the top of his lungs that he was exactly that, innocent. *At least before you convince him to the contrary.* If the doorman hadn't protested, chances were he wasn't clean, at least not one hundred per cent. *There's something there.* The sweatiness meant he was almost ready: Alzada liked his subjects medium rare.

Estrático stepped forward and stood in the inspector's way.

'Estrático, please. We don't have time for whatever this is,' Alzada dismissed him.

'I know, sir. But his lawyer hasn't arrived yet.'

'What are you talking about?' Alzada scanned him. The deputy was standing taller than usual. Not hunched and tentative, like he would on the upper floors or while running errands, but in actual defiance. *I can't believe this.*

Estrático elaborated: 'I did exactly like they taught us. From the start, I treated him kindly. I offered him something to drink. Spent some time with him in the cell to feel him out. Tried to get on his good side, you know?' *Well, this explains why the Federal's solved crime numbers are so low.* 'But as soon as I asked the first question, he clammed up. So, I called Pomada.'

'You did what?'

'I called the public defender's office.'

'No, I know who Pomada is, Estrático,' Alzada said. 'Now we *really* don't have time for this. How long ago did you call him?'

'But the procedure indicates—'

'Drop it, Estrático. Don't you understand he's *not* innocent? His job is basically to stare at a door for twelve hours and record every instance of someone walking in and out of the building. That's literally *all* he has to do. At some point last night, he saw this woman—'

'Norma.'

'Yes, Norma. Thank you . . .' Alzada tried not to lose his train of thought, 'He saw Norma Echegaray leave – *maybe* not on her own – and he didn't move a finger. He just sat there, staring at the door, until you arrived. Probably counting the dolaritos they slipped him to make him look in the other direction. So, unless the important thing you had to tell me is that he's blind, he has no "good side": he only has *one* side, the side that will lie to you to your face and take advantage of the fact that you have respect for the law. And by the way, what are you so afraid of? I'm only going to ask him some questions. And for that I *definitely* don't need Pomada.'

They can all do the math. Alzada always acted on the assumption that they all had, especially the young ones. He had read somewhere that in Bosnia the first thing people did upon meeting you was guess your age: not out of vanity, but to know where you were during the war. Were you old enough to grip a gun? And if so, for which side? Even Estrático – straight and orderly Estrático – must have figured out where he had been in the 1970s, what being a police officer had meant in those days. It didn't require a genius.

'With all due respect, sir . . .' Estrático was almost ashamed to speak the words: 'If we do this, we'll be like *them*.'

Alzada managed to steady his voice, then replied quietly: 'You have no idea what you're talking about, son.'

This young, smart, decidedly prepared generation – he so wanted to put his faith in them. But there was something smug about their primness, their rectitude, their behavior beyond reproach. Alzada wasn't even all that sure it was intentional: they just exuded an innate self-righteousness. They liked to give speeches about how the law is always to be upheld, how if *they* had been there, they would have acted differently. Of course *they* wouldn't have allowed it to happen.

But the truth was Estrático would be completely lost without the manual. He didn't know what it was to interrogate a man who had nothing left to lose, or to discover the animal that lives within oneself and have to strap a muzzle over its jaws. He didn't know what it was to wake up from a nightmare, only to discover it was not a dream, but a memory. 'No idea,' he repeated.

Alzada leaned in, patted Estrático on the shoulder: 'Nothing's going to happen to him. Now stay here and watch. This is how it's done.'

'GOOD MORNING, SIR. I'M INSPECTOR Alzada,' he said with a confident gesture, holding his hand out to the doorman.

The doorman remained seated, his arms crossed. *Fine. Have it your way.*

'As you prefer.' Alzada brought closer a metal chair, scarred with the memory of handcuffs, and sat across the table from him. He must have been around thirty years old. *Definitely not from Buenos Aires. An Indian, so probably from the north. El Chaco?* 'Have you been watching the news? The barricades, the riots? Have you seen them for yourself? I drove past one on my way to work this morning. What a mess, huh? Let me tell you—'

'I already told the other one. I don't speak until my lawyer gets here.' *Smart enough to be silent but not smart enough to cash out and disappear?* The doorman put both his hands on the table. Most people in the same situation would keep their arms close to their bodies. Sometimes they even crossed their legs. This one was a step above confident. *He's too calm. He's been in a cell before.*

'I don't think you're listening to me.' Alzada spoke in a voice lower than normal. Behind the door, he could imagine Estrático leaning in closer. 'I'm not trying to make small talk, you piece of shit. I only bring it up because in this chaos, do you know how long it's going to take for your lawyer to arrive?'

The inspector watched him making a calculation, sure that in the arithmetic of his survival the doorman hadn't taken into account two significant factors. First, time is relative, and severely subjective. *One minute. If you only think about surviving the next minute, then the next one, and so on, you're good. But if you start thinking about further than that, you're done for.* Second, there is a reason why there are no windows in the interrogation rooms of Buenos Aires. Sure, someone had finally caved and installed an audio system, but it was next to impossible to discern the true nature of a situation just from a grainy recording. *As long as I don't leave any visible marks . . .* Estrático might disagree with his methods, but he still wouldn't rat out a fellow officer. For his own sake.

Alzada's ribcage expanded, his shoulders rose up to his ears, his head tilted forward. A cat ready to pounce. With his right hand, he grabbed the doorman's left across the table before the latter had time to react. Alzada firmly held it down on the metal. The doorman's eyes widened.

'See, that wasn't actually a question. My guess would be . . . considering the demonstrators and all . . . thirty to forty minutes. If he leaves his office right now. But here is the *real* question.' Alzada pressed further on the doorman's hand. 'Do you know how many fingers I've broken in my life?'

The doorman tried to free himself from Alzada's grip, unsuccessfully. He stretched his bulging neck out of the collar of his uniform and grasped for air.

'I mean. You're no stranger to interrogation rooms, are you? You know what happens in them,' the inspector continued. 'Still, we don't like things to get messy. It gets us in trouble. "Democracy", you know? These days we have to at least keep up appearances. That's why at some point my boss had to forbid me from coming into these cells. Can you imagine?' Alzada gave him a full smile. 'Today's your lucky day, though: he's too busy giving out instructions to crowd control – the protesters are approaching the Casa Rosada. He has *no idea* what's going on within these walls. So please,' he cleared his throat. 'Please don't make me waste my time. I'd hate to think you would anger me on purpose. I would interpret it as you preferring to be held in a room with a sink . . . You know what I want. Just pick up that pen and write down whatever comes to mind.'

The doorman looked at the pen on the scratched metal table, then at his left hand, pale under Alzada's. 'I'm left-handed,' he protested meekly.

'I know.' With that, the inspector released his hand and sat back. He wasn't going to explain that most people position their belongings closest to their dominant hand. In the end, Estrático's glass of water had been useful.

The doorman hastily reached for the pen and started to scribble. Alzada leaned in. Three letters and three numbers. A license plate.

'Is that all?'

The man nodded.

'It wasn't the first time that car came by, no?'

The man nodded again.

'Because of course, you saw nothing yesterday evening. Like after dinner? No one come in, no one come out?'

'Nothing out of the ordinary, sir.'

Alzada was afraid to ask what exactly 'ordinary' meant in a high-end apartment building. 'Very nice. Now get out of here.' The inspector found himself considering the man's probable future. In his experience, snitches only talked because they thought themselves smarter than their peers. They thought they were going to make it out alive. *No one is the exception.* 'I don't think I need to tell you this, but I'll say it anyway. You don't wait for your lawyer to get here. You leave the station and go directly to your apartment.

Directly. You don't stop for coffee. You don't visit anyone. You don't tell anyone where you're going. You grab your stuff and take a nice, long vacation. I'm sure you have a cousin somewhere, out of the city, where you can lay low for a while?'

'Yes, sir. My family's from Resistencia,' the doorman admitted, suddenly malleable. *El Chaco. I knew it.*

Alzada rose immediately, his chair scraping the cement floor, and walked out of the interrogation room.

On his way past Estrático and Pomada – *that was fast* – who knew better than to upset him, he pushed the sheet of paper at Estrático's chest. 'I'm leaving for an hour or so. When I get back, I want to know who owns this car. And go down there in person, none of that polite over-the-phone bullshit you lazy bastards love.' Then he added, not dignifying Estrático with as much as a look: 'And don't stare. Has no one ever told you it's rude?'

'Was that true?' Estrático looked down at his own hand, while he lurched up the stairs after Alzada. 'About the fingers?'

'No,' Alzada turned around. 'My specialty was knee caps.'

8

(2001)

Wednesday, December 19th; 11:45

With two decisive strides, Inspector Alzada crossed the street and entered the closest café, slammed his hand on the counter. 'Un café con leche, por favor.'

At the bar, the deafening noise of the coffee machine, the parade of cups and spoons clattering like shivering jaws, the unused raincoats in a palette of cautious beiges, the smell of burnt toast.

Alzada positioned himself in a corner atop one of the chrome swivel bar stools and occupied the stool adjacent with his raincoat; he smiled remembering one occasion on which Sorolla had accompanied him to work and then to grab a coffee, eyes wide open during his immersion in this new and fascinating universe. His first of many questions – always a quiet child unless one needed him to be: why are the chairs glued to the floor? *The truth: café owners are terrified of an inebriated customer using one of the stools as a weapon.* To the seven-year-old, Alzada had said that it was so no one stole the beautiful seats. That, in Buenos Aires, had sounded believable.

Alzada took a sip from the Duralex; he liked his coffee in a glass. He could have easily done like many of his colleagues and found a subordinate to bring him coffee from outside the station, one of the many prerogatives, if not of his rank, then of his seniority; but the inspector had never felt comfortable with the number of personal errands one had to run as a junior and had sworn never to do that once he moved up. In addition, with Estrático busy with his research into the number plate, he could count on at least half an hour of undisturbed peace. Why spend it at the precinct? With the expertise of a man who has savored thousands of coffees in his life, he maneuvered his fingertips so that they barely touched the edges of the hot surface.

Menudo día de mierda. With such a bad start, God knows what the rest of his day might have in store. *Don't even think about it.* Alzada knocked three times on the wooden rim of the bar. At least he had gotten to see Petacchi again. The coroner was looking good – by his pasty standards – as if he were getting eight hours of sleep. *How* does *he sleep, knowing what he knows?*

Someone approached the seat next to him and interrupted his thoughts. A middle-aged man with a bad comb-over and a bulging briefcase whose leather gave in every direction. *Doctor.* Alzada removed his coat; under it, yesterday's paper appeared, folded on the chair; it had been a while since they had last been able to afford to buy the newspaper daily, the first of many consequences of the austerity measures. Before the man brushed it off, Alzada squinted to make out the headlines about Minister of Economy Cavallo's latest madness: 'During the holidays, the Central Bank will allow withdrawals of up to five hundred pesos'. Alzada stifled a bitter laugh, careful not to engage the doctor in conversation. *Five hundred pesos.* All things considered, the Alzadas were fortunate: their lives seemed like a million kilometers away from those of the inhabitants of Villa 21, a slum a mere twenty blocks away from their resolutely middle-class neighborhood. When Joaquín and Paula and Sorolla sat down in their living room in Barracas to watch the evening news, the images that came to them through their cream-colored television set felt almost otherworldly, like footage taken by a scuba diver in an underwater cave. Yes, they had reasons to be thankful. *You get used to everything except not eating.* Speaking of not eating: what exactly had happened that morning?

ALZADA HAD STORMED INTO THE kitchen, hungry and late. He didn't have time for a proper breakfast, but at least he could grab an alfajorcito for the drive. Sorolla was already gone and Paula was sipping her tea at the kitchen table. After a moment, she said: 'I took your alfajorcitos to school yesterday.'

Alzada had lowered his eyes from the cupboard shelf, where he was searching for them, and checked his reflection in the microwave door.

'They faint, ¿sabés?' Paula continued, staring into the void. From where she was sitting, it could have been into the garden, but even without looking Alzada knew her gaze was lost in the distance. He sat down across from her and took her hands, warm from cradling her tea mug.

69

'Paula.'

She was in a trance. 'It took me a while to realize that it's because they don't eat at home. I don't know how long this has been going on.' She looked right through him, her glasses increasingly misty: 'And I know that school is not a priority. I know that.'

Alzada pressed softly on her hands to calm her. She fell silent.

'It's because of the shortage of petrol,' Paula started again, 'It's more important to use the car to visit a cousin who keeps chickens. The family needs to eat. So, the children who still come . . . I mean. Fewer come every week. But the ones who come, they walk. When I first found out, I was quite upset – who knows what dangers await an eight-year-old on a country road to the city. I didn't want to think about it. What could I do, anyway? At least they come to school, and that's better than nothing. What is that saying? "Perfect is the enemy of good". But then, on Monday, I'm reading out the multiplication tables I have just written on the blackboard, my hand still holding the chalk over the numbers. They class is silent, well, as silent as is possible when I have my back to them. That's when I heard it. A thud. Silvina in the second row.' She shook her head gently. 'I sent everyone else out to play. That's when she confessed that she hadn't had a proper meal since before the weekend. That's at least three days, Joaquín . . .' she said, as if he didn't know.

Alzada tightened his grip over her hands.

'They faint, Joaco. They faint.'

'Listen to me. I don't care about the alfajorcitos.'

'And I know bringing them biscuits isn't going to solve the problem. And we don't have money to feed twenty-seven hungry children. But does that mean I have to watch them starve?'

What do you reply to that?

Fortunately, the phone had rung.

DISTRACTED, ALZADA WIGGLED AROUND ON the café stool and almost fell over. Instinctively, he clutched the counter, pressed his left foot on the floor, and twisted his body to keep his balance. And there he was: by the window, at the most prominent table, his back to the room in a gesture of vanity and contempt. Galante. *Commissioner Galante. So sure of himself he doesn't feel the need to watch the entrance.* Alzada would have recognized the broad back of his old partner in any café in Buenos Aires.

Good news: he was on time. At the station, you were only considered late if you weren't at your desk by the time the commissioner arrived. And that was never early. Five minutes to midday. Seeing him chew on his croissant, Alzada knew he had a comfortable margin. He motioned the waiter to make him a carajillo. The man, in an impeccable bow tie, obliged and refilled the half-drunk coffee with brandy.

Alzada welcomed the burn of the liquor, imagined it cauterizing his insides. Discreetly, he eyed Galante. He was having a quiet, almost surreptitious breakfast with the archbishop of Buenos Aires. The priest was dressed in rigorous black and Alzada was almost certain he had used public transport to get there. His long, solemn nose crinkled and expressed the worries of someone who was in charge of so many impoverished parishes in the city, where the recent financial cutbacks had hit the hardest.

Alzada watched the crowd outside through the glass that looked onto the street, with its traditional hand-painted fileteado letters that spelled 'café' in light blue and white. In the last couple of days, the number of buses arriving in the capital filled to the brim with people from neighboring provinces had risen exponentially: new blood for the war. At some point they would realize they had enough to take over and bring the system crashing down, and that point was not far off. But not all was orchestrated: on the opposite side of the street from where Alzada sat, a young man was using his skateboard to smash up a cash machine, even though they had been empty for weeks – contradicting Cavallo's insistent message that Argentinians' savings were safe. Next to him, another young man: the lookout.

Wait – Sorolla?

Alzada immediately rose from his stool to see over the letters on the window. The man had his back to him; same indomitable black curls, same denim jacket, same backpack. *No. It can't be.* It was almost noon, which meant Sorolla had been at work for at least three hours now. And he wasn't the kind of person who would attend a cacerolazo . . . or was he? *Come on, turn around.* The young man remained still, transfixed by his companion, whose weapon had begun to splinter against the display screen. *Could it actually be him?* It was one thing was getting incensed about the state of affairs over dinner – Alzada had been political in his youth, he understood all about the all-consuming flame of idealism – but this? Vandalism? *That's how his father got started.* Alzada pulled his wallet out of his pocket; as he looked up again, a group of thirty people, their faces covered, had taken the street by storm. *Fuck, they're gone.* He had lost him in the crowd. *I better get back to the station before the revolution.*

'Thank you for my papers, Inspector.'

Alzada turned to meet the voice. The woman behind him, waiting to take his seat at the bar, was la Dolores. He smiled. 'You can't blame them for enjoying the pleasure of your company, and taking more time than necessary to process you.'

'I know, Inspector. That's the reason I'm thanking you.'

'¿Cafecito?'

'Sure, Inspector.'

They switched positions; she'd be more successful garnering the waiter's attention. In her black tube dress, Dolores looked utterly out of place. *Are people staring?* It didn't seem to bother her.

'How is your day so far, Inspector?'

'I've had better ones . . . Yours?'

'The business of passion never sleeps, Inspector.'

'I can imagine . . .' Alzada said, hesitant.

'Would your mood have perhaps something to do with the fact that la Echegaray was at the station this morning? And not the one who's normally in trouble?'

'Do you know her?'

Dolores smiled. 'Don't worry, Inspector. She'll be back.'

'From your lips to God's ears, Dolores,' Alzada laughed. 'I would love to spend the morning with you but . . . duty calls.' He nodded his head in the direction of Galante.

'I understand, Inspector. One more thing: if you're looking for a fancy car that might have picked someone up . . .'

'How do you—'

'You might be good at your job, Inspector, but I'm damn good at mine. And that's one of the first things I tell the young ones:

never get into a stranger's car. For people like her, that means the car is driven by someone other than the owner.'

'Exactly my thinking. The make and model will corroborate that.'

'Have you run the plate?'

'I sent—'

'Don't tell me you made the handsome one go in person . . .' Dolores chuckled. 'You'll have no luck with the Dirección General de Tránsito. Not even *you* will be able to access that information. Not even if the civil servant were hanging by his ankles off the roof of a ten-story building.'

'I wouldn't know what you're talking about.'

'Of course, of course. Still, my money is on "restricted" or "government" or something like that. La Echegaray doesn't go out with just anyone, Inspector . . .'

'You spend too much time at the police station, Dolores.'

'I couldn't agree more, Inspector.'

'So where would I find such a car, say, on a day like today?'

'Hypothetically?'

'Sure.'

'Inspector, you must know there's a cabinet meeting taking place right now . . .'

'Right,' Alzada said, distracted. He eyed the street again. No Sorolla in sight.

'Everyone who is anyone will be there . . . and if one indeed drove to that cabinet meeting, which one would certainly do, where might one park . . .?'

'I need to go make a phone call.'

Alzada placed the required fifteen pesos under his saucer. The waiter waved him away, signaling the two coffees were on the house and Alzada took his money back. Especially during tough times it was worth it to them, having their establishment full of police.

'Take care of yourself, yes?'

'Always, Inspector.'

'I mean it: no making the rounds tonight.'

Alzada half-expected a mordant remark, but Dolores only nodded in agreement.

The inspector took a last look at the commissioner. He was glad Galante had company, it meant that they didn't have to engage in conversation. Back in the day, he would have said hello. No. Back in the day, they had been partners, and friends, and each other's best men. Back in the day, they would have sat together having breakfast practically every morning: if one were to examine the legs of one of the tables in the back of the café closely, they would find both their initials, etched in hesitant chicken scratch. That was almost thirty years ago. Alzada winced. Back in the day, they had both been in the business of looking the other way.

9
(1981)

Joaquín started the car and drove like he had nothing left to lose. On a normal day, the same trip would have taken him anywhere between thirty minutes and an hour. The route was quite similar to his commute: he had to get from Barracas in the outskirts of Buenos Aires, where he lived with Paula in a modest house with a yard, to his brother's apartment downtown.

Joaquín remembered the first time he had worried about Jorge. Actually, there had not been a "first time": worrying about Jorge had been a constant in his life. From the moment they had lost their parents – Joaquín had been ten, Jorge four – and even though they had been well taken care of by their grandparents, Joaquín had felt the weight of watching over his little brother upon him.

No. Joaquín could remember when worry had become fear. Right after Paula and he had moved into their new house, Jorge and Adela had come over to help them unpack boxes and build kitchen cabinets. *The military junta had barely come to power then, so five years ago?*

None of them had been particularly elated at the thought of the freshly appointed triumvirate, after all, a military government was a military government. But no one wanted to be the boy who cried wolf: this was not the first military dictatorship they had come across in their lifetimes. They had survived the first one; they would do the same now.

How could we have known?

THE NORMAL DAYS WERE OVER. No more than a quarter of an hour later, Joaquín landed in Palermo, his brother's neighborhood. It helped that the roads, as prescribed by the military curfew, were deserted. It also helped that, hiding behind the protection granted by his badge, he had run every single one of the fifty red lights he had come across on Avenida Entre Ríos – his right foot on the gas, his silver Renault 6 roaring like the car it was not. Had he actually grabbed his badge? Joaquín reached for the clip on his belt. *Shit.* A cold sweat overcame him: without it, he was defenseless. *What do I do now?* If he drove back . . . No. There was no time.

He approached number 2742 on Aráoz and slowed down to remain only slightly above the city speed limit. Any car racing through the night would attract unwanted attention, but so would one driving too slowly. He eyed the rabbit's foot dangling under the rear-view mirror: Paula had gifted it to him on the first day on the job and he had kept it there since, in spite of despising the idea of a good-luck charm, and in spite of Galante's constant mockery of her superstitions. Today, Joaquín was glad to have it with him.

He decided to delay his arrival for a couple of minutes and first canvas the adjacent blocks. *I don't want any surprises.* Joaquín was more familiar with the extraction procedure than he wished to be. First, the police station closest to the target received notice of an upcoming intervention, in the shape of a telex signed by a high-ranking officer in the Navy. Lately they were so frequent a simple call sufficed. Then, the conniving switchboard operator assigned a neighboring patrol car the doubtful honor of sweeping the area beforehand and remaining at a safe distance throughout the 'event'. This offered the military task force a zona liberada, which was code for total impunity. Finally, after approximately twenty minutes, and employing the same method of communication, the police car was sent out to confirm that everything was 'in order'. Fortunately, Joaquín had made inspector just in time to avoid being part of such patrols more than once or twice, shortly after their creation. Those had been the quietest nights of his career.

He turned onto Scalabrini, the street parallel to Aráoz, and saw two men sitting in the front of a parked, unmarked car, three blocks down from his brother's place. A navy-blue sedan. *Cops.* As he reached the corner, he let the car rock to a stop next to them and rolled down the passenger window.

'Buenas noches, chicos.'

What the fuck, Joaquín? One minute he had been trying to attract the least possible amount of attention, the next he was boldly announcing his presence. *You just can't help yourself, can you?* This was the rashness Commissioner Vukić had constantly mentioned in his rants at the police academy. 'Alzada, think! But not in your brainy way, you idiot! This attitude of yours is going to get you killed one day! It's stupid and dangerous and—'

'Immature?' Joaquín had quipped.

Vukić had sent him out to run seven times around the precinct block. One lap for every Argentinian the commissioner's mother had brought into the world after leaving Dalmatia. A Buenos Aires block was 129.9 meters both wide and long, as per the Spanish colonial decree of 1876, which meant every time Cadet Alzada spoke out of turn he enjoyed fifteen minutes of brisk jogging to calm down. If he couldn't curb his impertinence, at least he would regain his composure. Vukić's words.

Tonight, he'd have less time than that to do either. *Think, Joaquín, think.*

The driver, closest to him, was smoking and had rolled down his window a couple of centimeters. He turned to examine Alzada, wide-eyed and not a day over twenty, his white shirt, even on a stakeout, prim and starched. *Fresh out of the academy.* On his face, a too-immaculate moustache and the preoccupation of trying not to fuck up. *If only you knew how quickly that fear fades.* The fact that Joaquín had spotted them so easily seemed to have rattled him.

'How did you—'

'Ah,' Joaquín waived his hand dismissively, thanking God for having stumbled across a pair of rookies. 'Don't worry, you're doing nothing wrong. A couple more night shifts and you'll be able to recognize a brother in arms in an unlit tunnel.'

Brother in arms? For fuck's sake, don't overdo it, Joaquín. It's probably wiser not to show them up and risk embarrassment. Otherwise he would have explained that when on a surveillance job, the car should never be positioned at the front of a row of parked vehicles. Of course, parking on the corner was comfortable. Plus, it took advantage of the fact that Buenos Aires streetlights left much to be desired, even with a full moon like tonight, and simultaneously granted a clear visual advantage over two streets. At the same time though, one could easily be found out: two men sitting in a car at this hour? And visible from four different angles, no less.

'So, quiet night for you, too?' the one in the driver's seat offered. He seemed nervous, trying not to lose eye contact with Joaquín while fishing a new cigarette out of his shirt pocket. Too nervous by any standard – even rookie standard – and definitely too nervous for a routine night watch in a neighborhood such as this one. Of course it was a quiet night for these two: they hadn't seen anything. That was their whole purpose. To not see a thing. And then – more importantly – to report back at the end of their shift that they had not, in fact, seen a thing.

There are none so blind as those who will not see. The idea sank from Joaquín's mind into his chest, like sand in an hourglass: they were in on it. It took him a strength he didn't know he possessed to crack a smile. He had recently taken on the herculean task of reading all the *National Geographic* back issues they had gotten over the years; they crowded their living room and imbued it with a particular yellow hue. In one of them, he had stumbled upon an article on Arctic expeditions and one detail had stuck with him. Apparently, when corpses of ill-fated explorers are found on frozen trails, they always display what is known as the 'smile of death', caused not by a sweet, peaceful, hypothermic slumber, but by a painful contraction of the jaw muscles. A final, excruciatingly painful reflex. Joaquín relaxed his cardboard smile.

'Yeah, heading home,' he nodded. 'Have a good night.' Before he rolled up his passenger window, he added: 'The badges, chicos. In the glove compartment.' Puzzled, both looked over at their shiny safe conducts sleeping on the dashboard, blatantly on display.

Leaving the two men to fight over their carelessness – something Joaquín and Galante had done repeatedly during their endless nights of patrol – he hurriedly turned onto Aráoz. There, his first instinct was to check for unfamiliar cars. The grupos de tareas, the task forces, were famous for roaming the city in Ford Falcons the color of red wine bottles, but if any car had answered to that description this evening, it had already left. Joaquín leaned his head on the steering wheel and looked up: the whole building was pitch dark. *For the last time in my life, I've been late.*

10

(2001)

'Glad you called, sir. Perf— Good timing, too. I had just returned from the DGT,' Estrático greeted Alzada as the inspector crossed the street towards him.

'Any issues getting here?'

'No, sir,' Estrático stepped aside to allow room for a man to emerge from under the roll-down metal shutter of a shoe store. 'They've created barricades with burning trash in barrels over on San José, but other than that . . . What exactly is it that we are doing here, sir?'

'In a minute, Estrático.'

While they waited for the man to leave, Alzada took the pulse of the neighborhood. Across the street, 'el pueblo unido jamás será vencido', a popular tag these days, was spray-painted over a wooden board that protected a storefront. The people united will never be defeated. He found it odd that the shoemaker had come downtown. Certainly not a day to welcome customers. He was probably there to rescue the last valuables items before the riots broke out.

'So,' Alzada said, when the man finally locked the metal gate and hurried away, 'Any leads on the license plate?'

'Not per se, sir.' *'Per se'?* 'I went to the DGT myself, like you told me, to "apply my powers of persuasion" . . .' Estrático seemed uncomfortable with the implications. 'And?'

'Still nothing.'

'What excuse did they give you?'

'Gobierno.'

As Dolores had predicted. Alzada wondered whether he should confess he had made him go in vain. 'What make of car is it?'

'Mine? An Alfa Romeo.'

'Really, Estrático?' Alzada tilted his head. 'Just when I was beginning to think that we could make a good police officer out of you.'

The deputy hastily fished out his notepad. *Estrático's meticulously scribbled notes on every single detail he encounters.* 'It's a BMW X5. From 1999.'

'Impressive.' *Actually, truly impressive.* He had done some old-fashioned footwork and walked the surrounding blocks until he had found it. *Someone is a fast learner.* 'Color?'

'Cream.'

'This is too good to be true.' Alzada rubbed his hands and smirked mischievously. 'Is it nearby?'

'It's double-parked a little further down, on the next block,' Estrático said, pointing in the direction he had come from. 'Who is crazy enough to bring a car like that downtown—'

'I knew it!' Alzada interrupted. 'Dolores was right.'

Keeping an informant alive in this city had proven to be a considerably difficult task, especially an effective one like la Dolores. Alzada had learned that the hard way. From the moment he had met her, they had agreed he would never deliberately contact her outside the precinct.

'Dolores? The same Dolores who—'

'You can't possibly be surprised she's an informant . . .'

'A little bit, yes,' Estrático stuttered.

'Why else do you think that in spite of the constant arrests she never gets charged? Why do you think she's always let go before the end of the morning? If you tried to read her file – because there is a file – you'd find it empty. Nineteen years, and never a bad tip.'

'Nineteen years? But that would make her—' Estrático started counting in his head.

'Much too old for you.'

The deputy blushed but made no remark.

'She told me about this place once,' Alzada continued, looking up. Bar La Favorita. Desde 1964. 'And of course, dedicated to desk duties as I am now, I'd completely forgotten about it. A lot of chauffeurs come here. Good coffee. Less famous, less crowded, and less expensive than Tortoni. 'And it's close enough to Congress. When a congressman contacts their driver, they can pick them up in under two minutes. Traffic police in the area know better than to give tickets to any of the better cars. Now, before we do this, please tell me your visit to the woman's apartment was more productive.'

'There was nothing.'

'Nothing, *sir*,' punctuated Alzada.

'There was nothing, sir.' The deputy pulled out his notepad again. *Why can't he just memorize stuff like a regular cop?* 'About the building. No back exit. Carriage entrance. Marble staircase. Dark wood balustrade. Classic, but renovated. She had—'

'*Has.*'

Estrático didn't skip a beat: 'She *has* an elevator that leads directly from the front entrance of the building into her apartment, activated by a special key. I ran into an old lady who complained about the doorman being absent since this morning—'

'Don't tell me: security cameras with no tape in them. Faith in the magical power of deterrence.'

'Indeed, sir.'

'And the apartment itself?'

'Both the sister and the brother-in-law were there. The apartment is enormous. It looks majestic from the street, but the inside is even more impressive. My guess would be it was decorated for a tenant older than Norma Echegaray. A lot of gold. A lot of antiques. Some very, very valuable. But also a lot of quite expensive gadgets, a black leather lounge chair, a sixties wooden cabinet covered in old LPs, inside of it a fully stocked bar . . . she even had angostura!'

'*Has.*'

'Has,' Estrático reconsidered.

'So, your conclusion is . . .'

'Last thing: I also went through the closets.' *The thin line between good policeman and good stalker.* 'All the clothes belong to a woman. So no boyfriend who could be a lead, etcetera. I'd conclude that she must have inherited it and made some minor modifications to adapt it to her taste. She clearly lived – *lives* – there. Alone.'

'Thank you. But we're not writing a profile for a style magazine.'

'I didn't know you read those, Inspector.'

'Estrático . . .' Alzada admonished the deputy, but smiled. 'So, nothing terribly useful to our investigation, no?'

'Nothing seemed to indicate there had been an abduction.'

'Right,' Alzada said, letting the deputy chew through his statement. *Let's see if he can figure it out for himself.* 'No sign at all, then . . .'

'No, sir,' Estrático confirmed, drumming on his notepad. 'In fact, it might be the cleanest place I have ever been to. Not a dirty glass in the sink. Not a book on the nightstand, or even a night cream. Not one towel in the laundry basket. It looked straight out of a real estate brochure. As if she'd never lived there.' *If people only listened to their own words.*

'Have you considered that maybe there are no signs *precisely* because someone made damn well sure there would be none?'

'You mean . . .'

'Yes, Estrático. *I mean.* They knew we would look.'

'That makes sense.' The deputy stood firm, waiting for a cue.

'Well, in any case,' Alzada was impatient. They needed to act fast before fame-hungry Galante realized they had a case involving an Echegaray and took it over. 'Did you explain to them?'

'That given her social and economic status we would make this case our priority, drop everything else, and dedicate all our attention and resources to finding her? Or that they should under no circumstance surrender their hopes, even though with this lack of traction it's highly improbable we'll ever find her, and if we do, she'll most likely be dead?'

Alzada smiled. 'I hope you chose more tactful words, Estrático.'

'I did, sir. I was also careful to omit what rates a young, white, beautiful woman would elicit on the black market. And their life expectancies once they enter such circles.'

Alzada heard himself swallow; his Adam's apple bobbed reluctantly. *Change the subject.* 'It's time to do what we came here for.'

'Sir?'

'We're going to search the car.'

Before Estrático could begin to object, Alzada started walking through the crowd in the direction the deputy had indicated, subtly eyeing the demonstrators. *Had it indeed been Sorolla this morning? Could he still be around here somewhere?*

'Sir.' Estrático immediately caught up to him. 'Might I remind you that we don't have a search warrant?'

Alzada could barely hear the deputy above the blast of fire truck sirens. 'Look around you.' A young man walking down the street was hitting the hood of every car he encountered with a baseball bat. 'Do you think anyone is going to object?'

'But everyone can see us, sir.'

'Have you ever heard of the bystander effect? It will be painless, I promise. Count to ten.'

Estrático looked as if he didn't know if Alzada was serious.

'Here you are,' the inspector spoke to the car.

Alzada pulled a wooden wedge out of his suit pocket, and in one swift gesture chocked it into the top corner of the driver's door. Then, he jammed it further in with one dry hit of the bottom of his palm. He produced a slim metal rod that could have been a coat hanger in a previous life.

'Do you want to?' he offered the deputy.

Estrático cleared his throat.

'Fine, I'll do it.'

Alzada inserted the metal through the space he had created and aimed at the inside lock. It took him only two tries to push the unlock button. Ironically, the more modern the car, the easier to break in.

'There we go.'

The inspector opened the door and dumped the wedge and the rod to the curb. The car smelled new. *Someone has taken it to the cleaner's.*

'How often have you done this, sir?'

Alzada ignored the question. 'Don't just stand there.'

Estrático went around the car and opened it from the other side.

'Let's find something that looks even remotely like a print so we can get him in a room.'

'But sir—'

'Yes, Estrático?' Alzada leaned in and opened the compartment under the gearshift. A couple of pesos, two toll receipts from the Perito Moreno highway, a pack of cigarettes, coffee cups, chewing gum.

'We're not going to find anything, are we?'

Alzada smiled, pleased. 'Exactly.'

'Do you want me to check the trunk?'

'Don't bother. If she got in the car, she did so voluntarily. Who do the papers say the car belongs to?'

Estrático pulled out a folder from the glovebox. 'It's registered to . . . a company.'

'Okay, that's enough.'

Alzada slammed the car door shut, Estrático did the same.

'What now, sir?'

'On to plan B.' The inspector started to make his way back to La Favorita. 'Come with me. I think you might even enjoy this.'

'But sir, I thought the idea was to write him a ticket and see who pays for it?'

Alzada was almost impressed. 'You understood the principle. That's good. But since we're operating with a considerable time constraint, we're going to use a shortcut: we're going to rattle the driver just enough that he complains to his boss. The boss, being some entitled little bitch in government, will call someone in the police to moan about how he's being unfairly treated. Then we'll know who it is. Besides . . .' The inspector stopped in his tracks. 'I want to look this guy in the eyes. And we don't have many other options.'

From afar came an unmistakable smell: a tire fire. The inspector made a 360-degree turn and didn't find what he was looking for. There had to be a column of black smoke somewhere. *It can't be more than ten blocks away. Otherwise we'd be able to see it from here.* Alzada knew that this was the work of someone truly committed to the cause. *It's not easy getting rubber to burn.* And at a cautious distance, someone with a brain: they were communicating their position to the other protesters without having to worry about the police jamming their signal, and at the same time the smoke prevented police helicopters from getting a clear view of what was happening on the ground. *Smart.*

He entered the bar.

11
(1981)

Saturday, December 5th; 00:40

The entrance to the building was open: these bastards had grown so sloppy, so quickly. Joaquín knew from previous visits that the elevator took its sweet time, so he climbed up the three floors. Paula was right: he was getting out of shape. One more flight of stairs and he would have been panting.

Joaquín took two deep breaths to calm himself down and knocked softly on the neighbor's door. He knew she wouldn't have dared to call him until she had heard the boots stop moving carelessly through the hallway. *The noise they must have made.* If she had stood directly behind her front door during the extraction, as Alzada imagined she had, that meant she knew very well the balaclava-clad squad had already left, and it was safe to open. Still, Joaquín granted her time to verify his identity. He wondered how he looked when examined through a fisheye lens.

'Joaquín,' she finally called, her voice muffled by the door.

She opened and hugged him. Joaquín was surprised by her effusiveness. They remained like that for a while, static, in silence, ribs against ribs. Many years later, Joaquín would still remember the dark blue apron with white anchors – why she had been wearing an apron so late at night, he couldn't figure – reminiscent of fried fish. He had told Paula that his sudden aversion for calamari had stemmed from a late-onset allergy.

'It was horrible,' she said. 'Horrible.'

Joaquín turned around and looked at Jorge's door. For a second, he hesitated – it was not too late for him. He could walk away, knowing without a doubt what had happened, but never having to see it with his own eyes. Because if he decided to step into the apartment, all his efforts up to that point would have been in vain, and he had worked so hard to keep himself at a distance: whenever someone brought up the subject – ever so tactfully angling for his opinion – he had dodged the conversation with the excuse of freshening up his drink; every time a military van stopped at his precinct to put their prey in temporary holding en route to hell, he had left through a side door and spent the afternoon at a cafecito. Had he really thought these tricks would be enough to shield him from this mess? What did Jorge always say? 'It's not only the things you do, it's also the things that you don't.' Joaquín checked to see whether the door was warped. He reached for his gun, well aware that he was not going to need it. Ironically, at this moment, Jorge's apartment was one of the safest places in Buenos Aires.

REPENTANCE

WHEN THEY WERE FIRST CREATED, the grupos de tareas had been under a strict mandate of speed, stealth and anonymity. The military didn't have any moral qualms about dispensing killing orders like candy. Still, the government was determined to keep the news of the latest 'security protocol' away from the public. People wanted results, not the dirty details that came with eradicating subversives. What were they supposed to do, kill them with kindness? Alzada himself had roughed up more than one suspect to solve a murder. What was the harm in that?

In spite of the efforts to keep these incursions on the down low, it had very soon become common knowledge that people were disappearing. And to make things worse, the communist revolutionaries hadn't relented in their belligerence; on the contrary, they had regrouped in exile and returned with everything but a peaceful ceasefire on their agendas. In reaction to that, the government's strategy had shifted; they recruited 'the best of the best', formed new squads with anyone who volunteered to inflict violence, including convicted felons, and unleashed its beasts with quite a different goal in mind. Now, instead of targeting specific Montonero ringleaders or political adversaries, the squads were sent out to create chaos and sow fear in a population that no longer respected them. By then, the police had already surrendered the keys to the Buenos Aires metropolitan area to the army and become little more than a reluctant bystander who offered no objection, no obstacle, no resistance.

Joaquín pressed the five fingertips of his right hand on the lacquered wood – it was about time to file his nails – and felt the weight of the door resist against them. He pushed and the hinges squeaked as if they had been tortured. The door opened to show a dark hallway. A streetlampbathed the living room in a tentative light. Had Joaquín never set foot in the apartment before he would have needed a flashlight to move around, but he had patched up these walls when Jorge Rodolfo and Adela had moved in, helped his brother move the couch back and forth until Adela had finally decided on the right spot, hung paintings in this hallway. Chore after chore, weekend after weekend, he had given his scatterbrained, idealistic brother what he had considered to be the definitive push out of the chaos of his student union activities and into a professorial, comfortably middle-class life. What Alzada remembered most was the amount of books. There were books in piles in the hallway; books on the living room table, and not the heavy kind with abundant pictures of architectural monuments, no, real ones; books on the shelves against the walls; books in the kitchen, only some about cooking; books on the bathroom window ledge; books in the bedroom. Then, the first – and so far only – next-generation Alzada had arrived. Joaquín had thought it the final nail on Jorge's revolutionary coffin and spent a whole afternoon assembling a baby-blue cot. He couldn't bring himself to imagine the state in which he would find that room. Not one painting remained on the walls.

He moved forward slowly. No one called the police after 'a visit' – no one in their right mind, at least: the neighbors didn't; the families didn't; the disappeared certainly didn't.

Joaquín had never actually seen the fruit of such particular labor; he had been in drug dens and brothels and the morgue, but this was a different animal. He remembered the exact phrasing of the government decree that had authorized the excessive use of force against the revolutionaries: 'annihilation'. From the Latin, '*nihil*', to reduce to nothing. It smelled of hard work.

The armchairs had been turned over and looked like yawning yellow dogs stretching their legs after a long siesta. *Gratuitous.* At this point in their 'investigation' it was unlikely they had been looking for something other than Jorge Rodolfo himself: by the time a mission got the green light, judgement had already been passed. They had probably found that the couch weighed too much for their taste – or physical prowess – so they had decided not to lift it but stab the cushions until the stuffing emerged like milk foam. Viciously. Unnecessarily. A clever operative would want to get in and out quickly, they would want to avoid or at least minimize confrontation: some 'pacifists' had been known to resist the intrusions with sawed-off shotguns. Find them, restrain them, and into the car. Fast, fast, fast. This task force had not been in a hurry.

The bookcases had been ripped from their brackets on the walls. '*Where books are burned, in the end, people will also be burned.*' *Was that Thomas Mann?* Many of the tomes had proven to possess a rather feline instinct for self-preservation and had landed on their sides, but others hadn't been quite so lucky: they had fallen face up, confessing to those favorite passages, or face down, their pages folded into subversive waves.

Joaquín trod to the bedroom, which had received similar treatment. The drawers had been emptied conscientiously and were now leaning out towards the mattress. The mattress. He looked out into the hallway. His eyes were growing used to the darkness. On the white walls, Joaquín discerned two types of marks: on a lower, steady level, in blue and green and orange, the crayon artwork of baby Sorolla, who had surely taken advantage of one of his mother's momentary distractions to decorate on his own terms. And then; dark, sporadic rubber marks not confined to the lower reaches.

They had fought back.

JOAQUÍN FOUND THE PHONE, WHICH was no longer on the kitchen wall. He reconnected it with a soft click. The cord now hung low, all the way to the floor. *I'll have to come back and fix it. Thank God they haven't snipped the wire.* He attempted to dial home and realized that he called his own number so rarely he didn't know it with absolute confidence. It took him a couple of tries before he finally achieved the right combination.

'Joaquín?'

He didn't know where to begin. 'Paulita.'

That was all he needed to say. From the other side, a prompt: 'I'm coming.'

Joaquín didn't have the energy to object. He hung up the phone, leaned his back against the wall and closed his eyes as tightly as he could. It suddenly dawned on him: he had been right to look away all those times before. *This* would be harder. He would need to unsee. He would need to erase, erase, erase, what had happened: the ring of the telephone, the grinding of glass under his shoes as he entered the apartment, the living room littered with books, the not knowing where they had taken them.

Because they *had* taken them. His brother. And Adela. And the baby. The baby, the baby, the baby. Joaquín's lungs demanded more air than his ribcage could take in. The more he thought about it, the longer the list of things to erase got. Erase the rare times when someone had called the police station, the voice on the other side complaining, begging, crying, and the even scarcer ones when somebody had barged into the precinct, loud and outraged. Erase the politely detached answer given to every single one of them: 'I can't tell you more than what I know, madam.' Because it was always women – mothers, wives, daughters, grandmothers, sisters, girlfriends – overcoming their own fear of being next for asking. 'If it's a misunderstanding, as you say,' he had calmly explained, 'it'll be all cleared up by morning.' And the firmer correction: '"Arrested", señora. People don't just disappear like that in Argentina.' *Always the semantics.* Erase every time he had smiled confidently at these people.

Every time he had felt superior to them. Joaquín had felt safe, standing on the right side of the law. But what fucking law were they talking about when people were being disappeared in the night.

'Joaquín?'

Only then, hearing his wife's timid voice in the distance, did he realize that he was on the floor; his own weight had made him slide down along the wall until he had sunk his head between his knees.

'I'm here.' The cold kitchen tiles that minutes ago had felt like sweet relief now were making him shudder. 'Don't flip the switch.'

Joaquín didn't need to open his eyes to know Paula was crouching in front of him. He had heard her ankles crack when she lowered herself, he could sense the heat emanating from her, smell the Comfort fabric softener in her clothes. Minutes ago, the presence of another person in the room would have prompted him to draw his weapon. Now, he was glad he was not alone.

A noise in the distance.

Joaquín instinctively reached for his gun. It was coming from inside the apartment. Something shuffling on the parquet. He locked eyes with Paula. Could it be? Both rose to their feet and ran to the only room Joaquín had not checked.

'Sorolla?' he said.

He was nowhere in sight.

Paula motioned under the bed.

She sat on the floor and extended both hands, palms up. 'Joaquín, gordo.' Almost no one ever addressed the boy by his real name, to avoid confusion with his uncle.

Silence.

Joaquín went to the window. He saw a blue car unhurriedly roll down the block and thought he recognized one of the rookies. *There they are.* Keeping the lights off had been a good call.

'It's me, tía Paula.'

They held their breaths for what Joaquín felt were hours. And then: sausage fingers on a chubby little hand. The pajamas they had gifted him on his third birthday, a couple of weeks before. The boy curled up in Paula's lap. He didn't even look at him.

'Bring him a glass of water,' Paula said.

IN THE KITCHEN, THE FIRST light of the morning was coming through. *Already? How long have I been here?* Time had slowed almost to a standstill the moment he had entered Jorge's flat. Or had it been before that? When he had run up the stairs? Maybe when he had grabbed his gun at home. Or when they had received the call. When exactly had time stopped for the Alzadas?

'They forgot about him,' Joaquín muttered under his breath as he turned on the faucet and waited until the water cooled down. *It has to be an oversight.* When gathering intelligence for this incursion, someone had forgotten to make a note in Jorge's file about a toddler in the apartment. Heads would roll in the barracks. *They wouldn't come back for him.* Joaquín held his breath. *No. That would be too much of a hassle. Even for them.* His mind drifted and he briefly pictured a parallel universe, one in which the boy hadn't hid under the bed and had taken a peek out instead, to see what the screams were about.

They wouldn't have been cold-hearted enough to finish the job. Joaquín shook his head. *No. They would have handed him off to a superior who couldn't have children. There'd be a little Alzada somewhere, not knowing he was an Alzada, growing up with other people.* Joaquín's stomach turned at the idea.

Other people.

That was how *he* had thought of them. That was how *he* had survived for so long. That was precisely what he had been doing all along: keeping his distance from what was happening around him until it felt far enough to feel manageable. Because by that point, they were 'other people'.

Of course people disappeared. Or should he say, people *were* disappeared. Morally, it could be considered an objectionable policy, but there was a perfectly rational explanation for it. Something that justified even the most brutal of measures: they were terrorists. They built bombs and detonated them haphazardly, they kidnapped and killed respectable businessmen, they robbed stores at gunpoint to finance their fight, they shot at the police. They deserved it.

Other people.

It would never happen to someone he knew. It would never happen to *his* family. It would never happen to *his* brother. *It's always someone else's brother.* Joaquín cupped water in his hands, and let it run over. The truth was Jorge wasn't a saint. God only knew what exactly he'd gotten himself involved in, whose address book featured the younger Alzada's details, who had yelled out his name while his fingernails were methodically extracted, a pair of pliers slippery with blood.

Joaquín filled the glass. He imagined the bastards already far away, both Jorge and Adela blindfolded, his brother in the trunk, his wife hidden on the floor of the back seat, under their shoes. *Where are they by now? What will they do to them?* Joaquín stopped short. From now on, he would have to be more careful about where he let his mind wander. He shuffled down the hallway, taking the utmost care not to spill, and handed Paula the water. She took a sip. The boy had fallen asleep in her arms.

THEY TOOK SOROLLA OUT SLOWLY; he was still sleeping.

What now? There was hardly a handbook for such a situation. What did people normally do? The Ministry of the Interior had a window dedicated exclusively to answering queries about the disappeared. *The lengths these people are willing to go to maintain the charade the government isn't involved.* Joaquín knew he would get nothing more than a 'Come back next month, if they haven't reappeared of their own volition.'

Then there were the Madres, who for a short while had intrepidly gathered in front of the Casa Rosada demanding the safe return of their children. Almost immediately, the junta had made their leaders disappear. They had been quiet lately.

And he certainly couldn't make any sudden moves at the police station. Commissioner Vukić might officially keep his hands clean of what was going on with the military, but an inquiry like his would make the rounds quickly and almost certainly mean the end of Alzada's career. And he didn't need anyone prodding further into what had happened and find out the boy was with them.

The boy. What were they going to do about Sorolla? Act as if the stork had dropped him off on their doorstep? Paso a paso, Joaquín.

As they walked out of the apartment, Joaquín tried to hold Sorolla in his arms and relieve Paula of the weight. Both felt the boy's grip on her tighten. She immediately dismissed it as nervousness. 'Maybe in the elevator,' she said. But not in the elevator, nor as they stepped out onto the street. Not when they got to the car, not when they parked at home. When Joaquín impatiently tried to grab him from his wife, Sorolla looked up to him, then back at Paula, and said: 'Con él, no.'

He felt as though someone had punched him in the stomach. He turned towards the kitchen door and was blinded by the budding sun. He held on to the bougainvillea bush that so many times had scratched him on his way out and for once was thankful for the thorny welcome.

12

(2001)

The bartender at La Favorita was a man who had seen it all. On these stools had sat every established politician, every tentative revolutionary, every plotter with aspirations. These stools were popular. And every single visitor was greeted without distinction by the wet-dog smell coming from the mop perennially in the corner.

The bartender welcomed them by wiping clean two spots at the bar. *Here's someone who's learned to look without looking.* He had surely scanned them the moment they had walked through the door and made mental notes to report back to some high, dark authority. Something along the lines of: 'Two federales, one young, one old.' Alzada knew he was more recognizable than he'd like to be, and he knew that this particular bartending job most certainly paid off, in bulging envelopes of cash: there was a lot that could be overheard in a place like La Favorita.

Alzada grabbed one of the dark wooden stools and considered its height.

'Jefe, I'll have to do a Fosbury flop to sit on one of these . . .'

'You bet,' the bartender smiled at the 'jefe' reference. 'Coffee?'

Alzada hesitated. 'Cortado, please.'

'Make it two,' Estrático jumped in, taking a seat next to Alzada.

The bartender eyed him and nodded.

'How's the day so far?' Alzada started.

The bartender came closer to grab two coffee cups and plates from under the bar but didn't answer. *Am I losing him already?*

'I know *my* day has been hell. I can't even begin to imagine what it must be like standing only a couple of blocks away from—'

The bartender stood in front of Alzada and leaned on the counter. 'If you're here to get me talking about a certain cabinet meeting, you're asking the wrong person.'

Alzada saw an opening. 'So, it's still going on?'

'Yes.' The bartender looked resigned. *You know you want to talk about it. It's the only thing on everyone's mind.* 'How difficult can it be to decide which way they're going to fuck us over next?'

'Well, you know, they've tried almost everything. Now they have to come up with new ideas. Get creative. Consult the Politician's Kama Sutra,' Alzada gestured the title and subtitle of the imaginary book as if he were seeing it in front of him. '"One hundred new ways of fucking over your constituents."'

The bartender coughed up a rough laugh. *There you go.*

Alzada snuck a look behind him. Nothing on the walls but a palimpsest of cigarette smoke. Six crowded square tables made for a perfect echoing drum: every word he uttered would resonate to the four corners of the room. One would be more than able to follow their conversation at the counter even from the bathroom in the back and despite the background noise provided by the discreet chatter. *Exactly how I want it.* The rules of engagement dictated he couldn't shoot unless they shot first. *And if you do, don't let anyone see you.* There were too many witnesses at the bar. He would have to use them in his favor.

The inspector addressed Estrático without turning to meet his eyes. 'Have you seen the collection of cars parked outside?'

'How well some of us live . . . Can you imagine?' the deputy said.

'Yeah,' the bartender chimed in. 'I dream of driving every single one of them. At least once around the block. Feel rich even if it's just for a moment, you know?'

'Totally.' Alzada paused to take a sip of his coffee. There was a kinder approach that would yield the same result of identifying the driver: admire the car until he couldn't resist bragging about his imported BMW. But that wasn't enough: they needed him to get his boss involved. And do it quickly. For that, they needed to rough him up. In such a crowded bar, they would have to provoke him.

Showtime.

'Except for maybe that X5.'

The reaction was immediate. 'What about the X5?' A voice in the back.

Alzada smiled and turned around to scan the monochrome crowd. He had expected the driver to be inexperienced, yes, and gullible, sure, but not such an amateur. *You're going to get into a fight over a car that's not even yours? Asshole.* All the young men wore different versions of a wrinkled, ill-fitting black suit and the stiff cockiness of their chauffeur's uniforms. All a little more impatient than usual to end their shifts and get home. Which one of them had spoken?

'Nothing, nothing,' the inspector answered nonchalantly, turning his back on the culprit. Then he added: 'And in cream. Cream! I mean, what a great color . . .' he savored every word, '. . . if you're a mamá.'

The bartender's pupils widened. He set the customary glass of water next to their coffees and locked eyes with Alzada. *I know, I know. But I know what I'm doing.* The bartender didn't seem convinced.

Alzada again faced the tables. The driver must have known – at least by now – that he should not engage. Someone who confronted you so openly, so blatantly, so unreasonably, either had a plan or was a lunatic. In either case, not an adversary you wanted to confront. But most people understandably hire drivers for their skills behind the wheel, not for their ability to read anthropological cues.

'A mom?' Estrático asked. He had been quiet until now, and Alzada had begun to wonder if he was going to contribute at all.

The inspector swiveled back to his position facing the bar. 'Yes, you know: a luxury SUV is *ideal* for driving the kids to school. I hear it has also enough room in the back for all the groceries . . .'

'Just what you need to go shopping and then have lunch with the girlfriends,' the deputy added.

A chair scraped the fake terracotta floor. It was outside Alzada's peripheral vision, but he was definitely to his right, closer to Estrático. *Come on, cabrón. You know you want it.*

'And that color goes well with every handbag in your closet.'

'What did you say?' the same voice from the back.

Finally. The policemen looked at each other: they had him. Alzada saw a man in his early thirties rise from his chair. He seemed young for his receding hairline, and had grown his hair out and combed it back to give the appearance of a fuller head. Having been blessed with remarkable hair, Alzada couldn't help but instantly feel superior. The driver's suit didn't help: with a too-loose collar and the too-long sleeves, he looked like an amateur magician.

Now. The police handbook didn't suggest applying physical force as a viable means to obtain information. At least not anymore. On the contrary, the new manuals strongly advised against testosterone-fueled games and instead encouraged persuasion, confusion, or false promises. The truth was the new methods were cumbersome, and not as effective as the old, but they had been put in place for one beautifully logical reason: violence's fallibility. *One can know how a bar brawl starts, but never how it's going to end.* The inspector reconsidered the situation. Estrático looked like he had never lifted a weight; as for his own body, it had evolved confidently into middle age. *What are we getting ourselves into?* Maybe this hadn't been the best idea. He could see it clearly now: the 'conversation' they would have with Galante later. Because there was a hundred-per-cent chance that that conversation would happen, no matter how the situation evolved.

The books never mentioned what to do when someone had no other option. *The Echegaray woman is out of time.* He squared his shoulders.

'You heard me,' Alzada pushed. 'Are you both deaf *and* stupid?'

'At least I'm not sitting at the bar having a cappuccino with my boyfriend,' the driver answered, waving at Estrático.

The chatter stopped abruptly.

Both policemen dropped from their stools. The inspector hadn't been aware of his own imposing presence – even in his sixties– until he detected the driver recoiling ever so slightly, tilting his body sideways.

'Do you want to repeat that?' Alzada said.

The driver took a moment to consider the holsters on both men's hips. Then again, probably everyone at the bar was carrying.

'You heard me, maricón,' he sneered.

ALZADA WAS FAMILIAR – ALL too familiar – with things that happened in the blink of an eye. How many times had he heard people talk about the moment the animal inside takes over, without needing permission, without asking for it? About how time seems to stand still? About how every frame welds together to form a high-definition movie, for ever seared in your retina, a crisp, crystal-clear, indelible memory? Every time someone spoke about that, Alzada had wanted to call them out. He knew reality to be much blurrier. *Take any crime. A simple mugging. Or something more complicated like an abduction.* If things were done right, the whole matter could have a running time of under four minutes. In and out. *Painless.* But Alzada had seen it a million times at the station: witnesses giving exhaustive depictions of an event, only to start mumbling when confronted by another person's testimony of the same situation. Suddenly incapable of remembering crucial details, much to the police's despair – or relief. When this was over, how would the barman tell his side of the story? What would the driver remember? What would Estrático write in the report about their trip to La Favorita?

And yet, this time, Alzada blinked and indeed it was done. He heard it first: the unmistakable sound of four knuckles and no hesitation. A punch well thrown. His body felt it as if it had been his own arm. The hips rotate. The ankles give. The ribs grow forward. The shoulders charge. The thumbs curl under the fists. The hand flies. The motion comes to a halt. Alzada clenched and released his fingers instinctively. He opened his eyes.

He saw the driver on the floor, both his hands before his face.

He saw Estrático's back, tense and ready to meet his opponent.

He heard the deputy's voice, slow and deliberate: 'Who are you calling a faggot?'

Who is *this man?*

THE BAR WAS EMPTY. EVERY single customer had found a perfectly reasonable excuse to promptly leave the premises: a sudden appointment, an urgent phone call from their boss, the unfounded fear of getting a ticket for double parking. Even the man with the bleeding nose had scrambled together a couple of paper napkins from the bar to cover his shame and begrudgingly made his way to the exit. *We got what we needed from you.* The bartender had lost his smile.

The inspector approached Estrático, who was leaning on one of the tables in the back, staring at the floor. *Is he embarrassed?* 'He doesn't like us anymore,' Alzada motioned to the bartender, attempting to cheer the deputy up, and put a shot of something the color of sherry in front of him.

'Sir,' Estrático squirmed.

From a pocket Alzada produced two white pills. 'Have these, too.'

'I don't think I need them,' Estrático said defensively.

Alzada gave him a stern look. 'It's never about *needing* them. They'll just make your day a lot easier. And shorter.'

The deputy instinctively pressed his lips together.

'Estrático, don't be a—'

'About that,' the deputy interrupted, then cleared his throat. 'Inspector.'

'Yes?'

'Sir, I want to present you with my most sincere apologies. My behavior was unbecoming of an officer of the law and—'

Cute, but no.

'Let me stop you before you say something you'll regret,' Alzada interrupted. 'First, raise your arm. It reduces the swelling. I know it's nothing, but you don't want the girlfriend asking uncomfortable questions. I've been there.' He took Estrático's hesitant arm and lifted it. 'Second. With that attitude, someone was – sooner or later – going to break that imbecile's face, and I'm glad it was you. It was a beautiful swing. Did you break his nose?'

'I don't know, sir,' Estrático said.

'Did you hear it crack?'

The deputy looked puzzled.

'In any case, have the shot.'

Estrático obeyed.

From the moment Alzada had been introduced to his new deputy, he had been meaning to get rid of him. Estrático insisted on following rules when Alzada had long abandoned them, he persisted in following a protocol that had them flooded with paperwork. Instead of not disturbing the status quo, he asked the multitude of uncomfortable questions from which other agents shied away. He was green. But one day he would make a decent cop. Alzada decided against telling him. *He'll be insufferable.*

'I would hate to think that I've compromised the outcome of an investigation,' Estrático insisted. 'I don't know what got into me.' *Yes, you do.* 'Also, we're going to get so much shit for this.' *His first swear word!* Alzada could have hugged him.

'What's done is done. Now all we have to do is wait. You'll see.' Alzada circumspectly put his hand on his deputy's shoulder. 'As for Galante, I obviously don't need to explain to you the consequences of your actions. But considering how preoccupied he'll be with the riots, the amount of shit will only be moderate. And it'll be mostly directed at me. The only thing you need to worry about now is explaining how the driver could have possibly been so clumsy as to slip and fall face forward . . .'

The deputy looked at him, his jaw still clenched. 'Maybe he didn't realize the bartender had just mopped the floor?' Then, he burst out laughing. Alzada was caught by surprise: unlike his regular voice, soft and poised, a gravelly roar reverberated through the bar. Estrático laughed and laughed; Alzada couldn't help but join him.

Suddenly, the deputy's phone rang. It took one look at the screen for him to return to his sober tone: 'It's the station.'

'That was fast,' the inspector smiled. *The owner of the car must be more important than I had thought.*

Both attempted to regain composure, rubbing their eyes and drying their tears. A wheezing sound oozed from Alzada's lungs.

'The chief. He wants to see us,' Estrático reported when he hung up.

'Did he say when?'

'Pintadini said his words were: "ten minutes ago".'

'Don't just sit there.' Alzada hurried out. 'He's still our boss! Let's go!'

13
(1981)

'**W**here have you been?'

Paula was in her early thirties and yet, when Joaquín dragged his feet through the kitchen door that late afternoon and saw her, he couldn't help but be reminded of his late mother. It might have been that she was wearing an apron with polka dots similar to the late Mrs. Alzada's, or that she was sitting on a low stool, her back arched in the same shape as he remembered from his own childhood: wide apart, her knees pressed against a dark-blue plastic washbowl to keep it from squirming on the tile, her hands immersed in the suds, nonchalant but careful not to spill. *Yes.* It was their shared light-hearted approach to housework, the energized commitment of someone who performs household duties seemingly without effort.

'I was worried.' Paula didn't look up from the bowl.

'Not even a hello? To your loving husband?' he tried, theatrically, almost immediately hating himself for inhabiting the stereotype he had disdained for so long. 'Don't you want to know how my day went?'

She had obviously heard him struggle with the keys outside but was not going to mention it. No, she was one for long-term strategies: she would first extract the information she needed out of him, then make a scene. In a practiced rhythm, Paula scrubbed the dirt off the hems of the other pair of pants Joaquín liked to wear to the office. She deliberately brushed off an auburn curl dangling on her forehead with the back of her hand, now red and swollen from being soaked in hot water. Experience had taught him to remain quiet until she betrayed her hand, and then – only then, react. Most of the time, this was enough to placate her, but tonight he had a sense it would not be enough. *The danger of marrying a smart woman.*

Only silence.

'I called the station,' Paula finally spoke.

She can't have. She wouldn't . . . would she? He examined her. *No. She can't have.* She had to know about the consequences of her call, especially if her questions didn't match the version of events he had given. *She wouldn't put me in danger just to make a point. No, she can't have.* Still, he decided to go along: 'And? Did the boys tell you I couldn't take the call? I had to close a case. I've been killing myself to get that promotion and so far, Galante is already principal officer and has the upper hand to become commissioner. You see—'

'I don't need to hear it,' she cut him short.

Joaquín fought to keep the balance required to take off his shoes while standing, which was proving to be more difficult than expected since he was also trying to hide his right hand from Paula. Turned to the side, he brought his left foot closer to his upper body and felt his tie tightening around his neck. The more he struggled, the more he resembled a toad – a handsome toad with insolently green eyes, but a toad nonetheless. *I can't do both.* He lowered the leg, momentarily abandoning his endeavor to focus on the conversation. 'Do you really want to know where I was?'

'I don't know, Joaquín. Do I want – do I *need* to know where you were for hours on end? Today of all days? Probably not,' she sighed. 'But at least do me the favor of not insulting my intelligence.'

Paula's strained voice signaled she was losing her patience. Still, she was making an effort to keep her voice down. *For the neighbors.* She hadn't yet gotten her head around the fact that they now lived in a house, separated by trimmed hedges and a small path from the closest family. *You can scream all you want. No one will hear you.*

'I can see you've been drinking,' Paula went on.

'I'm not drunk,' Joaquín replied, too quickly.

'I've also noticed that you've been trying to hide your hand from me since the moment you came in.'

'This?' He raised his hand to reveal his right palm. Hours had gone by and it still hadn't gone back to its normal size. 'It's nothing!' *Too defensive. And too loud, Joaquín. Too loud.* If they had still been living in the apartment they rented when they got married his voice would have echoed against the narrow, tiled walls of the kitchen.

'Shh,' Paula met his eyes with a darting gaze, 'he's asleep.' Joaquín was startled. She had uttered those words as if she'd been practicing every day since his birth, as if it were normal for them to have a toddler sleeping in the next room. She stood up without distancing herself from the bowl. 'Nothing? Really?'

Joaquín shrugged it off and hoped she hadn't noticed him wince in pain. He went back to attempting to take off his shoe, this time using the rim of the kitchen cabinet as a lever, well aware she was watching him closely. His hands grew pale on the edge of the sink. He bit his lip in concentration. He could see Paula out of the corner of his eyes, smiling despite herself at the spectacle. And then, he slipped. The sole left a conspicuous mark on the cream-colored wooden panel.

His shoe was still on. Her smile was gone.

'Joaquín!'

'What?'

Paula joined him by the sink and pointed out the black arc he had drawn on the cabinet. 'It's going to take for ever to get that out.'

'Maybe I *am* a little drunk,' he conceded.

She readjusted her apron and fell back on the stool. 'Come here.' She motioned for him to place his foot on her thigh. 'Come on.' She waved, seeing him hesitate. Cautiously, he agreed.

Joaquín wobbled to keep his balance. Paula held him steady.

'Where were you?' she asked again, while she untied the laces of the left shoe.

'I never know what you want me to say.'

'How about the truth?'

'I was at work.' Then, with renewed confidence, he added: 'Where do you think I was? Of course I was at work.'

Joaquín knew the trick to sounding plausible was to embed the lie within the veneer of a wider truth. Indeed, that morning he had left for the station. *That* wasn't a lie. He smiled at the possibility of having gotten away with it.

'You're telling me that after the night we had, you walked into the station, sat at your desk, and worked for eight hours as if nothing had happened?'

'Yes.'

'On a Saturday.'

'Yes.'

'I've been married to a police officer long enough to know how the tercios work, Joaquín. You don't have to go in until Monday.'

'If you've been married to a police officer for that long, then you know not to ask questions,' Joaquín snarled.

Paula raised her eyebrows. 'If that's your answer, I really don't want to know. The other one.' She motioned for him to give up the right foot. *Why don't you just tell her?* 'There you go,' she offered.

He shifted his weight from one socked foot to the other, hesitant about how to read her. He was going to have to tell her eventually. 'I hit Galante.'

Paula looked up.

'He had it coming,' he insisted. As if his statement didn't require any further context. As if they were characters in a movie in which people actually talked like that. *Do you think you're in* The Maltese Falcon? Joaquín walked over to the fridge, opened it to find milanesas – thankfully a staple in their home – took one, grabbed a chair at the kitchen table. 'Sit with me, will you?'

She agreed.

They remained in silence while he chewed.

After a while, she said: 'You can't tell me you punched Galante and leave it there. I hope it wasn't in the face – Joaquín, tell me it wasn't in the face.' He looked down. 'For heaven's sake, Joaquín. We're godparents to their child!'

'Do you think I didn't know that?' he hissed, and immediately: 'Sorry. I'm sorry. I know.'

Satisfied with his change in tone, Paula said: 'So . . . what exactly happened?'

THAT MORNING, PAULA HAD BARELY put Sorolla to sleep in their bed when Joaquín had announced: 'I'm leaving early so I can talk to Galante as soon as he gets to the station.'

'I'm sorry about this,' his former partner had replied, half asleep in front of his coffee, before immediately suggesting: 'Have you thought about filing a habeas corpus?'

'A habeas corpus?'

'Yes. I thought you were a lawyer.'

'In five years of dictatorship,' Alzada lowered his voice – the office was starting to get crowded, 'have you ever heard of a successful habeas corpus?'

Galante was silent. 'Well. Let me know if I can do anything to help. Because I get the feeling you have something in mind.'

This is the moment. Politics might have created a rift between them: to survive the dictatorship, Joaquín had chosen to bury his head in the proverbial sand; Galante had taken the opposite route, rubbing elbows with the military, and had consequently risen among the ranks to principal officer. But he was right to have trusted his best friend. Joaquín had taken a deep breath and explained.

Horacio had remained impassive, then said: 'You know I would do anything for you. Anything . . .' he repeated.

'Just not this,' Joaquín finished Galante's sentence. Later, whenever he replayed the conversation in his head, he scolded himself for having let him off the hook so easily. For handing him the perfect words on a silver platter.

'Just not this,' Galante echoed, stressing every word. 'Do you know how much trouble I'd be in? The trouble *you'd* get yourself into if you decide to go through with this? How do you know they're not going to disappear you, too? And Paula? Are you really so naive to think they're going to respect you just because you're with the police? You're not untouchable, Joaquín!' After the initial stumble, Galante had now found a rhythm in his speech that comfortably supported his excuses. 'And even if, *even if* – let me tell you, Joaquín, it's a *very* big "if" – you were to make it out of there alive, that is the *end* of your career, Mr. Youngest Inspector in the history of the Policía Federal! You can say goodbye to becoming commissioner, superintendent, or anything you ever dreamed of. Do you think there'll be no consequences? Best-case scenario is that they decide not to fire you – which is improbable, or have you not met our boss, Commissioner Vukić? – and then you're going to be stuck filling out paperwork at your desk for eight hours a day, every day until you retire. And that is best-case scenario!'

Joaquín had taken a second, as if to reflect on Galante's words, but he'd already come to a decision: 'He's my brother, Horacio.'

'Please think about this, Joaco. Don't make the same mistake he did.'

Joaquín was startled by the comment: 'What are you saying . . .?'

'Yes, Joaquín. I'm saying exactly what you think I'm saying. I know it. You know it. For Christ's sake, *he* knew it. He was a boludo. And he had it coming.'

That had been it for Joaquín.

'Did this happen at the station?'

Joaquín nodded.

'But no one saw you.'

Joaquín stared down at his hand.

'Oh, Joaquín . . .' She didn't need to say more. At the very, *very* least, he would be suspended. Most probably, fired. Assaulting a superior officer? On the premises? In front of multiple witnesses? He had left Vukić no option.

'Well, yes.' Then, in an effort to change the subject, as if it had just occurred to him, he asked: 'Did you talk to your father?'

The Alzadas had briefly discussed whether to bother him at all. Granted, Jorge Rodolfo had never been a favorite of Señor Aranguren, to put it mildly. 'If the air we breathe weren't free, if we had to work for it, many people in this world wouldn't exist,' had been his words when Joaquín had first introduced them. *Subtle.* 'Your brother-in-law, God forgive me, Paula, is one of them.' With that, he sentenced the younger Alzada to be a persona non grata in his presence.

'This is different, no?' she had tried to reassure herself mid-dial.

Paula caught him before he went on his daily brisk morning walk. 'You should try it sometime. It's good for your spirit, and your shape,' he had advised Joaquín once, elbowing him a little harder than necessary in his incipient belly. Paula had rolled her eyes. After his daughter had stuttered through her plea, he said: 'I saved him once, you remember?' Of course she did: Jorge had been caught during the raid on a renowned safe house, dropping off fake passports for guerrilleros who wanted to return from exile to fortify the counter-offensive. 'I warned him then, and I warned your husband then, too. They knew it was a one-time thing. I see now that unfortunately the scare didn't last enough to keep him alive.'

Joaquín knew his father-in-law meant well, in his own little fucked-up way: he was trying to protect Paula, and that meant keeping her at a distance from all of this. Whatever the reason, however, it must have hurt her to hear those words coming from her own father. It was hurting Joaquín now. He pictured Paula putting down the phone on the kitchen counter while her father spoke, to listen to him only in the muffled distance. A tinge of bitterness in her voice when she repeated her father's words: 'When are you finally going to understand that you cannot save someone who doesn't want to be saved?'

'YOU KNOW HOW HE IS . . .' Paula settled the matter. She cleared her throat in an effort to keep the tears in her eyes from spilling. 'What do we do now?'

'Querida, I thought you'd never ask,' Joaquín was glad to leave the subject of Señor Aranguren behind. 'I have a contingency plan. Although I have a feeling you might not like the idea . . .'

'Surprise, me, Joaco. Because at this point—'

'Vukić.'

'What do you mean, "Vukić"? *Commissioner* Vukić? Your boss? The most dangerous man in Buenos Aires?'

'He's not *that* scary in the daytime.' A pathetic attempt at cracking a joke. She was right: he *was* terrified of his chief. *For good reason.* The commissioner of the city of Buenos Aires. The dark prince. Nobody moved in the light or in the shadows without him knowing about it. Without asking for permission first. Joaquín swallowed. 'He's agreed to come over later and discuss it.'

'Discuss? Discuss *what* exactly? Wait . . .' she realized, 'you invited him into our home?'

Joaquín rubbed his hands together to remove any trace of breadcrumbs from the milanesa and placed them both face up on the table, hoping they would not shake. 'What was I supposed to do? Ask him to break the law right there, in his office? While he was yelling at me about Galante and I was trying to keep my job? I don't know, Paula. I thought I'd wait until after dinner.'

'How about not asking him at all? Did you consider that?'

'He was going to know sooner or later . . .'

'Of course. As if he's not involved!'

'First of all, you don't know that.'

Paula rolled her eyes.

'Second, fine. What was I supposed to do? We don't have that many options. Or more accurately: this morning we had a couple of semi-decent options and now we have none. And we're running out of time.' Joaquín realized he was trying to convince himself, not her. 'I haven't told him anything yet. I only said I wanted to talk about a private matter. It was he who suggested coming here.'

'A ver . . .' She didn't have an answer. 'You invited him, so you must know what you're doing. I just hope for all our sakes you realize that this is Hernán Cortés level of recklessness.'

Cortés was actually quite successful in his endeavors in the New World. In 1519, upon arrival in what today is Mexico, he burned his ships as 'motivation' for his men. Without the option of returning to Spain, they had undertaken a march into the jungle, and hence begun the conquest of the Aztec Empire. All had ended up turning out well for him. But Joaquín knew Paula was right. *We have definitely burned our ships now.*

'What if you tell him your plan and he reports you? Or better yet, what if he makes you disappear? Or all of us? What if he discovers we have the boy, Joaquín? Did you think about *that*? There's no going back from this.'

He was silent. *There's no going back from this either way.*

'Good. If he's coming,' Paula looked at the kitchen clock – almost eight o'clock – 'he won't be long.' She stood up, took the apron off, and handed it to him. 'You can finish washing your pants. And Joaquín, shower before he arrives, yes?'

She walked out of the kitchen, then leaned back in and pointed at the mark on the cabinet: 'And that better not be there when Commissioner Vukić arrives. I don't care if you have to lick it off.'

14

(2001)

Wednesday, December 19th; 14:10

'**A**s soon as he gets here!'

...The commissioner's booming voice could be heard from the entrance of the precinct. *This is how he sounds three floors down?* Alzada remembered Paula's words when he had first complained about his friend's volatile character. It had been when Galante had become his superior, and Joaquín wasn't able to yell back at him anymore, at least at the station. 'Let him blow up,' Paula had said. 'Imagine a pot filled with milk on the stove. Instead of replying, let him boil over. No matter what he says, don't say a word. *Not a word.* Not even to agree with him. He'll calm down eventually. And then, you're good. Remember: like milk.'

Galante had preferred to install himself amidst the advertising people whose agency occupied the upper part of the building. He had convinced his superiors, arguing it was necessary if not for him – humble servant of the city of Buenos Aires that he was – then for the sake of his visitors. To represent the office he held with 'dignity and decorum'. *His fucking words.*

Alzada reluctantly approached the set of stairs that separated the commoners from the 'executive' floor. Estrático followed. They weren't going to take the elevator: Alzada knew that when the commissioner was in a particularly bad mood, he liked waiting for his underlings in his hallway; once the elevator doors opened on the third floor, he cornered them inside it. The acoustics inside that metal trap made you feel as if someone were yelling directly into your brain.

Here we go. Three flights of reinforced concrete stairs, each double-jointed through a landing. He'd seen so many people fall down these. Some accidentally. Alzada held on to the railing as if he didn't need it. As they climbed, the inspector broke into a sweat. He never got to do anything remotely physical anymore. Today, between the rush of the morgue and the excitement at the bar, he'd got a long-lost adrenaline boost that almost made him miss the days before he was on perpetual desk duty. Alzada pushed the emergency exit to the third floor.

'Where is that asshole?' Galante wouldn't fire him so close to his retirement, would he?

The commissioner had left his door ajar. A beam of daylight escaped from his office and cut the darkness of the interior hallway like a saber. Estrático walked past him. The deputy hadn't overtaken him until then – probably out of deference, since he seemed completely unfazed by the climb. Galante was not one to favor an open-door policy – instead he travelled downstairs whenever he felt the urge to make his opinions heard – so it was highly likely Estrático had never been up here until this very moment. *He must be terrified. We've never been called into such a 'meeting', have we?* Alzada decided to enter first.

'I'm here, chief,' he began.

The office looked just as grand as he remembered. Unlike the offices on the lower floors, this space was completely free of clutter: no boxes, no mountains of paper. A gargantuan ebony desk in the middle of the room. On it, a single file lay unperturbed on the desk, the dark-blue leather top underneath accentuating the folder's timid apple green hue. Almost chirurgical. Two idle paperweights completed the décor: on the left, a marbled sphere the size of a fist, on the right, a bronze statuette which had accompanied Galante since the beginning of his career. Its shape looked vaguely anthropomorphic – at least it had a head, a core, and what could be interpreted as limbs – but it lacked human proportions. The inspector had never dared ask about it.

'I'm here, chief,' the commissioner mocked him. '"*I'm here*"?'

Galante was wearing a prim, starched shirt. *Impeccable as ever.*

'Where were you when you were *actually* supposed to be here? Here at the precinct is where you should have been all along. What do I write departmental guidelines for, if you're not going to respect them?' It was common knowledge Pintadini, Galante's right hand slash lapdog, was the author. The commissioner couldn't possibly have been bothered to use such politically correct terms as 'dissuasion techniques to resolve disturbances'; his version would have been something closer to 'Beat the shit out of those motherfuckers, don't leave a mark.'

'When I said, "stay under the radar", what did you think I meant? Are you the only officer in the force who doesn't know we're spread thin – *very* thin – because of the riots? Are you not aware that I had to send every single man I have out there? That I've had to prioritize the urgent calls to the point that we're currently no longer acting against property damage? I thought I was doing you a favor, keeping you out of all of this. Just sit at your desk in case there was an emergency,' Galante continued. 'But no. You couldn't even do that. The *great* Inspector Alzada,' the chief announced him like he would a world-renowned magician, 'the great Inspector Alzada is beyond good and evil. Does he feel like taking on a silly little dossier that isn't even a case? He wastes his time and the department's instead of solving one of the *actual* cases sitting on his desk. Is he having a bad day and wants to punch someone in the face? He goes downtown and does exactly that!' Galante slammed the table with both hands, causing the marble ball to vibrate in its elegant pod and threaten to roll over the edge.

Out of the corner of his eye, Alzada saw Estrático hiding his hands behind his back. 'In my defense—' the inspector began.

'No, you don't get a defense! You don't deserve a defense, Joaquín.' To this day, the commissioner was the only person in the precinct to call the inspector by his first name. He lowered his voice and assumed a tone of familiarity, a nostalgic smile on his meaty face. 'I consider you a man who knows how to conduct himself, especially when executive decisions need to be made. And I expect you to set an example for the younger ones.' Alzada nodded. *That's why you assigned me a babysitter.* 'This situation might prove too much for a novice such as this one, but not you, Joaquín. We have been through much worse than this, don't you remember? And we managed.'

The inspector drew a painful smirk. *All too well.* By the time they had turned thirty, Alzada and Galante had lived through four successful coups d'états and half a dozen failed ones. How had they learned to be policemen in that time? From the moment they had stepped out of the academy, they had instantly been caught between two belligerent sides. The names had evolved, but the essence had remained unchanged: on the one hand, always, the military government with its hard-line approach to keeping order. For them, any police officer who refused to participate in their dirty work was judged on a scale from 'weak' to 'enemy of the state'. In the opposite trench sat different iterations of the same underground guerrilla: to them, the police was on the oppressive regime's side, and hence deserved to be the target of their endless attacks. Both rookies had navigated those treacherous waters as graciously as their limited experience had allowed. *I didn't manage at all.* Alzada had shown a well-developed survival instinct, which he had used to remain out of the spotlight. It was Galante who had managed. More than managed, he had thrived: his former partner had meteorically risen to both commissioner of one of the hottest precincts in the city and liaison to the Ministry of Defense. He was currently one step from becoming General Commissioner of the Argentinian Federal Police.

'Today my complete focus should have been on the revolution that is about to be ignited a mere few blocks from here, and how the police as an institution will answer to protect its citizens. But instead, let me tell you what happened to me: I'm sitting at La Biela, enjoying my huevos gramajos; I have half an hour to unwind before a conference call with Presidente De la Rúa, in which he might finally deign to give us either concrete instructions or carte blanche on how to handle the situation.' *Carte blanche sounds nice. More like a meringue dessert than the prelude to indiscriminate violence.* 'Which I hope he does sooner than later because they are burning the palm trees in the garden in front of the Casa Rosada. It's not looking pretty.' *He fears what will come with nightfall.* 'Now, returning to the point: I receive a phone call. A fucking phone call, Joaquín. You should thank God I was alone. Telling me that one of my men has punched Congressman Pantera's driver in the face!' *Bingo.* 'Do you happen to know who Congressman Pantera is, Joaquín?' Galante didn't leave him time to respond. 'The correct answer is: it doesn't matter! There are two hundred and fifty-seven freshly appointed idiots sitting in Congress and I don't give a fuck about any of them! What I *do* give a fuck about is getting a phone call from the Minister of Industry – the *minister*, Joaquín – complaining about how his friend's driver has a broken nose, courtesy of a police officer. A police officer!' Galante regained his composure: 'So I ask you, and by this I don't mean to violate the presumption of your innocence, since I know you to be a serene, responsible, cool-headed man who would *never* dare commit such an imprudence. But just in case: would you happen to know *anything* about this?'

The inspector silently hoped Estrático would have the good sense to avoid eye contact with the irate wild animal currently sitting across the desk. As for him, he fixed his gaze on the statuette. *Is it a titan?*

132

'Do you have *any* idea how this makes me look, Joaquín? Oh, excuse me. I forgot,' Galante faked deference. 'You don't give a flying fuck about any of that shit. You're a free spirit. You don't answer to anyone. I mean. You answer to me, theoretically – sporadically, I might add – but we both know you basically do whatever the fuck you want. And that's okay by me. It's been our particular agreement for I don't know how long now.' *Nineteen years.* 'You sit downstairs, you solve cases, you keep out of trouble. You. Keep. Out. Of. Trouble. Now you can't even do that? How difficult can it be? Joder, Joaquín.' Galante paused and considered his old friend. 'No wonder you got stuck being an inspector.'

They both knew that wasn't true. But Galante had to tell himself a version of events that would let him sleep at night. *Tell a lie a thousand times . . .* Alzada smiled at the reference.

'What the fuck are you smiling at, Joaquín?' the commissioner asked. Alzada was smart enough to stay silent. 'I think I can say I know you well enough. I'm serious. Not *one* more mistake. I'm not going to give you the pleasure of firing you. You would love that, wouldn't you? "Alzada the misunderstood." I warn you: don't make me do it. Don't make me do it, because I will! Do you hear me, Alzada?'

Alzada looked up. Galante had never called him that before.

The commissioner seemed suddenly exhausted; he held his chest as if to calm his own heartbeat. 'In conclusion, because believe it or not I have other things to do. I'm going to blame your actions on the fact that "exceptional circumstances", blah, blah, blah. I want whatever nonsense is still pending closed before you leave for the day. You're going to write the report—'

'I have Estrático for that,' Alzada interrupted.

'No. *You* will do it. And you will sign it, too.'

Signing the document was the ultimate punishment: it would prevent Alzada from making later claims against the report. How could he object to something he himself had signed? Galante handed Alzada the file.

'Actually, strike that. I want *two* reports. One on the "incident" at La Favorita, so I can present the image that I still maintain *some* degree of control over my station . . .'

'Yes, sir,' Alzada replied.

A feeble something from Estrático behind him.

'You,' Galante motioned to the deputy. 'I'm not going to dignify your behavior with a comment. I pair you up so you're a good influence on him, and this is the result?' *I knew it.* 'And about that Echegaray woman. Because you had to drop a second hot potato in my lap today, no?' Both knew that accusation to be unfair: if he hadn't paid special attention to the Echegaray case, he would be in Galante's office being screamed at for the exact opposite reason. *Heads you win, tails I lose.* As if he had read his mind, Galante switched gears: 'Do we know why they came in, instead of letting their private security handle this matter?'

'I think they're disappointed with them.'

'Disappointed.'

'Yes, sir. She slipped her detail.'

'Ah, I see. And why did they come in through you and not one of their contacts?' Was Galante jealous that it wasn't him rubbing elbows with the Echegarays? *You could have had them all to yourself if only you'd been in the office.* The commissioner frowned. 'In any case, those people are not going to rest until they have an answer. Or until the woman returns, whichever comes first. So, in the meantime, you're going to give me all that you have on her, all the notes from the interview. This isn't even your department. I want something that I can hand over to Flores when he comes in on Monday in case that woman hasn't reappeared by then.' He shifted into a perfunctory tone: 'I want them both to be short. I want them to be typed. And I want them to be done before you leave for the day.'

'Will that be all, sir?'

'No, Joaquín. That will *not* be all. Don't you dare go anywhere near a congressman, or driver of a congressman, or grandmother of a congressman—'

'But, sir. We *know* that he's involved in the Echegaray disappearance.'

'I'm going to pretend I didn't hear that. There *is* no disappearance. Do we understand each other?'

'Yes.' Alzada was suddenly cold.

'No. Tell me you understand.'

Alzada sat up. 'I understand, sir.'

'Now get out of my office.' The commissioner crossed his arms to signal he was done. 'Both of you.'

Estrático couldn't have walked faster towards the door.

'Joaquín,' Galante said casually, as if the idea had just occurred to him, 'stay for a moment.'

Alzada, who was already one step out of the room, turned and feigned surprise. He saw Galante open a drawer and pull out a bottle of Glenlivet and two glasses.

'There are whole weeks when we don't cross paths, and today I see you twice? We need to drink to that.' *He did see me this morning, even with his back turned.*

'Do you have time for this?' Alzada shot back. He knew *he* didn't: if he had to write the report, he'd be late for lunch.

Galante looked at his wrist; there was no watch. 'Sure.'

Alzada approached, still hesitant, and sat across from him. 'So,' he said, as he took the first sip of scotch, 'is he going to declare it?'

Galante sipped his in silence. 'I don't know, Joaquín. I really don't know. But even if he does, I think we can agree that declaring the state of siege isn't going to be the silver bullet. Not anymore. Because sure, it would have been useful – a couple of days ago. This morning, perhaps. But not now. How do we enforce a curfew now? The reports we are getting on the hour speak of thousands and thousands on the streets. These parasites have taken the city.'

Alzada swallowed. *Parasites.* That's what the subversives had been called twenty-five years ago, too. 'Well, it better be over soon because you look like shit, Horacio. Remember the days when you were the pretty one?'

The inspector wore his hair in proud silver tufts, while the commissioner was completely bald. Fortunately, and unlike many men in the same predicament, he had chosen to shave his head the minute his hairline had receded to the point of no return.

'Thank you, Joaco.' Galante smiled. 'With friends like these . . . But you're right. I haven't slept in weeks.'

'Some habits die hard.'

Galante chuckled half-heartedly. Since Alzada could remember, his partner had been a consistent insomniac. The endless sleepless hours had finally taken their toll: the image of the Señor Comisario should have been one of prestige and power in his own natural habitat. Instead, it was heartbreaking. His old friend was stooped over his desk, the weight of age and responsibility heavy on his shoulders. Galante rubbed his irritated eyes and combed through his non-existent mane. *The shadow of a man.*

'Listen. About before,' Galante's tone sobered. 'You know I have very little room for maneuver. I get a call from two different – two *very* high-up – officials, who tell me to overlook a certain situation. What options do I have?'

'I understand.' *I understand how you got to be commissioner, and I the oldest inspector in the force.*

'Seriously. You know how it is.' Alzada was silent and scratched his incipient beard. 'And then your deputy was present . . . I couldn't possibly make an exception in front of him. It's just that—' Galante searched for the word.

'Upstairs . . .' Alzada pointed at the ceiling, employing the mocking gesture people in the lower floors used to refer to their superiors. The commissioner too had once been downstairs. With him.

'Yes,' Galante smiled, relieved. 'Apparently now *I'm* upstairs. Just write the Echegaray report so I have something to show, and get out of here safely, ¿sí?'

Alzada stood.

'Are you going home for lunch?' Galante said.

'I'm going to try . . .'

'There should be no problem in that direction. Say hello to Paula and Sorolla for me. He must be what now, twenty-two?'

ELOÍSA DÍAZ

'Twenty-three.'

Galante smiled. 'We should get together sometime, with the boys. Maybe now over the summer?'

'Yes.' Alzada felt a twinge in his side. He knew it would never happen.

15
(2001)

'You were right!' Estrático blurted out as soon as Alzada entered his office.

The inspector motioned the deputy to be silent until he closed the door: he knew hallway acoustics to be treacherous.

'Now,' Alzada indicated he was safe to speak.

'He just handed us the name on a silver platter!' Estrático's fear of reprimand had vanished. 'All that we have to do now is find Congressman Pantera and—'

'And nothing,' Alzada interrupted brusquely. 'We don't "have to" anything. Perhaps you weren't in the same room as me a moment ago. Did you not hear when Galante said to forget about the congressman? Not only to forget, but to actively overwrite the connection? Handing over a clean dossier is the only thing we have to do.'

'But what about—'

'I don't think you understand.' Alzada dropped the file on his desk. *Fuck.* His plan, as eccentric as it might have seemed, had worked. How he hated to be right – sometimes. *It worked.* The only thing he hadn't anticipated was how important the 'mystery man' would be. Someone who in such short order can conjure up the police chief of Buenos Aires? *This is not good.* If Pantera had an address book that allowed him to almost instantly convince the police to stay away from the matter, what else was he capable of? His hand would not hesitate to reach out and certainly sway a prosecutor, indispose a witness, dissuade a judge. *There are powers in this country you don't want to mess with.* The responsible thing was to leave this alone. 'We're writing this report. Or should I say, *you* are writing the report. No matter what Galante said.'

'Of course, sir.' Estrático's wooden chair in the corner complained when he sat back down.

Where had the deputy's sudden desire to go against a superior's orders come from? Alzada refused to admit that he was actually proud of him for it. *Don't worry, Estrático. There will be other times to fight the system.* 'And remember: nothing extravagant. I want to go home for lunch eventually.'

'Of course, sir.'

'Good,' Alzada smirked. 'How is the report on the incident at La Favorita?'

Estrático stood and handed it to him. *Already?*

'This is fine,' Alzada concluded after a cursory glance. *What a damn shame about Estrático's pristine writing. If I don't type it up, the chief will know immediately. Not that he's going to pay any attention to it.* 'Get to the other one.'

Alzada looked past the deputy and into the common area. Through the horizontal stripes of the blinds, he assessed the deserted landscape: everybody was gone. *Not quite.* One desolate desk lamp had been kept on in a corner cubicle, a heron under which two officers smoked. The tender sub-machine gun sound of the telex, burning with news from the outside, drowned out their conversation. Revolution-proof technology. What time could it be? It was certainly much too early to catch another glimpse of la Dolores. From where he sat, the inspector didn't have a clear line of sight over the entrance, but he could see the security guard standing up from his rickety post. Basilio's routine was as reliable as Immanuel Kant's: just as the inhabitants of Königsberg had been able to set their clocks by the philosopher's daily walks, the guard closing up front meant it was 14.30 sharp. The remainder of his shift he spent inside, looking at the ceiling; all part of a program to make the force more efficient. The commissioner had decided that since their station stood in a district littered with other law enforcement options, the afternoons would be dedicated strictly to inside business. Like a bank, only less ethical. Walk-ins had to pick another station. But to enforce that policy today, with most of its officers patrolling the streets? Either Galante had forgotten about this particular snag – unlikely – or he knew they were declaring the state of siege. *He's waiting for the cavalry. Literally.*

Alzada considered catching up with Basilio and crossing the street to the nearest café. Here they were, on what could become a crucial moment in Argentinian history, sitting inside. *Some things you want to miss out on.*

'Sir?' Estrático's question brought him back. 'I think I have an idea.'

'You "think"?'

'I do, sir.'

'Be so kind as to enlighten me, Estrático.'

'You might not like it, sir.' Estrático rose to his feet, unsure.

'I don't bite, Estrático.'

The deputy approached. 'This morning you instructed me to take a complete inventory of the existing Jane Doe profiles in Greater Buenos Aires.'

Alzada had only a vague recollection of the never-ending list of orders with which he peppered the deputy's days. He certainly hadn't expected him to follow through on such a useless task – and so diligently, too.

'There are at least a dozen who could fit Norma Echegaray's physical description.' The deputy paused. 'The woman from this morning among them.'

Now *I remember*. 'Forgive me, Estrático. I was under the impression we'd already settled this matter.'

'Yes, sir.'

Alzada watched the deputy gather the courage to continue.

'But that was this morning, and this is now.' Estrático took a little step closer. 'This morning we didn't know there was something that wasn't sitting right about the Norma Echegaray situation. I went with a hunch and I should have known better. But now we *do* know.'

'I hate to repeat myself, but it appears you're experiencing considerable trouble understanding the instruction we've been given . . .'

'I've understood, sir.' Estrático cleared his throat. 'We know Pantera had something to do with it. I'm not saying that they are the same woman. I'm saying they *could* be . . . for the investigation's sake. It's the perfect—'

Alzada raised his eyebrows.

'It's a *convenient* way of continuing with this line of inquiry. Otherwise we'll never be able to catch him. Even if indeed he's behind it, we know for certain that a man so powerful will have been careful. No matter how hard we try, we'll never be able to tie him to it. And, even if we managed to link them, if we don't find her, either dead or alive, the most we'll be able to charge him with – if anything – will be illegal imprisonment. That's six months to three years . . . for taking a life. We need a body.'

He's right about this last part. Without a body there would be no conviction.

'Wait until you hear about how beautifully they match.'

'"Beautifully", now?'

'Yes, sir.'

Alzada's interest was piqued. 'Fine, let's have it.'

'The timeline fits. The doorman's testimony fits.' *As if that poor bastard would testify.* 'The distance between abduction site and where she was found falls within a viable radius. If you allowed it, *of course*, we could say Norma Echegaray "woke up" this morning in a dumpster. We'd have one fewer Jane Doe case, and one reasonable report to satisfy the Echegarays and get started on Pantera.'

Nothing about this is reasonable.

Alzada picked up the picture that Mrs. Echegaray had given them that morning. It was uncanny how much they looked alike. Could it be that the girl with the golden future had ended up in the trash – literally – behind the municipal morgue? Was it too wide a leap? After all, they were talking about Norma Fucking Echegaray. No, it wasn't possible.

Then again, Alzada knew reality to be often stranger than fiction. There was an example of it in his own family: Jorge, the unrepentant revolucionario, had not started out on that path. On the contrary, he had spent a large part of his formative years reading the very reactionary Heidegger, before deciding to shape his life – and his facial hair – in the image of the Che. It had been Joaquín who during Onganía's dictatorship had become active in student politics and shown support to the ongoing revolutionary processes in other Latin American countries. It had been Joaquín who had invited his teenage brother to one of his union meetings at the Colegio Nacional. It had been Joaquín who had forged Jorge's ID so he could join the group in spite of his young age. It had been Joaquín who had suggested he travel with him to a farm in the Pampa on the pretext of a conference on community organization strategies. There, they had learned how to shoot and, more importantly, duck. Enter the irony: the exact moment Joaquín's political fervor had faded – disillusioned with the turn to indiscriminate violence – the younger Alzada seemed to have found his calling. His experiences as a teacher in the villas had cemented a conviction that only through said violence might one affect change; he had delved deeper and deeper into the clandestine branch of the grassroots movement. The teacher turned revolutionary; the rebel turned cop.

Why can't these two women be a match?

No, IT WAS CERTAINLY NOT reasonable, but it could be made to fit. The physical resemblance, the plausible timeline . . . *We don't need it to be true, we only need it to* look *true.* In all probability, Norma Echegaray was already dead. What if under the gravestone at the family mausoleum in Recoleta lay a godforsaken drug addict? Alzada frowned. *It's a good solution.* Perhaps a little too cynical, even for his taste.

'Sir?' The deputy waited like a dog who had obeyed the command to stay, but couldn't wait to burst into movement.

'Yes. Give me a second.'

Then there were the practical considerations of the plan. The Echegarays *would* be a problem. That she had been found like that? Even with the chaos as an excuse, they wouldn't accept it. *Although, if we gave them a hypothesis supported by evidence . . .* A drug problem. Clichéd, definitely; disgusting, most certainly. But also, plausible. And plausible was what they needed.

Alzada knew they had to be careful: the case needed to be watertight. Not only for the high-profile nature of the victim, but for the inquisitive nature of her sister. She would protest when the deputy called her in to explain the cause of Norma's erratic behavior and subsequent disappearance. She would not acquiesce and take the lab report at face value. Tomorrow – no matter if army tanks sprawled over the streets of Buenos Aires and a new order was established tonight – tomorrow, like every Thursday at 15.30 for decades, the Madres would be at the Plaza de Mayo. *They never give up.* She would order an independent tox report. She would want to see the body. Most people didn't: they were just happy they had one to bury. But *she* would. *Fortunately, there are ways around that, too.*

They would need Petacchi. It wouldn't be the first time the coroner had been approached for that purpose. Alzada would have to convince him to introduce the necessary modifications to the report he was writing, incorporate traces of recreational drugs in the blood to reflect the new situation, make any other needed alterations for the profiles to match. 'How come?' Petacchi would inquire. *Obedient, but nosy.* The inspector would then answer something along the lines of: 'Someone came in and asked about a woman with the exact same description. We just need a little nudge to make it easier for the family. Do you understand what I'm trying to say?' 'Yes, sir,' Elías would reply. *Nosy, but obedient.* Alzada would finish with a cheerful comment, to lighten the mood: 'We found a match. Can you believe our luck?' The inspector shuffled around the folder on his desk. *Luck has nothing to do with this.*

'And this would mean . . .' Alzada wanted Estrático to say it out loud.

'Yes,' the deputy confirmed. 'This would mean we could still go after Pantera.'

Alzada considered Estrático. *Look at him, losing his moral compass.* He wondered if his young colleague had fully understood the consequences of that action. Two women would be sentenced by way of one blue ballpoint pen in the deputy's right hand. One woman would never be searched for; another would never be found. A man would be convicted for a crime he didn't commit. *So intent on doing 'justice' you haven't realized what just happened.* Without notice, without ceremony, without fanfare. Only one tiny detail made to fit a narrative. *That's how it starts.*

Alzada pressed further. 'Pantera would pay for something he hasn't done.'

'Well . . . technically, yes. He would "pay" for the wrong woman. It would balance the scales of justice, so to speak.' Estrático cleared his throat. 'And I know what you might be thinking . . .' *Doubtful.* 'This isn't what justice ought to sound like – short. Clean. Rhythmical.'

That was *exactly* how justice ought to be: a decent solution to a grim situation.

The plan had its glitches. For starters, there was Galante. *He's not going to like this.* The commissioner would lose the favor of the minister, but score major points with an important family. Where would that leave him in the equilibrium of dark forces of Buenos Aires? Hard to tell.

Then, Pantera. The man who seemed twice untouchable. First, because as a congressman he enjoyed parliamentary immunity: they wouldn't be able to question him or initiate an investigation without passing it through a vote in Congress – and chances were low to non-existent that they would convene an extraordinary meeting to throw one of their own to the wolves. If that weren't obstacle enough, they were talking about a man who hadn't hesitated to make an Echegaray disappear. An Echegaray. Had he not known who she was? No, they knew each other: that was why she had gotten in the car. Still, he must have known that there would be consequences. What sense of complete impunity he must have felt, to do something like this? Or perhaps it hadn't been premeditated. But still, that was one hell of a risk to take in the spur of the moment; what could have triggered him? What would make a probable future contender for the presidency lose his mind like that? 'Cherchez la femme', *as they say in all the old mysteries.*

'Is he handsome?'

'Sir?'

'Is he handsome, Estrático? Is Congressman Pantera hot, or is he one of those seventy-five-year-old mummies who pass out in their leather armchairs during parliament sessions?'

'He's one of the younger ones . . . Statistically I guess—'

'Do you not have eyes? Come on, Estrático.'

'Well, I guess . . . Yes, one could say that he's hot. But I don't follow—'

'Thank you.'

An affair. They had an affair. They had been together.

But then why would he have his lover killed? *Occam's razor: the simplest hypothesis is the correct one.* She had gotten pregnant. From there, all very Greek tragedy; the dishonor to the family, the end of a promising career, the inevitable question of 'what do we do'. Then, the inevitable answer to the inevitable question.

'Sir?'

'Estrático, we'll never finish if you keep interrupting me.'

If Pantera has the power to disappear an Echegaray, what will he do to us? Two little policemen would certainly not be an obstacle. He would fight them tooth and nail, like a cornered cat. He would not hesitate. He would squash them like little flies. Alzada noticed his hands shaking. Not even the commissioner would be able to protect them.

'Estrático,' Alzada finally said, 'we better let this one go.'

The deputy's face dropped. *Where have I seen that disappointed face before? Oh yes: every night at dinner with Sorolla.* 'How can you not care?' was his nephew's perennial accusation. Care had nothing to do with it, or maybe that was exactly it. *All I do is care.*

148

'It's not a bad idea, Estrático. Not a bad idea at all . . . Anyway, we might have done enough for today, don't you think? I'm sure she'll be back in no time.' This last part more for himself than for the deputy.

'But sir—' Estrático began to object.

'Look,' Alzada said, 'I've thought this through. And it's not my favorite solution either, but it will have to do. There are things that are bigger than us, and this is one of them. On Monday, this will be Flores' problem.'

Quarter to three. Normally, if he hadn't left the station by two, he would have called Paula to say he would be late for lunch. He picked up the phone. The answering machine again. 'Paula, it's me. I'm still here. I know what you're thinking. I'm late for lunch. Galante has me writing this report. Yes. I'll be there as soon as I'm done, yes? Is Sorolla home with you? I'll see you in a while. Chau.' He hung up, tired.

Estrático was scribbling away. Tomorrow Alzada would tell him to clean out the entire office. No wonder they couldn't find anything in this mess. And this notwithstanding he was probably the only cop who had no personal effects whatsoever in his office. *We have time for a quick one.* Alzada opened the key drawer of his desk, pulled out his flask and offered it to the deputy: 'A sip?'

Estrático was visibly torn. His conscience surely reminding him of the rules regarding drinking on duty, although of course the strict prohibition was waived for the regulation glass of wine with lunch. But the ban was still there. And Estrático was a lover of rules. On the other hand, did he not want to become the first deputy to share a drink with the elusive Alzada?

'I know of someone who died holding a flask in the air like this.'

'Of course.' Estrático hurried to grab it and took a sip without letting his lips touch the rim. Further surprise in the deputy's eyes.

Alzada smiled without teeth. Out of all the types of alcohol Estrático might have expected to encounter, Pedro Ximénez was the least probable. An intense dessert sherry from Southern Spain that hijacked the taste buds with the insistent sweetness of molasses. The only alcohol Paula ever indulged in.

'Can I ask you a question, sir?'

'Do you mean another one?'

'Yes, sir,' Estrático smiled and handed back the flask.

Alzada drank. He pictured Congressman Pantera at his mansion, desperate to solve the problem of a lover turned inconvenient. He pictured Norma getting into the car, trusting the driver and ready to be whisked off. He pictured the driver, hesitant to finish the job. All figments of his imagination.

'I didn't know you had a son, sir.'

'He's not my son,' came Alzada's immediate reply.

'Oh, I'm sorry, sir.'

'No need to apologize, Estrático. It's a common mistake—' Alzada was about to enter into an elaborate explanation when the radio switched from music to the news. *Shit. It's three.* 'Now I really need to go,' he said, locking the flask back into the drawer. 'You know what you have to do, no? Call Petacchi for the photos and the tox report and complete the dossier. When I get back from lunch, we can have a quiet conversation, yes?'

'Of course, sir.'

'And leave it on Flores' desk when you're done. I don't want to see that file ever again.'

16

(2001)

Wednesday, December 19th; 15:45

The house was dark. The house was quiet. It had been built with Buenos Aires temperatures in mind. The narrow white hallway and stone floors meant to keep the humid heatwaves under control. Many a summer siesta they had slept with Sorolla lying directly on the marble in a pillow fort. This quiet was strange. Coming home for lunch normally meant Alzada was greeted by the smell of a delicious meal, the sound of Paula humming a song that was hard to recognize, and Sorolla watching the news in the background. Today, he could hear the refrigerator whirr. The inspector retraced his steps to the entrance to switch on the light. The red-and-white checkered oilcloth on the table lay bare. A cold shudder went down his back.

¿Dónde está Paula?

Alzada felt his knees weaken. He checked his phone. Nothing. He leant with both hands on the kitchen counter. Cool relief for his palms. Then he saw a note in Paula's meticulous handwriting: 'We're going to therapy. We love you, P. & S.' *Today is* – mierda – *Wednesday.* Every Wednesday Sorolla had a regular appointment with Dr Emmerich, a renowned therapist. One would think that at twenty-three Sorolla might perhaps be embarrassed by the fact, or at least wish to go alone. But at his express request Paula and Joaquín walked him there. *Every single week. How could I have forgotten?* It had turned into a family tradition, the one thing in their increasingly insane lives that never budged. First, an early lunch, which he had distractedly missed. Then a stroll to the doctor's office. He would chat with Paula until Sorolla's appointment was over and, on their way back, the three would stop for ice cream at Chungo. *Joaquín, Joaquín . . .* He had been so distracted by another family's tragedy that he had neglected his own.

Alzada looked at his watch. 15.47. He could still make it. What was he going to eat, though? On the fridge he found a second note. As always, Paula was one step ahead of him. 'These are for you.' On the top shelf, what he assumed must be a mountain of milanesas. Sorolla's favorite. He reached down to grab a beer only to notice another note on one of the Quilmes bottles. 'Only one . . .' *No beer, then.* He didn't have time for it anyhow. If he drove out this minute, and infringed all existing traffic rules, he could catch up with them just as they arrived. But that meant he would have to skip lunch. Decisions, decisions, decisions. With two expert fingers, he snatched a breaded steak from underneath the complicated topography of the tin foil. *Back to the car.*

Alzada turned the corner and found Paula and Sorolla standing outside the doctor's office. From afar his nephew looked like the young man the inspector had seen that morning. He was wearing the same denim jacket, without the backpack. *He could have dropped it off when he went home for lunch.*

'I have to go in now,' Sorolla said, with his usual terseness.

'Already?'

Paula impassively pointed at the face of her watch. 'It's four ten.'

'*Eight* past four.'

'Fine, Joaquín. Eight past four.'

'Thank you for waiting,' Alzada said. *How did they get here, and on time?*

'Okay. I'll see you later.'

Sorolla disappeared into the building.

'I see,' Paula brushed his collar once they were alone, 'that you have breadcrumbs on your suit. I assume you realized you were late, so you decided you had time for a milanesa?'

Alzada was not going to make matters worse by confessing he had eaten in the car – which they had agreed never to do – and not one but two milanesas. He decided to play dumb: like a teenager feigning sobriety upon his arrival home after a night out, he stood as still as he could manage.

She eyed him. 'Or was it two?'

Alzada knew denial would hardly help his cause. 'No,' he said, like a hiccup. After a moment, he added: 'Did you consider that today might not have been the best day for this? Nothing would happen if he skipped *one* Wednesday.'

'Not everyone likes to suffer in silence . . . He needs it.'

Don't I know it. That was the only reason for the enormous sacrifice this weekly trip meant to their finances.

'I realize it's a big ask, that you split your hours and come join us for lunch every day.'

'They allow it.'

'That's not what I mean. You might not see eye to eye on politics and perhaps that's why lately things have been tense between you two, but he still likes you to come. He appreciates the effort. Especially on Wednesdays.'

Who would have thought it?

'You were once political, too. Or has your memory started to fail you, viejo?'

'It's not that,' Alzada replied, wondering what it really was. 'I'm swamped at work and yes, it might have slipped my mind that today was Wednesday. And yes, I was hungry. And yes, I grabbed a milanesa for the road – so sue me,' he snarled, then, surprised by his overreaction, immediately modulated to a softer: 'I'm here now, aren't I?'

'Yes.' Paula took a long breath. 'Yes, you are. Let's walk.'

'Let's.'

'Joaco, before I forget . . .' she said as they made their way down a quiet, residential street. Why couldn't *he* have become a psychologist? These people were loaded. *It requires the exact same skill set as my job. Minus the violence.* They could have resided in a neighborhood such as this one, with tree-lined streets instead of toppled-over cars. *We can't be very far from where Norma lived. Lives.* 'Orestes called.'

'Who?'

'Orestes.'

'It will come to me,' he hesitated.

'Your deputy?'

'Oh, he's not *my* deputy,' Alzada waved the idea off. 'He's only been "assigned" to me temporarily, under the guise of helping me with the workload. In deference to my "old age", I suppose. The truth is that *someone*,' he pointed to the sky – he rarely said Galante's name out loud anymore, 'must feel at least a tinge of guilt for not letting me retire and on top of that having me in charge of a disappearance.'

Paula opened her eyes wide but remained silent. *Shit.* He had always been so careful to conceal his assignments from her whenever they were particularly gruesome.

'In any case,' Alzada coughed, 'I'll be glad to return him as soon as the situation goes back to normal. He's of no help. At all. More importantly,' he snickered, 'his parents named him Orestes.'

'That doesn't change the fact that he called me.' Paula looked hurt.

'He called *you*? But how does he—'

'How does he what, Joaquín?'

'I just can't believe that boludo called *you*. Is nothing sacred anymore?' *Why does he have your phone number?*

'Are you done?'

'I don't know,' Alzada growled. 'What did he want?'

'To talk to you,' she said matter-of-factly. 'He said you wouldn't answer your phone.'

'I don't understand. I—' Alzada reached for his jacket's inside pocket. 'I – I must have left it at home. I was in such a hurry.'

'You know they say haste is only for delinquents and bad toreros,' Paula teased him.

Alzada frowned. 'Did he say anything else?'

'He said to tell you the tox report you ordered this morning was clean. A glass or two of wine with dinner. Wait . . . and one little anomaly: high levels of CHG.'

'HCG?'

'Yes, that. What is it?'

'Human chorionic gonadotropin,' Alzada huffed. *She was pregnant.*

'Joaquín . . .'

'Oh, it's a hormone. A pretty solid indicator of pregnancy.'

'Not good for your case, I assume?'

'It's not that exactly.'

They were reaching the limits of their tacit agreement; normally he remained elliptical about the details of his work; Paula was cautious never to pry further than polite small talk. No. They were not going to have a conversation about his job, and especially not one about this sort of case. It would blow open a door Alzada wasn't sure they would be able to close ever again. A door that would lead right to how Sorolla had come to live with them, and why they were right here, waiting for him to come out of therapy. And yet, he was tired. The shrapnel of all the secrets that had accumulated over forty years of marriage had started to weigh on him. If only there was a way to expose it all without disturbing their delicate balance. An offering at the altar of the god of coexistence.

'It's this woman who has . . .' Alzada stumbled over the word, 'disappeared.'

'I see. And she's pregnant? But if you can't find her then how can you have her tox report . . .'

'Okay so . . . this woman. She was last seen walking out of her building, so we got the doorman, and he's given us nothing. Well. Not nothing: a license plate. We know who the owner of the car is, but he's obviously not "the owner", so we have no way of tying the two. I don't see what we can do. Or should I say, not in a time frame that will be helpful to that poor woman. God knows where she is by now.'

'The Second Commandment, Joaco.'

'Of course,' Alzada conceded, although he believed that if taking the name of the Lord in vain should ever be allowed, it would be precisely in a circumstance such as this one. 'What I meant is that the more time passes, the slimmer her chances. And if they have done things "right"– which I assume they must have given the social latitudes we're talking about—'

'Always with these words, Joaco! "Social latitudes"?'

'She's from a very, very, *very* good family. Owning half of Buenos Aires good.'

'And the tox report, then?'

Alzada hesitated.

'Come on,' she nudged him gently. 'I know we normally don't do this, but I'm intrigued.'

We might just as well . . . 'A corpse found this morning. This is what I meant when I said I was swamped. But anyway,' Alzada took a deep breath, 'we can't move forward in the investigation of the disappeared woman: without a body there is no crime.'

'That reminds me of Videla, when they asked him about the disappeared at that press conference – how did he explain it? Do you remember? "The disappeared person is an *unknown*. They are not an entity. They *are* not: not dead and not alive."'

'Are you quoting Dictator Videla at me? Seriously?'

'Yes.' Resignation in her voice. Sometimes Alzada wondered how she mustered the patience required for the full-time position of Señora de Alzada.

'You're right,' he conceded, 'and Videla was right. It's exactly that: the unknown . . . How can you obtain a conviction for murder relying exclusively on circumstantial evidence? It's almost impossible to make those charges stick without a body. That's precisely why Videla is living in his beautiful apartment in Recoleta and not rotting in a cell.'

'I see. But that is precisely my point.In mathematics, an unknown is solved by a rule of three. Do you remember that, from school?'

'The "solve for x" thing?'

'The "solve for x" thing,' she repeated, stressing every word. You need a body to continue the investigation, so find a body to act as a placeholder. And then you solve for x.'

'Do you know you're not the first person to suggest that today?'

'Don't tell me Orestes is not a bad cop after all . . .' Paula nudged him. 'Besides, and don't think I'm saying a man should go down for something he didn't do, but maybe — isn't it time people were held accountable for their actions? Look around: the revolution is here!' She gestured widely, having picked the quietest street of Buenos Aires to make that statement.

Alzada smiled.

'You know what I mean.'

'I see Sorolla has convinced you.'

'Maybe.' Paula was embarrassed. 'I mean. I don't agree with the violence. But isn't it about time things change?' She paused. 'At least they try.'

'Even though they know from the very beginning that they're going to fail...'

'I don't know, Joaquín. Do you always only do things that you know will work?'

Alzada took a deep breath. *At this point...*

'More importantly: do they look alike?'

'Who?'

'Keep up, viejo. The dead woman and the disappeared woman, do they look alike?'

All people bear a striking resemblance once dead. 'They do.'

'Then what is holding you back? Galante is not going to fire you.'

'He will eventually,' Alzada laughed.

'Not today. He will not like it, perhaps, but you know in the end he'll have your back.'

Alzada looked serious. 'It's dangerous. Someone who has already killed one—'

'Allegedly.'

'Allegedly killed someone, and an Echegaray what's more . . .'

Paula did not react to the mention of the last name.

' . . .what could he do to us?'

'First of all,' Paula stopped. 'Orestes is now part of the "us"?'

Alzada ignored her quip. 'Estrático wants to risk it only because he doesn't have anyone.'

'You don't know that.' She was suddenly severe. 'Either way, find someone to protect you who is higher up than that mystery man. If you don't have a godfather, you don't get baptized. You'll be safe with the Echegarays on your side. There is no better protection than old money.'

'You would know something about that . . .'

Paula smiled.

Inadvertently, they had arrived at the old Aranguren house. Alzada bent his head back to admire the full splendor of the casa chorizo where he spent every Sunday of his youth courting young – and exasperatingly indecisive – Paula Aranguren. The early twentieth-century stone house was built in imitation of the French classics. On its façade two symmetrical windows framed two ionic stone columns, which in turn framed the central wooden door. The windows could almost be mistaken for doors, since they reached only a foot above street level. Aesthetically, the only difference between them and the entrance were two symbolic iron grilles, which made them look like ridiculous balconies perched atop miniature jasmine bushes. To the right of the door, and above the bell, the bulb of the lamp had blown out. Apparently, the new owners didn't display the same affection towards the house as the previous ones had. Alzada lowered his gaze and met his wife's eyes.

'If things get ugly today, you swallow your pride, take Sorolla to your father's gated community and wait for me there, yes?'

Paula was silent.

'Do you remember when you taught Sorolla how to suck the nectar out of jasmine flowers? He would spend hours sitting under those bushes.' Her way of agreeing, even if she didn't like the prospect.

'Yes,' Alzada said, too preoccupied to be anything but curt. It felt like an eternity since Sorolla was a boy.

'Now, about that woman . . .'

He smiled. *It's Paula who should have become an inspector.* Alzada reached into his pocket and didn't find his phone. Again. 'Can I borrow your phone for a second, please?'

Before Paula could ask he was already dialing. 'Estrático? Yes! I left it at home. Yes. I know. Too early to confirm. Okay. Listen. I've been thinking. I might have an idea . . . Do you have the pictures? Good. Did you leave it on Flores' desk yet? Fantastic. Grab the whole file and meet me at Norma Echegaray's apartment. Call her family and tell them to be there . . . Let's say in . . .' Alzada glanced at his watch. 'Can you meet me there in forty-five minutes? Yes. At the Echegaray address. Let's make it an hour. With traffic today . . . And don't be late.'

Alzada handed her back the phone.

'You're one to talk. "Don't be late."'

'What?'

'You've never been on time in your life.'

'Again, I apologize for being late. I'm having quite the day.' He paused to see if he had been convincing enough. 'So . . .'

'You need to go,' she finished his sentence.

'I'm really sorry.'

'Go,' she said, resigned.

A smile appeared in Alzada's stubble.

'But you're shaving that horrible thing off.'

'You're going back home, yes? After this?'

'Yes.'

'Both of you.'

'Yes, Joaco.'

He gave her a rushed kiss on the cheek, said, 'You're the best,' and started to run towards Castex 2640.

'I better be!' she yelled after him. 'I better be,' she repeated to herself.

17

(1981)

Outside it was night. Joaquín smoked, propped against the kitchen door screen that gave onto the backyard. 'You're always in the way,' Paula had said one day, and with that she had decided he couldn't sit in the kitchen while she cooked. She was right: he was intent on snatching a piece of entraña whenever the possibility arose. Or empanada. Or torta. Or milanesa. They ended up agreeing on the door frame. From there, they could still talk, and Joaquín could still smoke. Approximately halfway through their courtship, after months and months of smoking together, Paula had deemed it a disgusting habit, and quit, but by then it had been too late for her to fall out of love with him, and for him to fall out of love with her. So she allowed it – barely.

'Can you please put it out now?' she asked from inside. 'It's your third one in a row.'

Joaquín switched his cigarette to his left hand to check the time, attempted a gesture towards the ashtray, yet finally ignored her plea. 'I don't know whether this is the best idea we've ever had, or the worst.'

'*You've* had,' Paula specified, clearly still upset about the mark on the cabinet, which of course he hadn't been able to erase in its entirety. She motioned to the dark outside, where the roar of a car grew closer. 'We'll know soon enough.'

AT THE SIGHT OF HIS superior, Joaquín's immediate reflex was to throw the cigarette butt into a flower pot placed by the main door to that effect. He abandoned his slump, ran his fingers through his freshly showered hair to make sure it was in place, wondered if he still smelled of liquor, and stood very straight in the doorway to compensate for that doubt. 'Good evening, Commissioner.'

'Commissioner Vukić,' said Paula.

'Call me Fernando, please,' were the commissioner's first words.

As he passed the threshold of the kitchen entrance, he lifted his brimmed hat and took Paula's hand almost with reverence. *A wolf in sheep's clothing.* With that same gallant gesture, he was able to snap a hand in seven little pieces. Joaquín had seen it.

'Would you like some coffee, Commissioner— I mean, Fernando?' Paula offered, as Vukić approached the chair at the head of the table. He had chosen the one spot equidistant from the entrance and the door to the living room, where he wouldn't lose sight of Joaquín.

Before Vukić had the time to answer, or sit, Joaquín blurted: 'They have disappeared my brother.'

Still standing, Vukić turned to Paula, who was holding the Bialetti's shiny octagonal beauty. Seeing the espresso pot tremble in her hands made him smile. 'Is this true?'

'And his wife,' she confirmed. Her voice, until that moment steady, now trembled.

Joaquín's eyes were on the commissioner. Vukić opened the buttons of his jacket one by one and sat down at the table as if he hadn't heard what they had just said. The young inspector observed his boss and took precise mental notes just as he would have with a suspect. *Like I was taught. By him.* Instead of conforming to the fashion of the time – the beiges, ochres, burgundies and dark greens in odd geometrical patterns – he had remained a bastion of classicism: in an impeccable navy-blue three-piece suit, he looked almost absurd against the background of the Alzada's humble kitchen, which was, as per Paula's choice, tepidly beige. *Where is he coming from at this hour, and dressed like that? Or where is he going?* 'He doesn't live with his wife anymore, does he?' Paula had asked him once. 'How do you know? Joaquín had replied, worried the commissioner might have behaved inappropriately towards her. 'He hasn't told anyone.' In fact, Alzada himself only knew because as one of Vukić's most trusted subordinates he had once been sent to deliver some papers to his residence. 'His suit,' she had answered matter-of-factly. And upon seeing the confused look on Joaquín's face: 'No woman irons it for him.' *She would definitely have made the better detective.*

Joaquín noticed Vukić's golden signet ring – family coat of arms and all – clicking tenderly on the table. His perennially furrowed brow subtly revealed the existence of an ongoing thought process underneath. Joaquín knew that sharks can't survive without swimming on – not because of the singular placement of their gills but because they don't possess a gall bladder and they lack an internal oxygen bubble to keep them afloat. He wondered whether Vukić had a gall bladder. He most certainly had a plan.

Paula's voice by the stove brought him back. 'I told you I don't like it when you use "disappear" like that.'

'Like what?' Joaquín was still not shifting his gaze away from Vukić.

'As a transitive verb, you idiot,' the commissioner intercepted the question, then repeated, 'as a transitive verb'. A cavernous laugh emanated from his belly. He broke off eye contact with Joaquín and turned around: 'And sure, Paula. I would love that coffee.'

To Vukić's surprise, not only did she bring over the coffee pot, she joined them at the table. Joaquín knew the commissioner felt more comfortable in the company of men. And then, to Joaquín's surprise, Paula lit herself a cigarette. Amused, Vukić slid the ashtray she had set out for him in her direction.

'At least that explains this morning . . .'

Joaquín lowered his gaze, but immediately began where he had left off, half trying to avoid the subject of Galante, half trying not to lose his courage 'I've called you because we have no idea what to do. We don't know where to look. We don't know whom to ask. I—'

Paula put her arm on Joaquín's as his throat closed.

'But that's a lie, isn't it?' Vukić smiled. Both Alzadas looked puzzled. 'You wouldn't have called *me*, of all people. And into your home? That's one hell of a risk to take.' Joaquín swallowed with difficulty, hoping his boss wouldn't notice. 'So, I'm going on the assumption that you do have a plan. I assume again – please correct me if I'm wrong – I was not your first call.' Vukić paused for confirmation.

Joaquín shook his head.

Vukić continued: 'Please tell me you haven't reached out to the Madres.'

'No,' Joaquín said.

'Good. They're under constant surveillance. One phone call to them – one meeting – and you would have automatically become a widow,' he said, turning to Paula, then to Joaquín. 'What about their comrades?'

'What about them?'

'Alzada . . .'

'I don't think he was—' Joaquín protested.

'Have they been in contact?'

'No,' the inspector confirmed.

'So much for revolutionary values.' Vukić coughed without a hint of condescension. 'They're probably expecting them to break in the first twenty-four hours and are busy changing locations. Okay. Now that we've got the preliminaries out of the way, let's speak about the plan. You haven't called me here to merely inform me you have a problem. Or that you have an idea. No. I might not have known the details, but I could infer that from your behavior today.' Joaquín instinctively touched his hand, still tender. 'You've called me here because you *do* know what you want to do. And now you need something from me.'

Joaquín looked down. For so long his admiration for his superior had been tainted by the knowledge of his shady dealings.

'When I am commissioner, I'll do things differently,' Alzada had once sworn to himself. Once. What seemed a long time ago. This was now.

'That's right. Look down. Find your balls – pardon me, madam,' Paula seemed unfazed, 'and ask me. That's what you brought me here for, no?'

Joaquín hesitated. He had been thinking about this since the moment Galante had refused but simply acknowledging this would be enough to risk his career – if things went well – and his life – if they didn't. Joaquín swallowed. Spending the rest of his years in the force counting bullets in a moldy basement suddenly sounded like both a fair and manageable punishment for his audacity.

'Come on, Joaquín. Ask me,' Vukić insisted.

Had he just called Alzada by his given name for the first time in fifteen years? The commissioner was leaning forward, a hungry expression on his face. *That's why he used my name.* Vukić was right. The commissioner had answered his call. He was sitting in his kitchen. Was it not a little too late to worry? *It's only saying it out loud.*

'I want to go.'

Joaquín braced for impact. He observed Vukić taking his time to single out another cigarette from the pack, then smiling jovially: 'There you go! See? It wasn't *that* hard, was it?' He took a long drag. 'Okay. Now that we've got this out in the open, we can finally get to the good part.'

The good part. Of course he's known all along. Only so many reasons why a subordinate, one with a troublesome brother, would discreetly ask him for a meeting after having punched a fellow officer in the middle of the station, on his day off. Vukić had known what Joaquín was going to ask him. And yet here he was, sitting in his kitchen, a broad smile on his face. Why?

'I know you'll probably look back on this evening a million times,' the commissioner said, bringing Joaquín back from his musings. 'But that day is far away. For you, and for me. Stop dreaming. Stop thinking. For my part, I'd rather regret something I've done than something I haven't. So, let's talk business.' Vukić made the slightest motion towards Paula. *He wants me to tell her to leave.* In the Alzada household, the current seating arrangement would have to do.

'Fine. First things first, then. We need at least one other person. And I think you might be opposed to the one I have in mind . . . Hear me out before you object.' Vukić looked intently at Joaquín: 'Do you know the boy who works at the station – he's not on the force – I mean the substitute medic in the afternoons—'

'No.' Alzada cut him off, something he would never have dared to do at the station. He knew perfectly well about whom the commissioner was talking. *Over my dead body.*

'Who are we talking about?' Paula asked. Joaquín knew what she really meant to say was: 'Have I heard of him on the few occasions when you gossip about work at dinner?'

'No,' Joaquín repeated, half answering her, half rejecting Vukić's suggestion. He finished his cigarette and crossed his arms.

'He is . . .' Vukić tried to explain, 'Fine. I'll give you that. He is . . . eccentric.'

Joaquín, like a child who believes the intensity of his disgust is not coming across correctly, made a face and grunted.

'Joaquín, we've taken note of your disapproval,' Paula said, severely unimpressed by her husband's antics. And turning to Vukić: 'Is he any good, Fernando?' *'Fernando'? Really?*

'He *is* good,' Vukić said. 'His name is Elías. He's smart. He's efficient. He will know where they are. More importantly, he'll know not to say a word.'

'How can you be sure of that?' she asked.

'He . . .' Vukić hesitated to find the right word. 'He's . . . He's no foreigner to the system.'

'He's a collaborator!' interjected Joaquín.

Paula shot him a poisonous look.

'Technically, he's not,' Vukić said. 'What he does is . . . He makes sure . . .' explaining the situation made even the commissioner slightly uneasy, 'he makes sure they're alive.'

Had Joaquín looked at his wife, he would have been able to observe the information sinking in; her smile tightened, her breath shortened. Instead, he jumped up to confront the commissioner: 'He makes sure they're alive so they can keep torturing them! We wouldn't want them to die before we establish that they're innocent, would we!'

'What do you want me to say, Alzada? What would make you feel better?' Vukić rose to meet Joaquín's height, and in doing so towered over him. 'That he's an expert in pain? He is! That he knows how many blows a person can take before they faint? He does! How many days someone can go without food or water before dropping dead? How high the voltage needs to be so it hurts like hell, but it doesn't fry the brain? Because if it does, they can't answer any more questions? Reveal more names? He knows all these things, and more you don't even want to imagine. That is his *work*! Not everyone can be Socrates, Alzada, and drink the fucking poison! Some of us have to live in the real world!'

Vukić caught up with his breath and, for a moment, seemed rattled to have raised his voice. He looked around the kitchen and sat back down. Alzada followed suit.

In a softer tone, the commissioner continued: 'What is it that you need to hear? Would you be satisfied if I told you what . . . that deep down he's a good person? That underneath that rugged exterior lies—'

'He doesn't have a rugged exterior,' Joaquín quipped.

'No, he does not.' Vukić smiled, and leaned in. 'Listen to me. He's resourceful. He's willing. He knows the ins and outs of the detention centers. He has medical knowledge.'

Joaquín lowered his head and stared at the grounds at the bottom of his coffee cup. If anyone had told him that he would ever find himself in this situation, he would have laughed in their face. He moved the cup around, shifting the arrangement of the grounds. This wasn't real. There was time to change it. Could destiny be cheated?

'My mother would have read them for you,' Vukić said, nodding at Alzada's cup. 'A Balkan tradition. I can do better: one doesn't get very far in life in the exclusive company of saints, Alzada. I'm not telling you to become his best friend. But frankly, he might be your best bet if you want to get your brother and his wife out of whatever hell they're in.'

'I agree,' Paula said. And with that, the matter was settled.

As if her intervention had reminded Vukić of her presence, he commented: 'Not even the todopoderoso wanted to lend a hand? I would have pegged him as someone who would know whom to call to make it happen . . .' He side-eyed Paula.

Old Aranguren had been retired for quite some time but connections in Buenos Aires' better circles were durable. The perks of belonging to a dynasty in a city where the right name still meant something. The fact they were not on good terms wasn't public knowledge, and Paula would not betray how she felt about him, not in front of Vukić. Joaquín didn't worry; she was eerily skilled at that. Only someone married to her for many years could have read the distress in her smile as she stood up and said, leaving the room: 'Please don't raise your voices again. I don't want you waking up the boy.'

Shit.

Paula stopped in her tracks, turned around and looked at Joaquín, terror in her eyes.

What had Vukić said when he had explained to the rookies on his team how to obtain positive results during an interrogation? 'Fear has a smell,' he used to say, savoring every word. 'A very distinctive one. And not one you *ever* want to find yourself exuding. You just have to . . .' he would raise his nose as to sniff out the air, 'detect it. Then go and find what sets it off in that person.' A shiver went down Joaquín's back. *Can he smell it on me right now?*

'What boy?' Vukić asked unhurriedly. It felt worse than if he had screamed.

Now Joaquín could see his boss for what he really was. For what his wife so often had warned him against, but he had refused to acknowledge: a man who was not quite a gentleman. A thug with a nineteenth-century gold pocket watch. Patient, sadistic, opportunistic. A thug, nonetheless. *Why doesn't he arrest me? It would make his career.*

'We might just as well . . .' Alzada said, meeting Paula's eyes again. *As if we have any other option.* 'My brother and his wife have a child. A boy. He was in the apartment with them when they came. For some reason, they missed him.'

'What do you mean, "they missed him"?' Vukić's tone remained nonchalant. He seemed to almost be enjoying himself.

'I think he heard noises – I *know* he heard noises – and his first instinct was to hide. When we arrived at the apartment, he was under his bed.' Joaquín explained.

Without missing a beat, Vukić rose. 'Can I see him?' he asked Paula. *How does he know to ask* her?

If she was afraid, she no longer showed it. 'Follow me.'

As the three walked to the bedroom, Alzada wondered whether Vukić would have the same reaction he'd had when he first met his nephew: when they put Sorolla in his arms at the British Hospital, Joaquín had been surprised by how little he weighed, and how much heat he emanated. It felt like holding a tiny, pink hot potato, wrapped in linen with a light-blue cross. *To remind the parents to whom the baby really belongs to.* When Jorge Rodolfo and Adela told him they had decided to name him after his uncle, Joaquín had cried for days.

But no. Vukić leaned in briefly, took a quick glance at the lump resting among the many cushions on their bed and turned around. He passed Alzada on his way out, and only said: 'I just wanted to see who we're doing this for.'

BACK IN THE KITCHEN, THE commissioner seemed to suddenly be in a hurry. 'So, it's settled,' he said as he buttoned his jacket. 'No whining. And no bullshit like what you pulled this morning.' His voice softened. 'If you wanted to be on desk duty in aeternum, you could've just asked, Alzada. Now you've left me no option but to suspend you, and if Galante files a complaint . . .'

The inspector nodded in agreement.

'I'm going to call Petacchi.' Vukić raised his eyebrows at Joaquín, who stood still in silent resignation. 'He's going to find out where they are,' he continued, 'and he's going to take us there – tonight. We've lost enough time as it is.'

Joaquín stared at the floor. 'Yes, sir.'

'One last thing: it's going to be expensive,' Vukić added. 'The man is impeccable, but he *is* a mercenary.'

Paula spoke: 'We have some money saved up.'

'And you?' Alzada asked the question that had been on his mind all evening.

'Me?' Vukić said, as if he had never hurt a fly.

'Yes, you.' *What are* you *going to want in exchange for this?*

'We'll talk about that later. For the moment, worry about this. I'll pick you up in a couple of hours.'

'Yes, sir.'

'And dress for the job.'

'Yes, sir,' Joaquín said, without knowing what he meant.

Vukić grabbed his hat from the kitchen counter, half bowed before Paula, and was gone.

18
(1981)

Saturday, December 5th; 23:10

Like a dog guarding his usual spot, Joaquín leaned against the kitchen door frame. He had once read that it was the safest location in the event of an earthquake. 'Earthquake' had been their mother's nickname for Jorge Rodolfo as a child. One day, exasperated by his constant mischief, she had once again begged him to sit still. '¡Eres un terremoto!' the late Mrs. Alzada had yelled, half hoping he would change, half surrendering to the fact that he would not. Terremoto. From the Latin 'terra', earth, and 'motus', movement. What a perfectly fitting name for him. It seemed like the younger of the Alzada boys had worked every day since his birth to live up to and honor that description. He had been loud and raucous and wild. At a cousin's baptism, he had jumped from the roof of the house into a fountain, Sunday clothes and all. Joaquín smiled. At every turn of his life, Jorge had set out to shake the ground, and then waited impatiently – and with a certain morbid curiosity – for the consequences.

All Joaquín had ever wanted was to run for cover. He had run, and quite successfully, from the slum apartment above the train tracks where they had grown up, tight like sardines in a can. He had wanted to run from a law school that had failed to keep him engaged. He had run from whatever happened at the police station. 'The art of questioning a witness is precisely that: an art,' he recalled Professor Iraola explaining from behind a desk that barely covered the giant savant's thighs. 'A good lawyer only asks questions to which he already knows the answer.' Young Joaquín had imagined rugged, seasoned criminals confessing to Iraola on the stand, from the mere pressure of being in his imposing presence. Joaquín simply hadn't needed answers.

'You haven't eaten anything,' he heard Paula say from inside.

Sometimes he wondered how he could have married someone with so prosaic an inclination: keeping him warm and fed seemed to be her main objective in life. Joaquín peeked in and saw her covering the lasagna dish in tin foil.

'You've only had one serving,' she insisted. When she was nervous, she cooked. When he was nervous, he ate. That's *why I got married to someone with so prosaic an inclination.*

'Many health experts would recommend less than a kilo of lasagna for dinner . . .'

'That's true . . . for other people,' Paula said.

He could hear her smile without looking. Neither wanted to talk. Neither wanted to fight. Neither wanted to be in that situation, yet here they were. It wouldn't be long now until Vukić returned, Petacchi in tow. *I wish Jorge had been a little less courageous, and I a little more.* Had he just used the past tense to refer to his brother? Was that how it happened? Had he pre-emptively started to grieve?

Fortunately, Alzada heard the roar of Vukić's reckless driving. He flicked his cigarette, readjusted his tie and leaned into the kitchen to say goodbye. Paula was not there. *It's better this way.*

ALZADA CLOSED THE CAR DOOR behind him and swiveled in the passenger seat to examine Elías Petacchi. At the station, the inspector would never have devoted more than a passing glance to someone like him, just a small blip on his radar. A temp what's more. Petacchi had learned – opportunely for both of them – that there was one particular inspector's balls he needn't break. He stayed out of Alzada's way. That had been the extent of their relationship. Until now.

In the back seat, Petacchi looked uneasy. The young doctor lounged in a posture that looked both artificial and uncomfortable, his legs spread unnaturally wide, each touching one of the front seats. His dark, mercurial eyes didn't miss one detail of Alzada's movements as the inspector scanned him. A prominent, fine nose, not completely aligned with an unshaven jaw. Thin, dark hair – dark to match his eyes – parted like a drawn opera curtain, in a supple wave that reached his shoulders to meet a leather jacket and a mustard sweater. Underneath a perfectly starched shirt collar, a seashell necklace. *Half a man.*

Petacchi squirmed in his seat at Alzada's inquisitive gaze. *Not used to the scrutiny, are we?* A weasel like him benefitted from not drawing attention, lived to be unseen. Still, the medic readjusted himself, said 'Good, evening, Inspector,' and tentatively stretched out a bony hand in the direction of Alzada.

'Tell me something,' Alzada said, ignoring his gesture, 'have you ever considered combing some gel into that mane of yours? Or getting a haircut, perhaps, to match the dignity of the institution you serve?'

'Alzada,' Vukić interceded.

Although the commissioner's office was on a different floor, nothing happened at his station without his knowledge. He was well aware of how disliked Petacchi was among at least half his staff: his well-known evening collaborations earned him both defenders and critics. Still, everyone had to admit they would rather work in close quarters with a crooked medic than a leftist. *At least with him I know where I stand.* Alzada grabbed his outstretched hand. A claw came to mind upon contact. The inspector smiled a full smile. *If you can't convince them, confuse them.* Petacchi responded with a muddled grimace.

There was no time left for games. Vukić stepped on the gas, putting them both in their places. He reinterpreted traffic lights as suggestions and intersections as chicanes. He tailed the few cars they encountered on the splendid newly unveiled 25 de Julio highway so closely they swerved out of his lane. He devoted most of his attention to retrieving a little metal box of licorice candy from one of the multiple pockets of his impeccable double-breasted suit, out of which he hadn't changed, then proceeded to vehemently offer them some. They arrived at their destination in one-third of the expected time. Alzada was nauseous.

REPENTANCE

THE ESMA COMPLEX WELCOMED THEM from a distance. More than the sight of the structures on its compound, it was the sudden sense of emptiness that announced they had arrived. On Avenida del General Paz, there were still a few streetlamps, the occasional glimmer shining taciturnly in the neighboring apartment buildings. Beyond that, and stretching to their right for several blocks, the abrupt end of all light, and the start of a pitch-black space that extended to the bay of the Río de la Plata.

'Petacchi, whenever you're ready . . .' Vukić said.

Petacchi stuttered.

'Well?' Vukić pressed him as they approached the corner of the compound. Alzada knew that stopping the car in such close proximity, even if allowed, would draw attention. So would driving past and having to turn around.

Petacchi cleared his throat and replied mechanically: 'I would suggest turning right on Libertador and going through the main entrance. It's at the end of the block, at the corner with Comodoro Rivadavia. That one has more traffic. If someone comes in at this hour, it won't be anything out of the ordinary.' Cold sweat ran down Alzada's back as he took in the medic's words. *The ordinary.*

As they drove along the southern perimeter, the inspector looked past the commissioner to absorb the magnitude of the structure. Alzada had driven by it before, but not since it had been repurposed. Originally the space had housed the Navy Petty Officers School of Mechanics. The suitability of its vast quarters, its efficient layout and its excellent location – conveniently close, and yet far enough from the city center – had precipitated its rise to notoriety during the dictatorship: they were before the largest detention center in the country.

A cemetery would have been less eerie. Illuminated only by the motion-sensor floodlights along the perimeter fence, its stateliness was striking: past a clear esplanade lined with perfectly manicured lawns, dozens of cypresses and cedars and ceibos in full bloom distracted the eye from focusing on the actual buildings. They drove past 'Cuatro Columnas', the central pavilion, its classical Ionic colonnade projecting a pathetic shadow onto the courtyard. *Like prison bars.* Alzada suspected there were no prison bars inside.

'Here,' Petacchi said.

They turned left to face the entrance of the ESMA. Alzada was confronted with the quiet, sprawling monster inside the gates. He had counted at least eight or nine buildings across what he estimated to be something like thirty-five acres, all whitewashed and topped with red-tiled roofs. Were they holding people in all of them?

The medic tapped on Vukić's shoulder as the commissioner headed towards what could have been a railroad level crossing – if it hadn't been flanked by armed guards. 'Don't slow down when you wave at them.' *How often does he come here?*

The gate rose without resistance.

Petacchi pointed to their left. 'The building we want is at the end of this alley.'

Vukić drove deliberately slowly. On their left, a row of plane trees. On their right, a brick wall. The soundtrack was that of their tires grinding on the gravel.

Alzada ducked instinctively as they passed a watchtower, two barrels sculpted out of reinforced concrete, one stacked on top of the other, each with an identical, horizontal slit from which peeked two inquisitive muzzles. No one on foot. Vukić kept driving steadily and veered towards the last building before the fence.

'Here we want to do the opposite: let's take the back entrance,' Petacchi instructed the commissioner calmly. He could have been talking about a cinema.

Vukić avoided the circular driveway and took a side street into further darkness. They reached two symmetrical patios that shaped the rear of the building into a trident. Each of the legions of windows seemed to be staring down at them from different angles. Alzada knew it was highly improbable prisoners would be held up there: at such height, they would be too visible to the outside world. Not that anyone would dare approach the compound close enough to discern their presence.

So this is where they end up. This right here, this ugly, martial construction, was the answer to all the insistent questions asked at the station, all the futile habeas corpuses filed, all the desperate pleas to every possible acquaintance, all the favors called in to obtain a shred of information. 'Seriously, Joaco. How can you be so naive?' Alzada could hear his brother say. 'When the Madres meet every Thursday to chant outside the office of the president demanding to know where their children are, it's not really about not knowing *where* they are. Oh, no. They *know*. It's that they know they're not coming back.'

'Alzada, do you perhaps feel like joining us?'

The inspector realized both Vukić and Petacchi, the latter with an immaculate black leather briefcase in hand, had gotten out of the car. The commissioner stood a couple of steps ahead of him, motioning towards the entrance to the building. Joaquín was suddenly cold. He closed the two buttons of his suit jacket – as if that were going to make a difference – caught up with his boss and looked back into the driveway. On the gravel, surrounding Vukić's silver Audi, vans without markings or plates, parked in an unruly fashion, like loose batteries in a drawer.

Rubicon, here we go.

THE SINGLE-DOOR SIDE ENTRANCE THAT Petacchi had chosen for them gave way to a cavernous main hall. Alzada immediately pictured it in the old days, busy and loud, officers running down the stairs from the dorms, never late for a drill. Someone had chosen to illuminate the space by directing faded lights towards the recessed ceiling, probably hoping for a more elegant effect. In fact, it resembled a run-down 1920s hotel. *Dismal.* Only a single, impassive desk in the middle of the hall, a tired officer sitting under a small lamp that illuminated a thermos, a binder of sorts, and an overflowing ashtray.

Vukić spearheaded the crew walking with purpose, as if parting the seas; Alzada and Petacchi followed closely, painfully conscious of their steps echoing on the polished stone floor.

'Good evening. We're here to interrogate the Alzadas,' the commissioner barked with contempt at the soldier.

A knot in Joaquín's throat. *The Alzadas.* That could very well be he and Paula. In there. *In here.* If they had made different choices. If they had been less lucky. *If this thing tonight doesn't go the way we want it to.*

The officer didn't lift his eyes from the desk. 'Names.'

Vukić waved to Alzada on his left.

'Jorge Rodolfo and Adela,' Alzada said, as if apologizing.

'They're not here,' the officer replied without even opening the ledger.

Alzada looked around. Doors to the left and right and front and back. *Leading God knows where.* How were they ever going to make it out of here alive?

Vukić turned to Petacchi, who simultaneously raised shoulders and eyebrows. The commissioner pressed his lips together in disappointment and decided to focus back on the little man at the desk.

'Second Corporal . . .' Vukić leaned in closer until he could read the officer's nametag, '. . . Montalvo?'

'First – First Corporal Montalvo,' Montalvo corrected him. *Still, a nobody.*

'Montalvo,' Vukić repeated. He pronounced it slowly, as if searching his memory for an old familiar face. *He's indicating he'll remember the name when he files a disciplinary report.*

The officer nodded and remained unfazed.

'I'm sorry, *First* Corporal Montalvo,' Vukić said, and seemed – at least for a split second – to mean it. 'I truly am. Maybe you didn't understand me the first time I asked you. And that's a perfectly reasonable mistake to make. It's okay.'

Here he goes. So many times, Alzada had always wondered why he preferred any other superior's sermons to Vukić's. The popular approach to discipline in the force was to shout, often to the point of spitting in the subordinate's face, leaving him temporarily deaf in an attempt to drill obedience into his brain. No. Vukić was a very different animal. He favored the quiet, unhurried elaboration of a reasonable argument. He knew that a constantly deferred eruption of rage was far worse than any yelling: he took his sweet time to make you feel like the unfit imbecile you knew you were. Already, Alzada could see, Vukić's tone was having the desired effect. As the first corporal followed the speech attentively, he sat up and swallowed, his Adam's apple bobbing visibly against the knot of his black tie. He had realized his mistake. Vukić had his undivided attention.

'You might be tired. You might be sick of sitting at this shitty desk. Your mate has probably gone cold,' the commissioner pointed at the thermos, 'and so, perhaps, when we walked in you weren't at the peak of your mental capacity. Pay attention now: we . . .' Vukić paused and gestured towards Petacchi and Alzada. Both squirmed at the unexpected reference. '*We* are not people you say "I don't know what you're talking about" to. Or . . .' he searched for the expression the officer had used as an excuse.

To Alzada's surprise, it was Montalvo himself who completed his sentence: '. . . They're not here.' Imbécil.

'"They're not here". Yes. Thank you.' Vukić was a magician in action. 'We're not *those* kinds of people. Do you see where I'm going with this?' *Is Montalvo nodding in assent?* 'Here's what you're going to do, First Corporal: you're going to open that cute little ledger of yours.' Vukić drummed his finger on it. Clop. Once was enough. 'You're going to look up the Alzadas – Jorge Rodolfo and Adela – and you're going to tell me exactly where they are.'

Montalvo waited until Vukić had removed his hand to open the ledger and frantically flipped through the pages. Names, names, names. So many names, all written in blue ink.

'They got here yesterday,' the corporal offered, suddenly in a solicitous mood. *'Got'. What a nice way of putting it.* It made it sound like they had checked into a luxury hotel on the French Riviera.

'Oh, yes,' Montalvo looked up slowly, keeping one hand on the page so as to not lose the spot, 'I know *exactly* who they are.'

The familiarity gave Alzada a chill. *How many people come and go every day? Out of all of them he remembers the Alzadas?* That couldn't be a good sign.

'So . . .' the officer continued, 'her we interrogated properly . . .' He moved his tongue over his teeth. A venomous smile appeared. Seeing as his comment hadn't garnered the response he had expected, Montalvo withdrew it, and added: 'He's still here.'

He's still here. Thank God. He's still here.

Not having forgotten the second part of the instruction, Montalvo rose promptly from his chair. Its rubber casters made it stutter on the floor. 'Follow me, please,' he said, disappearing at a brisk pace down an unlit side corridor.

19

(2001)

Wednesday, December 19th; 17:20

The elevator screeched as it reached the fourth floor. Estrático stepped onto the carpeted landing.

'Here you are, sir.' The deputy smiled, relieved. *He thought he would have to do this alone.*

'Come on. Let's turn this into a murder investigation. Your memory is fresh on how to do this, yes? They taught you at the academy?'

Estrático nodded, not convinced.

Alzada needed him fully on board: it would be intrusive enough for these people as it was to have two police officers in their house, telling them their loved one was dead. At least they would feel more comfortable with one of their own.

'You explain what they're about to see. You keep the photographs face down on the table and slide them over one by one. Start with the headshot. Whenever they feel ready, they can flip the picture themselves, yes?'

'What about the tattoo, sir?'

'She could have gotten it without telling the judgmental sister. Have you never hidden anything from your family?'

Estrático cleared his throat.

'Speaking of family, don't think for a second that I've forgotten you called my wife.'

'I'm sorry, sir.' The deputy lowered his gaze to meet his shoes. 'You weren't answering your phone. I had Paula's number . . . I thought I would try her. I hope you didn't take offense.'

'Offense? Yes, Estrático, you caught me. I'm jealous of the conversation you had behind my back . . . If you'd spent more than twenty minutes in the force, you'd understand that wives and police business don't go together. One day, you'll have a wife, and then I'll give you the full speech.' The deputy flashed a childish grin. 'In the meantime, stay away from mine. And especially don't call her "Paula". It's Señora Aranguren to you. Or Señora de Alzada, in case you didn't know her last name.'

'Of course, sir. But going back to the tattoo . . . what I meant was . . . what if they're not a match?'

'I know what you meant, Estrático.' Alzada scoffed. 'She's not going to look that closely, trust me. Nobody does. All we need to move forward with the case is a warrant, and all we need for a warrant is the slightest doubt. Besides, no one ever died from looking at a picture.'

Estrático grimaced.

'And to address your question: have you ever heard of a cop being punished for fucking up a case? No! It's quite the opposite, actually. So if she really isn't the girl, no sudden movements, a curt apology, we return to the main door and leave, yes?'

If we're wrong, our heads would roll and be put on spikes. Galante would make sure of that. But I don't need him thinking about that now. The inspector laid his hand on Estrático's shoulder with a little more force than he had intended; the thump echoed off the cold stone around them.

Embarrassed, Alzada rang the doorbell.

The deputy pushed his curls back.

'Now show me what you've got, Estrático.'

THE APARTMENT WAS JUST AS Estrático had described it.

Mrs. Echegaray opened the door alone. She seemed quite comfortable in her sister's apartment as she led them through the hall into the living room. *She must spend a lot of time here.* Alzada was invited to sit in a dangerously low designer chair he knew would trap him but was too polite to refuse, and Estrático sat on an aluminum stool with protruding deer antlers at the sides. Sitting on a mouse-grey couch under a watercolor of the Amazon that stretched from the corner to a window overlooking Avenida Presidente Figueroa Alcorta, Mrs. Echegaray examined them.

Where is the engineer? They were probably under the impression that this was only a courtesy visit, with updates and perhaps even some good news.

'He's out with friends,' she said, as if she had read his mind. 'Would you like a whisky?'

'Thank you, madam.' Estrático shook his head.

Alzada made a mental note of the complex structure of old bookshelves that surrounded a tiny television set, the two orchids by the other window and a piano against the wall across from the couch.

'Let's begin.' Alzada turned to Estrático, who didn't skip a beat.

'Madam . . .' the deputy set the folder with the pictures on the low glass table that separated the policemen from Mrs. Echegaray, 'we have news.'

The woman leaned forward.

It's not too late. We can make up an excuse, we can leave.

'We fear we might have found her,' Estrático maneuvered around the words.

'Fear?'

Alzada felt his stomach rise.

'Before we start, let me preface this—'

'No preface necessary.' She didn't take her eyes from the folder.

Estrático reached for the file.

Alzada stood and gestured vaguely around the apartment. 'Would you allow me for a moment – the restroom?'

'Yes.' A string of voice. 'At the end of the corridor, to the left.'

Alzada saw Estrático begging him with his eyes not to leave him alone. But reacting in time was crucial: otherwise he would throw up on the beautiful hand-knotted kilim at his feet. The deputy must have sensed the urgency: his face shifted to resignation, then acceptance.

Alzada gave Estrático an encouraging nod and was gone.

HOW MANY BODIES HAD HE seen in his career? Hundreds. *It never gets better.* A pulsing headache grew in Alzada's head. He put his hands on the stucco walls along the corridor and moved forward supported by them, then jumped into the bathroom and locked the door behind him. A series of unproductive heaves. He hoped the sound didn't travel to the living room.

What he remembered most from the first one was the smell: like their childhood terrarium, when Jorge didn't look after his turtles with the required diligence. Alzada leaned on the sink with both hands and lowered his head. Why had he been on that call? It had been at least ten kilometers outside his district. Vukić had hand-picked him for the task. 'You do this – and don't wait for Galante.' By the fear on the faces of the fishermen when he arrived in the marshes up the Río de la Plata delta, it had been their first body, too. The two men, a little younger than him, were pulling bundles from behind the cattails and setting them down in a line on the edge of the water; the grass under them flattened by their boots, caked together with mud.

'Buenas noches, chicos.'

They had lifted their eyes with a mixture of suspicion and relief.

Alzada had approached.

Four bodies. Their hands tied behind their backs with copper wire. Clavicles broken to put them in that position. Feet tied together. Washed ashore after a couple of days, surely, from the way they were bloated. And those bruises? As if they had fallen from a great height. *Where did they come from?*

The brighter fisherman seemed to be thinking along his lines: he looked up into the sky. Alzada remembered the ten plagues. A thunderstorm of hail and fire. What was going to fall from the sky next?

'Like buoys, sir.'

They called him sir. They were scared to call their local police. They had probably seen them play cards at the bar and joke about this. They were afraid of him also.

'What did you say?'

'I found them floating, caught between the reeds.'

'Out there?' Alzada pointed out to the water and wondered how anyone could find their way in the pitch black.

'Yes, sir. This morning, when I was setting the nets.'

'Well . . . Drop them off at the morgue before it opens. And don't say anything about this, yes?' Alzada made sure to make eye contact with both of them. 'To anyone.'

'Is that a threat?' *The 'sir' is gone.*

Alzada had been surprised at the occurrence. 'It's a recommendation.' *A recommendation I'll have to follow myself.*

Dawn was arriving on the delta.

Alzada had pressed his lips together, just like he was doing now. He rubbed his face one last time in cold water and dried off with a peach-colored towel. He then folded it carefully back on the rack.

One last look in the mirror.

'NO PUEDE SER. NO PUEDE ser. No puede ser.'

When Alzada arrived in the living room, Mrs. Echegaray was saying only that.

'It can't be. It can't be.'

'I'm very sorry, madam.' Alzada rejoined the conversation.

What just happened?

Estrático was at a loss for words.

It is her after all. We only did it to get a warrant and it turns out to be true.

Alzada went on autopilot. 'Thank you for your co-operation, madam. We are now going to leave you to make the necessary arrangements . . . Of course we will continue to work on the case and keep you updated. We'll see ourselves out.'

Mrs. Echegaray recomposed herself at surprising speed; she stood, straightened her dress, and walked them to the exit. Only when she opened the door did she show a lapse in her fortitude: she suddenly held Alzada's hands in hers. 'Please let me know if there is anything I can do.'

It is her after all.

It is her after all.

It is her after all.

Back in the elevator, Alzada noticed there were scratches on the wooden floor by the entrance of the apartment. As if someone had rearranged the furniture.

20

(1981)

They walked up the stairs in a single file: Montalvo first, followed closely by Vukić, Alzada and Petacchi in the rearguard. Thuds as they stepped. The inspector looked down: they were walking on cork planks. *A makeshift access point? Maybe to accommodate one of the newer functions of the building . . .* Alzada shuddered.

Three floors up, they found themselves in front of another empty desk. *The boldness – no one on surveillance. Not boldness: impunity.*

'Mind the ceiling,' Montalvo recommended, tilting his head slightly and walking confidently into the darkness.

Alzada held his hand up and felt a beam at an angle. They were in the attic. *So they are keeping them on the top floors.* He could have sworn they were walking along an L-shaped passage, but in the shadows it was difficult to discern with precision.

They stopped. At first, the spot seemed arbitrary. But as their eyes grew used to the very little light that seeped through a slim horizontal window in the distance, Alzada recognized the outline of a door. Then another. And another. Suddenly he realized they were standing in a hallway, rows of doors on both sides. How many floors did this building have? And how many hallways like this one? How many Alzadas behind each door?

'This one,' said Montalvo, his two feet squared towards a corrugated metal plank.

'Thank you, First Corporal Montalvo,' Vukić said resolutely.

The officer hesitated briefly, before turning to Petacchi: 'Don't I know you from somewhere?'

The doctor froze. Did he really think he wouldn't be recognized? *That's the whole point of you being here.* And then Alzada realized Petacchi's surprise didn't stem from being recognized, but from being recognized only now. To the inspector, on the other hand, the timing made perfect sense: since the moment they had walked into the building, Montalvo must have been trying to place his face, only to brush the thought aside to focus on his conversation with Vukić. Then, at some point on the stairs it had stopped bothering him completely. Now that they had arrived in front of that door, the officer was questioning whether letting them in had been the correct choice. Had he made a mistake? Would he get in trouble? Alzada looked at Montalvo and could see doubt creeping in. The officer nervously pulled his collar. *A little late for regret.*

Vukić had arrived at the same conclusion. 'We'll be right down,' he said, trying to put the officer's mind to rest.

Montalvo – apparently still under the commissioner's spell – turned and made his way back down the stairs. Swiftly.

The moment he was out of sight, Vukić hastily pulled the door open. *It doesn't even have a lock.* Alzada crossed himself.

In the distance, wailing.

THE ROOM WAS DARK. A dark piece of cloth hung over the window. The only source of light was coming through a slit high up in one of the walls. On a rotten mattress, a man rested supine, half wrapped in a blanket, a hood over his head.

The sound of the steps entering the cell made the gibbering wreck wince; he would probably have retreated if his broken body had allowed him to conjure more than an ashen, terrified twitch. Or if the room's size permitted such movement.

The three stood, their backs against the door, afraid to step on him.

'Elías,' Vukić motioned Petacchi to approach.

With one agile movement, the young doctor knelt by the cot and started working swiftly. First, he placed his briefcase on the floor. Then, he took off the hood.

Jorge. It was Jorge. Even in the dark, Alzada could tell.

Petacchi pulled out a pouch with utensils from the inside of his coat and positioned them on the mattress. *Clever. He's used the briefcase as a decoy in case it got confiscated.* The doctor seemed unfazed by the state of his patient. Watching him, Alzada wondered how many people he had treated within the walls of this particular detention center. How many in others.

Joaquín approached his broken brother while Petacchi handled the stethoscope and opened what could have been, in another life, pajamas, and now were little more than shreds of cloth soaked and stuck to the skin. In spite of his light touch, every gesture of Petacchi's was met with a grimace of pain. Still standing, Joaquín discerned two long, thin bruises across his brother's torso. In the shape of the object they had used. *A strap? A cane, maybe? Probably upon arrival. Definitely a while ago.* The contusions had started to turn dark. On the canvas of Jorge's chest, Joaquín recognized the unmistakable marks of the picana: the electric cattle prod had left the younger Alzada with a third and fourth nipple. Cast like oversized spider bites, these wounds were open. *Fresh.*

Joaquín heard his brother murmur. 'What is it?' he asked.

The murmur didn't get louder.

Only when he crouched by his side next to Petacchi did he recognize Jorge Rodolfo's exhalation: he was calling for his wife.

Joaquín hesitated for a moment. But as his eyes grew more used to the darkness, he realized he wouldn't need to answer Jorge's plea. If anatomy is the branch of biology concerned with the study of the structure of live organisms, this was a lesson in anti-anatomy: there no longer was a structure. The only argument in favor of classifying Jorge as a living thing was a swollen, darkened abdomen that trembled at irregular intervals. His limbs were folded into impossible angles. The relief of his torso had been rendered unfamiliar. *What is that noise?* Alzada almost said out loud, before he realized it was the sound of his brother's hoarse breathing.

With urgency, Jorge lifted his head. 'Joaco.'

'I'm here,' Alzada said, coming closer to his face. Along Jorge's temples, a breach irrigated his closed eyes. His aquiline nose was broken. 'I'm here,' Alzada repeated, stroking his feverish forehead.

'I didn't . . .' Every word was an effort. Jorge opened his eyes: their whites were no longer white. 'I didn't say anything. *Nada.*'

'Shh,' Joaquín tried to soothe him. He knew that after being given such treatment, people confessed to things they had done, and to things they hadn't.

'I didn't tell them anything. I swear,' Jorge insisted.

Joaquín took his brother's hand. *Wet.* He lowered his gaze: one might have thought Jorge was wearing nail polish, dark prune. Joaquín brought the hand closer to his eyes. The dim light confirmed his fears: his nails had been meticulously ripped out.

'Adela,' Jorge said.

To avoid returning his attention to the hand – anything but the hand – Joaquín looked around. Vukić stood guard by the door. By his expression, Alzada knew he was getting anxious. *We're spending too much time in here.* Petacchi continued going through the motions of a slightly altered routine check. He had measured his pulse and carefully tried to lift the younger Alzada to put his ribs in a splint. But at this point – Joaquín could tell without any medical training – they would probably have to put the whole body in a splint. *The work they've done on him, and in only twenty-four hours? Impressive.* Alzada was sickened by his own appreciation.

'I heard Adela,' Jorge tried again, his lips barely parted.

Joaquín couldn't stand to look at him. On the wall, etched scrawls. Dates. Names. Only two years ago, the Argentinian government had agreed on a visit from the Inter-American

Commission on Human Rights. They had visited these premises with much pomp and circumstance. Had these walls not been here then? Joaquín decided to focus on the floor instead. The same terracotta tiles they had laid in Jorge Rodolfo's kitchen. Could it be, or was his mind playing tricks on him? Humidity – or something else – had created a capricious stain by the mattress. It was like one of those marks everyone had at home, which by dint of staring at them over the course of years took on the shape of a particular object. This one, too, had potential. If this stain had been found on Alzada's irregular worktop, or in the raw wood of the kitchen table, or in the sinuous crevices of the bathroom marble, it could have become a screwdriver, or maybe a slender giraffe calf. Perhaps a violin. The right choice had to be made from the start, Joaquín knew. *Once you see something, you can't unsee it.*

'There's not much more we can do here,' Petacchi announced.

He parsimoniously wiped every utensil clean and returned them to their rightful place in his pouch. *Had he said 'here' as in 'here at the ESMA', meaning he would receive the treatment he needed at a medical facility?*

Petacchi rose. 'His temperature is out of control. And I'd be remiss if I omitted his vitals are . . . all over the place.'

Hearing him talk so serenely made Alzada want to bash his smug face against the wall. Then he understood: the calm was for Jorge's benefit. Joaquín looked at his brother. Indeed, there was not much anyone could do. It would be a miracle if he survived the night.

Vukić understood. 'Let's go.'

'Sir, before we move him. I think we need to discuss the plan?'

'I can't help you with *that*,' Petacchi cut in. 'Before tonight I had never been up here. I normally see them in the infirmary. In the basement.'

'The basement no, please . . .' Jorge implored behind them.

'Well . . .' Vukić spoke now in a lethargic cadence. *This is how he delivers bad news.* 'This might come as a surprise to you, Joaquín, but this is the plan: we're leaving through the door.'

'The main door,' Alzada wanted to confirm.

Vukić nodded.

Is this a joke? Alzada paused to assess their circumstances. He rolled his shoulders back, his hands slack by his sides, and looked around. He didn't like what he saw.

First, there was his brother. Were those blisters on his feet? *Intentional.* He repressed the urge to vomit. That had been Joaquín's last cigarette. Those bare, battered feet did not belong to someone who could run for his life. *Is he even going to be able to walk?* Petacchi had been right: Jorge Rodolfo would have to be carried.

Next was the doctor. Petacchi would probably not be able to help with the heavy lifting. *Five, maybe ten meters.* After that, who could tell. And he would definitely not be a deterrent against anything that might await them outside the cell. Because Joaquín knew the real problem began once they opened that excuse of a door. To have thought they could circumvent – or overcome – any resistance from the Navy officers had been, to put it mildly, audacious. Vukić would be of little help in that department. *The man might be imposing, and convincing, but he's getting old.* Regardless, it was too late. They had to move. Now. What was the saying? 'The line between bravery and stupidity is so thin you don't know you've crossed it until you're dead.' *We'll know soon enough.*

A groan. Petacchi was trying to sit Jorge Rodolfo up on the cot. *We're never going to make it.*

'We're going to walk out? Just like that?' Joaquín asked, one last time.

Vukić nodded, confident.

That, for Alzada, was enough.

'I can grab my own brother, thank you very much.' Joaquín pushed Petacchi aside without effort and knelt in front of the cot as if it were an altar. He gently gathered Jorge by the neck and legs.

'Adela,' his brother said.

Alzada and Vukić exchanged glances. *This is it.*

21

(2001)

Wednesday, December 19th; 18:55

'Let's do this, then. Go find me one of those forms to request an arrest warrant,' Alzada said to Estrático behind him as he was stepping into his office.

'Hello, Joaquín.'

'What the—'

Alzada flipped the switch. Sitting in his seat, Commissioner Galante.

'Oh, good. It's you. You scared the shit out of me, Horacio. What the fuck are you doing here?'

'What the fuck am *I* doing here?' Galante looked old and tired. What only a couple of hours had done to his physique: the low shoulders and bloodshot eyes the visible effects of a persistent vigil. 'Chaos has taken over the city. There are a dozen dead, and more to come. So, I decided to take pity on you two and was coming down to give you the rest of the day off . . .'

Alzada approached and sat across from him at the desk.

'Did I say you could sit?'

Alzada had barely touched the seat when he rose again. 'I came back to file an arrest warrant against Pantera.'

'Excuse me?' Even with the height disparity produced by their arrangement, Galante was an imposing presence.

'Yes, sir. I have evidence.'

'Evidence? What evidence? That she got into a car, and that the car is his? Come on, Joaquín. No judge in his right mind will sign it. You know as well as I do that a murder conviction without a body is impossible.'

'We *do* have a body.'

'You have a body,' Galante repeated.

'Yes, sir. The Echegarays identified a body.'

'Are you kidding me?'

'No, sir.' Alzada cleared his throat. 'They identified . . . The body . . . is the one from the morgue this morning. I brought them pictures and they corroborated—'

'You did what? Are you out of your fucking mind? You tried to make them match? An Echegaray with a drug addict from a dumpster? You are out of control, Joaquín! But I will also say, and you must be damn well aware of this: you are one lucky bastard. What if they hadn't IDed her, Joaquín? What if it hadn't been her? Our careers would be over! What the fuck were you thinking?'

'I was thinking that I was doing my job, sir.'

'Don't mock me. And don't believe for a second I don't see what you've set in motion: now I have a murder to solve!' The commissioner slammed his hand on the table. 'But of course you do. This was your fucking plan all along, wasn't it? To force my hand and go after Pantera!'

'Sir, if I may . . .' *This is the moment you pick to interrupt?*

'You may not!' Galante pointed at Estrático. 'You—' The commissioner went silent. He took three slow breaths and readjusted his tie. 'Now . . . What is this all about? Who is this new and engaged Alzada? Frankly, I liked the old one better – saved me half the trouble. For fuck's sake, what's gotten into you?'

Alzada mumbled.

'The first time, this morning, I couldn't know you were going to be ridiculous about this. But this second time, this one's on me, isn't it? I should have known that you wouldn't be able to handle this case. With your history and all . . .'

'My *history*?'

Galante ignored him: 'And now, what, you thought you were going to pay a visit to Pantera?'

'I was coming to get a warrant.'

'Ah yes,' Galante paused. 'A warrant. You said.'

'It was a job, Horacio.'

'A job,' Galante repeated, incredulous. 'You're telling me someone put a mark on Norma Fucking Echegaray.'

'That's exactly what I'm telling you, yes.'

'You know this is not going to happen, no matter if you have the body, no matter if they are Echegarays; this won't fly in court. We're not in the business of vengeance, at least not anymore . . .' A little smile appeared on his face. '*But* they can always choose to solve the matter privately . . . You can suggest as much when you explain it to them. Yes, you. I'm not touching this shit with a ten foot—'

Glass shattering.

Almost like the sound of a clumsy waiter who had dropped a tray full of drinks. *Almost.* Alzada had heard the sound many times before. It was a different kind of cocktail.

FOR ALZADA, IT WAS THE silence. The initial shattering of glass could have been something else. A brick through a neighboring shop window, for example. But the ongoing murmur of the crowd outside had all of a sudden dimmed. Alzada only noticed it now that it was gone.

The first time he had witnessed a bottle bomb, Joaquín had had the same reaction of stunned admiration. *It was beautiful.* His privileged location at the time had allowed him to observe its journey from the moment it was launched by an energetic arm, then drew an arc in the air, then crash landed against a dumpster. Joaquín had joined the ranks of those fascinated with watching something burn. That's how Alzada knew at this very moment, without seeing them, that people in front of the station had cautiously stepped aside, but not too far: they were glued to the spectacle. They stood quietly. In awe. Staring at the fire spreading on the façade.

Alzada sprinted to the front door. When he reached the two officers who had been sitting in their cubicle, both made as if to stand up, cigarettes in hand.

'Do you need help, boss?' one of them offered.

Alzada wanted to yell at them to follow him, but he knew that if he spoke mid-run, he would betray his already fatigued breathing and he didn't want them to lose the vestiges of respect they apparently still harbored for him. Alzada raced past them without answering.

The Molotov cocktail had caught the security guard closing up. Seven o'clock. Basilio had left the keychain hanging from the outside and chosen to devote all his attention to admiring the spectacle. *He's so lazy he would rather go out front and face the fire than walk through the station and use the side door. That's private security for you.* The inspector slammed the glass pane with his palm until he got Basilio to turn in his direction. Alzada saw the guard's hands shake as he struggled with the lock.

The inspector rushed out to find himself the center of attention. As he had predicted, part of the mob had indeed stopped its march towards the Casa Rosada and become an audience. They had arranged themselves – at a safe distance, of course – into a perfect semicircle around the station's main entrance. Alzada stood at the empty space in the middle, arms on his hips, an exhausted orchestra conductor. ¡Qué calor! The temperature had not dropped, even as night approached.

'What are you still doing here?'

'There's a fire extinguisher—' Basilio started.

'Go home,' Alzada dismissed him.

'Do you not want me to—'

'I can do this,' the inspector answered, a fraction too fast. *No, I can't.* He wasn't even sure he'd be able to locate the fire extinguisher within the office, let alone put it to work efficiently.

Alzada looked around. The distance between the crowd and them was decreasing quickly, now that the novelty of the explosive had begun to wear off they had started encroaching on the two policemen.

'Give me your jacket,' the inspector instructed Basilio.

The guard was confused.

'You don't want to be caught with that.' Alzada pointed to the ironed patch peeking from under a fold on the guard's arm. 'Seguridad'. And underneath: 'Policía Federal'.

As well-meaning as Alzada had intended his comment to be it had the opposite effect: now Basilio looked scared. The inspector attempted to downplay it: 'A ver, you're not going to need it in this weather, no?'

The guard hesitated.

'Come on,' Alzada insisted. 'Give me the keys. I'll close up when I leave.'

Basilio handed him the jacket, nodded unconvincingly in appreciation, mumbled a rushed 'Buenas noches, inspector', and disappeared into the crowd.

WHERE WERE WE? ALZADA PIVOTED instinctively towards the heat source, only to stop and turn around again: not a smart move to have his back turned on the crowd.

Whoever was behind this had picked the perfect moment in the day to throw the Molotov cocktail. At dusk, the fire looked impressive. On the ground, the glass shards had given up any memory of their past life as a red wine bottle. Above them, at Alzada's eye level, the nineteenth-century plasterwork crackled under the flames, the baroque pastel yellow of the station façade already showed its first charcoal marks. The inspector found the exact spot on the wall where the bottle had landed. *Thank God for amateurs and their bad aim.* Only thirty centimeters higher and the projectile would have flown right through the window, and into the station.

Fortunately, it wasn't going to spread much further, nor burn much longer. That was the thing with homemade explosive devices: to begin with, they had probably not used the right flammable substance, and instead had filled the bottle with rubbing alcohol, or even rum. One of the few upsides of petrol being so expensive at the moment. And by the looks of it, they had forgotten to add a thickening agent to the mix before stuffing it with a piece of cloth to act as wick. The ethanol was starting to evaporate. Unless it caught onto another surface, it would fizzle out soon. Even so, Alzada understood he had to make *some* effort to put it out. *Where the fuck is Estrático?*

As if magically summoned, the deputy suddenly appeared, a fire extinguisher in hand. Alzada was coming to appreciate the moments in which Estrático popped out of nowhere. The inspector ripped the metal bottle away from him; one could not expect a man who very clearly got manicures to get things done.

Alzada struggled to pull the pin from the reverse grenade and pressed on the handle enough to check it allowed for movement. *I guess this is it?* He watched the flames, which seemed to grow from the stone, and felt almost sad to have to put it out. He aimed the nozzle at the waning fire, not without first yelling at Estrático to move.

The deputy positioned himself between him and the crowd, allowing Alzada to maneuver without worrying about having his back to the people. *Good boy.*

Alzada pressed the handle again, this time until his hands turned white. Foam the color of chicken broth sprouted from the nozzle and swallowed the flames completely. *This is heavy,* joder. He swept the fire extinguisher from side to side. *It looked easier when Paul Newman did it in* The Towering Inferno.

Alzada set the bottle down and was careful not to step on the foam. *The last thing I need is to ruin my shoes.* He leaned against the front door to observe the disappointment of the mob. *The culprit must still be around.* The inspector knew it to be an integral part of a pyromaniac's psyche: the pride in what he had done was too strong for him to hurl that Molotov cocktail and just leave. Even if it went against his own interest, he would feel the need to stay and watch.

Estrático joined him. 'Do you see him, sir?'

'Quiet, Estrático.'

Unlike in other demonstrations, the crowd was not only made up of the usual protesters. Every walk of Argentinian life was represented here. *We can exclude the grandmothers as suspects.* Alzada's eyes glided over the bystanders. *There you are.* The person most transfixed by the spectacle. A young man. Too attentive to the police's next move. Head to toe in dark clothes, neck scarf to conceal his face. *There must be others, they always travel in packs.* Not that it would make a difference: even if Alzada pounced on him, by the time he reached the spot where he had stood, he'd be long gone. At the end of the street, toppled-over cars had been repurposed as bonfires. *How am I going to get home?*

GALANTE APPEARED. *ABOUT TIME.* IN his three-piece suit, thecommissioner ceremoniously pondered the wall, then the fire extinguisher, then Alzada, then gave the situation an approving nod. *This is going to have consequences.*

'We're not going to be proud of today,' Galante sighed.

'Do you mean—'

'Joaquín,' the commissioner paused, as if trying patiently to explain in simpler terms, when both knew all Alzada wanted was to hear him say it out loud. 'This just gave me justification – no, this now *demands* I give the order to fire.'

'Rubber?' Alzada asked.

'For now.'

'Sir?' A voice from inside made the three turn towards the door. *Pintadini is still here? That means Galante is expecting a long night.*

'Just a minute, Pinta.'

'Sir,' Pintadini repeated, this time in a tone so grave that Galante waved him to approach.

'Is it official?' he asked.

'Not yet. But he's announced an address to the nation. Any minute now,' Pintadini smirked. 'Which probably means in around an hour.'

If De la Rúa declares the state of siege we can forget about finding Pantera.

Galante closed his eyes for a moment. 'That's all for today.'

'I can stay,' Alzada blurted, surprised at his own initiative. Why had he offered? What was there left for him to do? It wasn't even night yet, which always brought out the worst in people, and they were already throwing Molotov cocktails at police stations. What was next? Definitely not something six worn-out cops could deal with. No. The president was not appearing on national television to wish them goodnight. *He's sending in the military.*

'Me too,' Estrático echoed.

'No. Let's close the station,' Galante decided. 'Pinta can drop me off at headquarters on his way home. Where's your car, Joaquín?'

Alzada had to think for a second. 'Just outside this mess. I left it by the Echegaray apartment—'

'So, we're talking about a twenty-minute walk?'

'Yes, sir.' Alzada nodded. *Today it will be at least thirty.* 'But once I reach it, I can get directly onto the Panamericana highway.'

Galante seemed relieved. 'Be careful. They have built barricades along the villas.' He turned to Estrático: 'And you?'

'I came on foot.'

'Okay. Leave both your badges here. I don't need to get reports on cops being lynched.' *Need.* Alzada swallowed. 'Good night, Joaquín.'

When Alzada turned to leave, Galante grabbed him by the arm, as if he had only now remembered: 'And I never want to hear about that Echegaray business again, do you hear me? You drop it, yes?'

Alzada nodded.

Galante softened: 'It's time for you to go home.'

22
(1981)

Vukić opened the sorry excuse for a door and walked into the hallway, Alzada close behind him carrying his brother, Petacchi at the back. They had only advanced a couple of metres when Jorge Rodolfo's legs slipped from Alzada's grasp and hit the floor. *We haven't even reached the top of the stairs.* The commissioner turned around to identify the noise, and, without skipping a beat, grabbed Jorge by his right shoulder. Between the two policemen, his feet barely touched the steps down.

When they got to the ground floor, Alzada looked up to realize Montalvo had abandoned his desk and was comfortably surveying the operation from across the hall. *How long has he been standing there?* The inspector had been so focused on not dropping his brother that he had neglected his other senses.

Alerted by his presence, Vukić immediately stepped forward to meet him, leaving Alzada to carry all of Jorge's weight. From afar, someone could have confused them for two friends that had had too much to drink, leaning on each other, waiting for the night bus to take them home. But if that someone came closer, they would recognize there was something deeply wrong with the picture: one was relying too heavily on the other.

'We're taking him,' the commissioner announced.

'Wait, wait, wait.' Montalvo's tone was firm; in contrast, his body was loose, almost relaxed. *He knows we're at his mercy.* 'Visiting a detainee . . . I mean. Sure.' *Far from it: you've realized you made a mistake in letting us in, now you're trying to fix it.* 'It's not the norm. I'd even go as far as to say it's quite *far* from the norm. But we're colleagues, etcetera . . . An exception can be made.'

Alzada hoped Montalvo would just blurt out his objection. He wasn't sure how much longer he would be able to hold Jorge Rodolfo upright without help from Vukić.

Montalvo continued: 'But now you want to *leave* with him? That is a *completely* different situation. Why would you think you can just walk out of here? Not only is it a flagrant breach of protocol—' he let out a fake cough, 'but it is disrespectful to our efforts.' *So that's what this is.* '. . . to keep this nation safe.' *From your desk.* 'Are you even aware of the amount of organization it requires, to track down a parasite such as this one?' Alzada swallowed. He had used many unflattering words to qualify Jorge; never 'parasite'. 'Do you know the effort that goes into finding these subversives? The work that goes into carefully extracting them from society?' *Carefully, yes.* 'And now you want to take this one and do what? Return him to the streets? He'll be planting a bomb tomorrow!'

Alzada tried to imagine what options were going through Vukić's mind: he was sure the commissioner was using Montalvo's speech to plot his next move. Confronting the officer directly would have been Alzada's first choice. The imbecile would probably be so surprised that someone would dare touch him, that he would at worst calm down and at best acquiesce. But what if defying Montalvo had the opposite effect and only inflamed him further? Seconds seemed minutes. *Silence is the better option.* And indeed, the lack of retort was slowly having the desired result: the officer's rhetoric had started to deflate.

'Definitely against protocol,' Montalvo repeated, then finally fell silent. 'Don't move.'

He disappeared through a small side door.

'A VER, ¿QUÉ ESTÁ PASANDO aquí?' a voice thundered through the hall.

The commander walked towards them slowly, as if the world would only start to turn when he arrived. Alzada had only guessed his rank. *Difficult to tell in his green fatigues.* But if the size of a man's belly was historically considered an infallible indicator of his hierarchical status, then this had to be at least a general. Resting both fat hands on his belt, the latter shifted up and down as the commander approached with deliberation. Behind him, Montalvo had become barely visible.

Alzada took a step back; Vukić took one forward.

On his first day as a police officer, Alzada had committed the common mistake of dismissing the commissioner as a simple brute. It had taken some time for him to discern Vukić's killer instinct; at first, he had observed that he came up with effective solutions in seconds, like a born warrior. That was when his appreciation for his superior had started. Of course, one could argue that a lesser cop might have had the same reaction, following the primal urge to take the measure of one's adversary, and have him measure you in return: up close the commissioner was an imposing presence, and that would maybe deter the commander. But for Vukić that wasn't enough. *He's boxed in his youth.* Like the fighter who dodges a punch by counter-intuitively leaning forwards instead of backwards, the commissioner had clearly calculated that by stepping inside his personal space the man would not have the room needed to grab Jorge. He would have to maneuver around him. And in passing, he had also created a blind spot. The Alzadas were now no longer in the commander's line of sight. *Out of sight, out of mind.*

'Éstos. They say they want to take Alzada with them,' Montalvo explained from behind his superior.

Joaquín was not nearly as tall as Vukić, but over the commissioner's shoulders he could glimpse a tanned and ample forehead, on which time had ploughed the first few wrinkles. Black hair slicked back with gel so perfectly it might have been drawn with a stencil.

'Good evening, gentlemen.' *'Civilians', he must be thinking. I can smell the contempt from here.* The commander spoke without hurry. He was going nowhere. And neither were they. 'I'm Commander DeCervatelli.'

'Good evening, sir,' Vukić replied deferentially.

'I was disturbed in my sleep.' *That's a lie.* 'Only so that I could clarify one particularly important rule of the ESMA. And while it is a fairly obvious one, it seems like it has yet to be understood.' He regarded each one of them – *where is Petacchi?* – and paused at Vukić, as if the latter were a child who needed to be given time to process the gravity of his intrusion. 'People come into the ESMA.' He reveled in every word: 'They don't come *out* of the ESMA.'

Alzada swallowed.

DeCervatelli didn't look like a monster. On the contrary, he looked like a decent man – someone who had his priorities in order, and who kept a tight ship in the academy and was well respected. Someone who was good as his job. Alzada realized that he looked like someone with whom he could have a beer and probably agree on more than a couple of things. Jorge Rodolfo was getting heavier by the minute.

'This is a very particular case—' Vukić said.

'*Every* case is a very particular case,' the commander cut him short.

'Sir, if I may.' Without skipping a beat, Vukić leaned in and whispered.

Alzada hoped the echo of the hollow structure would work in his favor, but he barely managed to discern a couple of loose words. Did he just hear 'the bigger fish'? *We're dead.*

Jorge Rodolfo clearly was of the same opinion, because, like an inopportune drunk, he erupted a little louder than any of them would have hoped: 'I didn't tell them—'

Where will it hurt the most? Alzada tightened his grip around his brother's ribs. Jorge winced, and was silent.

The sound caught DeCervatelli's attention, who sidestepped Vukić to take a look at the heap of flesh in Joaquín's arms. Alzada shuddered.

'And if it wasn't clear,' Vukić intercepted him, 'I would be remiss if I didn't explicitly state that we are obviously enormously appreciative of the work you're doing for our nation.'

The commander leaned back and swelled with pride. *Thank God.*

'In no way do we want our visit to give the impression that we underrate the efforts you have undertaken – you *are* undertaking – for our safety.'

'Well,' DeCervatelli said. He brushed his moustache with his left hand. *He's impressed.*

'Well?' Vukić tempted fate.

'This is exactly what we were talking about the other day. We love to collaborate with our brothers in arms. Unfortunately, not everyone is of the same disposition. Just the other day I had to listen to someone yap about some "preso politico". Can you believe it? There are no political prisoners in Argentina, only common criminals! Ah, if only more police officers were as solicitous as you are . . . Y bueno . . .' He slowed down. *Here it comes.* 'If you think he can be of *any* use to you than he has been to us, my friend,' the commander put his hand on Vukić's shoulder in camaraderie, 'he's all yours.'

Vukić emitted a nervous laugh to match the commander's smile.

'Anyway, we have enough of them for the . . .' DeCervatelli paused deliberately mid-sentence, '*transfer* next Tuesday.'

Out of the corner of his eye, Alzada saw Montalvo struggle between a smile of satisfaction and a grimace of disapproval. *Thank God for military hierarchy.*

'Yes. That will be my final word on the matter. Take him with you,' the commander ordered. He seemed to be, after the initial annoyance, almost amused by the situation. *He wants to get back to whomever he was working on.* 'In any case, he's given us all he had: a couple of names and an address, and by the time we raided it, they were already gone. So good luck, gentlemen.'

DeCervatelli turned towards the door from which he had emerged. Montalvo reluctantly sat back down at his post. Was that Alzada's cue to aim for the exit? Should he perhaps wait for Vukić to take the lead? Why was he still standing there? The commander brusquely halted and swiveled back to face them. *That's why.*

'One more thing,' his voice remained quiet and composed, 'when you're done with him . . .' DeCervatelli lifted his right index finger in a reprimand gesture, 'you know what to do.'

Vukić nodded dutifully. Joaquín shivered.

'I don't want him to show up floating in the Río de la Plata.' The junta had never seemed to be worried about bodies surfacing on the river, never bothered by the set of uncomfortable questions; if anything, they were just slightly embarrassed to have to answer before an international audience, which they knew to have a short-term memory. 'Then it's *you* who will have a problem. What's your name?'

'Comisario Fernando Alejandro Vukić.' The commissioner stepped forward. 'Policía Federal.'

Alzada realized in that moment that all through the night he had not identified himself. What would he have said if someone had asked for his name?

'Bien.' The forthright answer seemed to please the commander. 'No loose ends. Do we understand each other?'

Without waiting for confirmation, he turned around and left. VUKIĆ STARTED MAKING STRIDES AWAY from the officer and towards the door. Alzada couldn't possibly ask him to return and help with Jorge Rodolfo; he didn't want to draw any more attention. There were twenty-five, perhaps thirty meters to the door through which they had entered. It was now or never. *Ahora*.

Alzada hoisted Jorge in his arms and prayed he wouldn't give. His brother's body was slippery, he was soaking wet. *What is he drenched in?* Alzada felt him slither. He found it more and more difficult to grip harder without hurting him.

Twenty meters.

The smell. In the beginning, he had attributed it to the poor sanitary conditions of the place. But now, leaning forward to try to hold Jorge Rodolfo, the origin became clear. All this time he had thought the morgue was the most unpleasant experience of his life. Alzada forced himself to think of a good smell, but nothing came to mind. Then he tried to think of another bad smell, one not noxious, fetid and rancid at the same time. A smell that wasn't the product of attempting to decompose a human being while alive. Alzada tried to repress the heaves.

Fifteen.

His steps had now acquired a squishy quality on the stone. Fluids had drenched his left side and were now dripping down his shoes. God only knew the color of the stain they were leaving behind. He felt Jorge grab on, and that encouraged him. *Vamos, Joaquín.* Only a couple of steps. They just needed a couple more steps.

Ten.

He had Vukić in front of him, was Petacchi following? Alzada was reminded of Lot's wife, turned into a pillar of salt for looking back. The doctor would have to figure it out by himself.

Five meters.

Joaquín saw Vukić opening the door and holding it for him. That was all he needed. He gathered strength from where there was none. He pushed past him, and into the night.

23

(2001)

S omething was out of place.

It was not unusual for Alzada to get home late from work. Not that he was the most dedicated officer at the station, far from it, but between errands and Buenos Aires traffic, he often arrived after nightfall. His perpetual lateness notwithstanding, he always made sure to be on time for the nine o'clock news. In comparison, today was early. Joaquín checked his watch. Twenty to eight.

It was also not unusual for him to find Paula and Sorolla sitting together in front of the television: after a lifetime of exclusively and religiously watching the news, she had recently been introduced by their nephew to the joys of TV dramas. And so, guided by her very own Virgil, they had delved into a new world. Both of them were now hooked on several American series and had tried several times to make Joaquín join them. One day, he had finally acquiesced and caught a few minutes of a series set around an American funeral home. But Joaquín didn't need that kind of macabre entertainment and preferred to use the time to read his Montalbano.

What was unusual was the quiet. Whenever Paula and Sorolla watched television together, there were always laughs, and comments, and gasps, and inside jokes, and the microwave ding announcing the popcorn was ready. Now, as Joaquín took off his jacket and tie and set them over a kitchen chair, no sound came from the living room. He leaned in. Paula and Sorolla sitting, perfectly still, staring at the TV. The rainbow-colored vertical stripes indicated no signal. Joaquín approached the couch. *Have I missed it?*

It couldn't be. The moment he had gotten to his car, Alzada had turned on the radio, even though he normally liked to drive in silence and even though it meant dividing his focus between the state of the road and the broadcast, which could switch to the official announcement at any moment. Still, the inspector had happened upon no barricades, contrary to what Galante had predicted, nor homemade spike strips, which worried him most since they were impossible to detect at night. Alzada knew steel pipes with nails had been widely used on that same highway to intercept trucks transporting food. He felt almost disappointed about the fact that he'd barely encountered a couple of isolated groups – teenagers, for the most part – burning tires on the sides of the Panamericana. *Is this the revolution? I've seen worse on a regular Tuesday.*

It must be about to start.

REPENTANCE

Joaquín stood behind Paula, his thighs against the cream-colored back of the couch. *Have they even noticed me coming in?* Suddenly, the light blue of the Argentinian flag filled the screen. In its middle white stripe, the anthropomorphic sun seemed somewhere between bored and tense, its brows furrowed, its lips pursed, wrinkling the corners of its mouth. The voice of a news anchor announced the president was about to address the nation, deferentially introducing him as 'Doctor Fernando de la Rúa', in the Argentinian tradition of granting that title to people with a law degree. *Just what the country needs: another lawyer.* 'You're one to talk, *Doctor* Alzada,' he knew Paula would quip if he had made the comment out loud.

De la Rúa appeared on screen. His image, rendered familiar by his repeated presence in the media – even more so in the last couple of weeks – retained its striking aura. It was the black caterpillar eyebrows, in sharp contrast with his utterly white hair. Or maybe his piercing professorial gaze. Or his nose, the shape of a stalactite persuading one last drop to join the calcareous formation below, and almost as prominent as his wise man's ears. The president started off with a succinct 'my fellow countrymen' and then proceeded to deliver the message. *He's got no time to lose. If I were him, I would already have left the city.* De la Rúa made mention of the delinquent factions, who he said were taking advantage of this 'difficult hour' for the Argentinian people to cause 'unjustified incidents'.

Someone must have recommended he put on his round, metal-rimmed glasses mid-speech to distract from the fact that he was explaining said commotion left him no option but to declare the stage of siege 'to guarantee the safety of the general population'. Only as a 'very temporary measure', he added. The specs worked: they covered the bags under his eyes and made the difference between a power-hungry maniac and a moderate technocrat seemingly only interested in the common good. In the background, the faux baroque gold leaf of the Casa Rosada.

It took De la Rúa a mere four minutes to strip citizens of every one of their civil and political liberties. Joaquín realized he was tapping his left foot on the floor. If Paula hadn't been engrossed in the speech, she most certainly would have told him to stop. *We live in a democratic state based on the rule of law.* And yet, for the next thirty days, De la Rúa wasn't obliged to abide by the Constitution. *It's not as if a state of siege ever went totally wrong in this country* . . . Joaquín expected Sorolla to jump up in indignation at any point now. *Nothing.* Sorolla didn't blink. The broadcast was over.

Paula turned to face him.

'Joaquín,' she said very slowly, the syllables slightly disconnected as if his name were unfamiliar to her, as if she were just learning how to pronounce it.

She stood and held him tightly. *Why don't we hug more often?* He pressed her harder against him, so hard that he could barely understand what Paula was saying, her voice muffled by his shirt.

'Joaco, it's happening again.'

24
(2001)

Joaquín let go of Paula with the same care he had used as a child to separate the stamps he wanted for his collection from their envelopes. He would first soak them in lukewarm water to release the adhesive gum, then hold each stamp with tongs to peel the paper off its back.

'What do we do now?' Paula sat back down on the couch.

Sorolla bolted up and disappeared.

'Where is he going?' Joaquín joined her on the freshly empty spot. He asked mainly to avoid the silence: it was a common occurrence for their nephew to retreat to his room. Since his arrival, the boy had been quiet – almost as if he believed that his mere existence was an imposition. Joaquín felt a twitch at the thought of Sorolla feeling like a nuisance in his own home.

'To listen to the radio, probably.'

With the official broadcast interrupted, amateur shortwave would be the closest thing to news for a while.

'I think we wait,' Joaquín said. 'No?'

'Nothing's going to happen to him.'

How can she—? Maybe she was referring to something else. Alzada was silent.

'They let you go home.' *She doesn't want to sit with her thoughts either.*

He nodded in response. 'Galante insisted.'

'Do you think they're bringing in the military?'

Joaquín nodded again. What other possible explanation was there? Why else would the commissioner close the station? He knew that he was going to get support, sooner or later.

'Do you think he sent you home because he owes you?' Paula's question brought him back.

'Because he once wasn't there for me? After twenty years?'

She curled her lip. 'Yes, no. Definitely the military.'

Joaquín sighed. History had a tendency to repeat itself in cycles, and their democracy had never been the most stable, but how often in their lifetimes would they have to discuss the possibility of living under a dictatorship? *When is enough, enough?*

'What about the case?' Paula left him no room to wallow.

'The—'

'Yes. The case from this afternoon. Did you get what you wanted?'

There seems to be no easy subject tonight. 'In the end, we had to drop it.'

'That's a shame.'

'Yes. A shame.'

SOROLLA BURST INTO THE LIVING room. 'I want to go.'

Experience and Paula had taught Joaquín she was more skilled at handling all matters concerning their nephew. The 'bull-in-a-china-shop doctrine', she liked to call it; he tried not to take offense. Joaquín picked up *Un mes con Montalbano* from the coffee table. Maybe he'd get some reading done.

'All of Greater Buenos Aires is mobilized,' Sorolla insisted.

Joaquín pictured his nephew in his room, a moment ago, standing tall, practicing how to convince Paula to let him go. *He's a grown-up. What kind of self-respecting man needs permission to leave his house?* Had they been too soft on him? Half of Argentina had survived trauma and they were just fine.

'Your uncle and I . . .' She could speak on his behalf. 'We think it's best if you don't go tonight.'

'Especially not to the center,' Joaquín added without looking up. *I hope you enjoyed this morning, boludo, because that's all you're going to see of the cacerolazos.*

'Especially not Buenos Aires, darling,' Paula softened.

'No reason? Just "no"?'

'Don't be impatient, Sorolla. Let me finish.'

'I'm sorry,' he apologized immediately.

'Thank you.' She took a moment to gather her thoughts. *The amount of patience it took to deal with these young people!* 'Well. For one, you'd be infringing the dusk-to-dawn curfew. Didn't they mention that on the radio?'

'I don't care about the curfew,' Joaquín heard Sorolla say. *Why do I have the feeling I'm not going to get very far in the book?* 'No one cares about the curfew, at least not tonight. There's thousands and thousands of people on the streets—'

'That leads me to the second reason: we're concerned that . . . that . . .'

Joaquín knew exactly what she was getting to.

'You know you don't do well in crowds,' she finally managed. 'Are you not worried about that yourself? Only the other day we were talking about how your practice of consciousness implies setting your own limits. Perhaps that should entail – what do they call it? – not overriding a justified concern owing to a sudden impulse. What do you think?'

Where the hell is she getting all of this from? Probably from the books she had told him to read but he'd dismissed as pop psychology. Joaquín caught a glimpse of Sorolla. The mention of his limitations had him biting his lip.

'Now we're under martial law. That means we're not only talking about crowds,' she continued. 'There could very easily be . . . an incident, *querido*.'

'An "incident"? Are those your words? Because they sound more like *his*.' Joaquín didn't look at him, but he could imagine Sorolla pointing dismissively. 'Do you mean the police are going to do the usual? Use brute force against unarmed civilians? That doesn't seem to bother you any other day. Is today different because that unarmed civilian might be me? The hypocrisy!'

'Sorolla,' Paula warned him. She must know Joaquín had given up on the page at which he was so intently staring.

'People are getting together at every corner,' Sorolla persisted. 'Everyone I know is going.'

'Maybe it's time to meet new people,' Joaquín quipped.

Paula gave him a look.

I know, I know. I'm not helping.

She returned her attention to Sorolla: 'There'll be other cacerolazos.'

Their nephew huffed. He looked nowhere near being done. 'This is *exactly* how dictatorships happen. First martial law. Then what? We need to stop this before it's too late. Don't you understand? It's not about making noise with a pot and a pan anymore. This needs to be a *revolution*. And it needs to be *today*!' Sorolla was getting heated. In part, because he was buying into his own rallying words. In part, because the fearless warrior wouldn't dare go anywhere without Paula's approval – *the reverence he has for her.* It wasn't looking good so far: she smiled and nodded; her arms were crossed. She would smile and nod herself out of the situation and Sorolla would return to his room. Joaquín could see Sorolla reading her too and running desperate because he wasn't convincing her. In no time, that restlessness would make him cross a line. 'If anything, I'm surprised *you* guys won't go. After everything—'

Paula's chin quivered.

'Leave your tía alone.' Joaquín had been silent, but no longer. He placed his index finger on the sentence he had been trying to finish for a while now.

'Finally,' his nephew turned towards him, 'he deigns himself worthy of this conversation.'

'See, that's where you're wrong. This is not a conversation. In a conversation, I'd actually be listening to you. In a conversation, I'd actually *care* about what you have to say.' Joaquín paused to allow Sorolla to respond; the boy just swallowed. He didn't need to look at Paula to know she was making her classical 'Joaquín, por favor' gesture. 'I don't know what could have given you the impression that that is the case here. Your aunt has very patiently explained to you why you're not going.' He cleared his throat. 'So, you're not going.'

'How very authoritarian of you. Why doesn't this come as a surprise?'

He had often had this discussion with Paula, about why she had bonded with their nephew while he hadn't. 'He's got a lot of quite remarkable things to say,' she had explained, unconsciously making him jealous. 'And I don't think you realize how much respect you inspire in him.' 'More like fear,' Joaquín had answered, half defensively, half pained. 'No,' she'd objected flatly. 'The way he looks at you, like a young red deer buck during his first rut.' Alzada had scoffed. 'And the way *you* look at him . . .' 'I don't judge him for that PSTD thing, if that's what you're implying.' 'Oh, no. I know. You judge yourself.' 'What can I say, Paulita, it's easier.'

Joaquín looked over to Paula, who nodded encouragingly.

'Bien.' He took a deep breath. 'Let's have that discussion.' He inserted the bookmark and hesitated before closing the book. 'Sit.'

Sorolla sat.

'Hit me with your best argument. But I warn you,' Joaquín set the book down, 'I've heard them all. What's it going to be? Perhaps a classic like "You want a better world, but you want other people's children to make it"?'

Sorolla was silent.

'That's it, no? Correct me if I'm wrong, but I think our disagreement isn't about *what* we want for this country but *how* we want to achieve it. That's precisely why we're having this conversation tonight and not any other night. This social unrest that you support, this revolution that you announce, have you stopped to consider if it's even viable? What it implies? You want to go out on the streets today and protest. What do you think we'll wake up to tomorrow?'

'So you *do* think something needs to be done.' *Well avoided.*

'Of course,' Joaquín said emphatically, only to specify: 'Just not by *you*.'

'If everyone were to think like that, change would never happen, tío.'

'Fair point.' Under any other circumstance, at this point Joaquín would already have made the transition from raising his voice to full-blown yelling. *Paula observing this interaction like an overzealous tennis umpire might have something to do with it.* 'But I don't think this family needs to sacrifice any more of its members to a cause.'

Sorolla bowed his head. 'That's low.'

'It might be.' *It is.* 'But you can understand that, no? Especially you?'

'"Especially me"? What is that supposed to mean?'

'It means . . . it means . . .' Joaquín struggled to find the words. How many times had he had a similar discussion with Jorge Rodolfo? How many times had he trodden carefully around the issues? And what had all that tiptoeing achieved?

'What your aunt was too polite to say before is, what if something happens to you? What if you have a panic attack and you're trampled to death by hordes of demonstrators?'

Sorolla turned pale.

'And that's of course leaving out the fact that yes, the police will be on edge and possibly overeager tonight. I can guarantee you that. I guess what I mean to say is "especially you" have the perfect excuse.'

'I don't *want* an excuse! I'm done talking and talking and not seeing anything get done! How are *you* not tired of it?' Sorolla rose.

Joaquín stood too and readjusted his belt. 'I *am* tired.' As he said it, the feeling invaded his body. 'We've paid our dues, now leave us alone. To you, I must look like a . . . what is the word for someone like me? How would the Elements of Revolutionary Style put it? A comfortable—'

'Bystander,' Sorolla said, spite in his voice.

'Yes. That's it. A comfortable bystander with a cushy government job, no? Well let me tell you: there's nothing dishonorable in providing for your family, hijo.' Joaquín realized he had unthinkingly called him son. Sorolla remained still. 'Do you think I'm not aware of the compromises I've made throughout my life?'

Joaquín stopped to glance at Paula. *Is this the moment?* Unlike adoptive parents, they had never had the luxury of preparing for the inevitable 'how to tell him' moment. The boy had been sprung on them, and they had been happy. 'We'll talk about those things as they come up,' had seemed a reasonable approach. Yet so many topics didn't arise in regular conversation. *Otherwise, how would we live?* Joaquín returned his attention to his nephew: 'Since you mentioned law-enforcement tactics, do you know I was in the riot squad when I was twenty-two?'

Sorolla seemed startled.

'Yes, I know it must be hard to imagine.' Joaquín smiled. 'I was fitter then. And do you know why I did it? I had already cashed in every possible favour within the force to keep your father out of trouble and this was not even the dictatorship that had him killed; it was during the previous one. I had to step in for a riot officer whose cousin agreed to "lose" Jorge Rodolfo's file. The intricate favor structure that keeps the system in motion . . . Anyway. For six months every one of my shifts started with putting on the protective gear. And I did so gladly. For your father, for your aunt, for you – who weren't even close to being born. And what's more, I'd do it again.'

'Were you scared?'

'Of course I was.'

'Good.'

Joaquín smiled. 'If you think me being scared would have given you any advantage over me, you must have less of a fucking idea than I thought—'

'Language,' Paula intervened.

'I'm sorry,' he bowed in deference, then cleared his throat. 'To the point. There's no greater danger than underestimating your opponent. You might think cops are slow and overweight and with horrible aim. The bad guys in an old Western lurking behind a cardboard movie set. Nothing could be further from the truth. They're in phenomenal shape, and well trained, and . . . You're standing there, and you see them coming.' Alzada had been terrified. He had stood in formation, barely filling that asshole's uniform, thinking 'This is the last time I cover for Jorge.' He had been thankful for the steel soles in his boots, which anchored him to the pavement and prevented him from running in the opposite direction. He had recited the tactical formations under his breath like a prayer. 'That's actually not true: first you *hear* them. It's something you don't see in the photographs. A colossal wave taking its time to reach the shore. So loud you can no longer hear the man standing next to you chewing gum with his mouth open. In that moment, you realize you don't really know what you're doing. You barely hold the line. And then,' Joaquín paused to check on Sorolla, who was engrossed in the narrative like when he was a little boy and his uncle re-enacted for him General San Martín crossing the Andes to free Argentina from Spanish rule. 'Then you hear your command, you close your eyes, and you charge.' Joaquín paused again, this time for dramatic effect. 'Do you think their strength comes from the courage of their convictions? No! Is it because they've been promised wine and women in Valhalla? No! The *only* fuel they have is their fear!' Now he was yelling. 'So, when you talk about being glad that I was scared, I think: there's no way he's going out there tonight. *They* have the upper hand. *They* have understood something you apparently haven't: there's sides to everything. And in that game of sides, it's them, or *you.*' With the last sentence, Joaquín pressed his index on his nephew's chest.

'Okay,' Paula said, 'I think that's enough. I'm going to make dinner.'

'Let me help you, tía. It's not like I have anywhere to be . . .' Sorolla stepped back until Joaquín's arm dropped, then walked with Paula into the kitchen.

'Don't pout,' Joaquín heard her say. 'He's only being like that because—'

'Yes, I know,' Sorolla softened immediately, putting his arm in hers.

Joaquín took a deep breath. *How does she do it?* Should he lay off the subject for a while? He'd been rattled by his nephew, to a higher degree than he'd expected. He would let the situation cool down before going at it again. *Have some gnocchi.* Whenever Paula was worried, there were gnocchi.

And yet, despite his best intentions, his first words as he entered the kitchen were: 'Please explain to me, what if there was a confrontation? What is your plan?'

'Common sense,' was Sorolla's nonchalant answer, while he arranged the three place mats on the table. 'It worked for you, didn't it?'

Paula placed a pot of water on the stove. From where Joaquín stood, leaning on the cabinet on the opposite wall of the kitchen, he could only see her back. *She's smirking.*

'And when they charge you with one million volts?' he insisted.

'Oh, that won't happen.'

Joaquín raised his eyebrows and waited for his nephew to elaborate.

'They're not going to catch me,' Sorolla smiled, setting down the plates and glasses.

'Obviously.' *Just like his father.*

Alzada felt a pain in his side. Sorolla had inherited Jorge Rodolfo's dark curls, and his love for coffee – *though, to be fair, that might come from Paula.* More surprising was the fact that he also shared character traits with his father he would have been too young to pick up from him. How could that be? Was nonchalance genetically transmitted?

Sorolla hated when someone, unaware of their family circumstances, mentioned his resemblance to Joaquín, especially when someone thought he was his father. Joaquín had long dismissed that reaction as something common to all children, but now it dawned on him: was he as embarrassed at being related to him as his father had been? Was that why they were having the *same* discussion with the *same* arguments, two, three decades apart? *I'm only doing what it takes to survive.*

'I think you should abandon your political inclinations while you can and go back to your quiet life. The birds, isn't it, chico?'

'Joaquín, please.' Paula gave him a cup of coffee.

He made a gesture as if to say 'Now? With dinner?' but didn't refuse.

'First of all,' Sorolla set the cutlery, 'don't call me "boy". Second, if you must know, I work in the South American mammals' section. So, if you want to insult me, at least make it factually correct: it's marsupials, not birds. Tiny marsupials. And third, if that's all you can resort to, I must be winning this argument.' He spun around to dip a finger in the sage and butter sauce and winced. 'I know how disappointed you must be. What was I supposed to become, police like you?' *The same reproach as Jorge.*

'What exactly is wrong with being a police officer?' His brother had eternally disapproved, but never answered.

Sorolla ignored his question and continued: 'Me working to rehabilitate injured monitos del monte so they can be released back into the wild must kill you. Do you lie when people ask about me? What do you say, that I work at a bank?'

'Come on, Sorolla,' Paula said, returning her attention to the boiling water.

'You have no idea what you're talking about.'

'Maybe that's because you never explain anything to me. I always get the same answer: "one day". The only person Joaquín allowed to imitate him did so with painstaking accuracy, down to the inflection. '"One day", you say. I don't even know where they are!'

Alzada looked at Paula. The only promise they had made to each other that they both knew they had broken.

'It was safer that way,' Paula said.

'If you want me to have more of an idea, you need to tell me.' Sorolla turned to Alzada. 'You can start with this: was my father also a disappointment? Did you tell *him*?'

'Sorolla, I think you should stop right there,' Paula tried again.

'No, no, Paula. Let him,' Joaquín conceded sardonically. 'Tonight might be the most I've ever heard him talk.'

'I'm not surprised he hated you.'

Paula insisted. 'Sorolla, por favor.'

'Will you please stop defending him?' their nephew turned towards her. 'And stop telling me what to do. You're not my mother.'

Paula stopped in her tracks, pasta strainer in hand. She opened her mouth as if to say something, changed her mind and tended to the gnocchi.

That's it.

'Do you really want to know the truth about your father? Why we don't talk about him?' Sorolla nodded, self-assured. 'He *was* a disappointment. But not for the reasons you might think. He was naive and reckless, and at times a downright idiot. He loved being in the middle of the action. He had to interfere in matters that were none of his fucking business. So many times I had to rescue him, so many times I got into trouble for him. And still, that's *not* why he disappointed me.' Joaquín hesitated. 'No. What I never understood was how he could love his political cause more than he loved you.'

'That's a lie!' Sorolla yelled.

'Not *once* did he ask for you!' Joaquín shouted back.

'That's a lie,' Sorolla repeated, softer, so he could hold back his tears. He looked to Paula for confirmation; she kept facing the stove. 'Well, I wish it had been you!'

I do too.

'At least he wasn't a murderer!'

'¡BASTA!' Paula shouted.

'Then what would you call what he did to your mother?'

Paula's voice thundered through the kitchen. '¡YA BASTA! That's enough!'

Joaquín and Sorolla watched transfixed as she progressively became smaller and smaller until she sank to the ground and curled up in front of the oven, the bowl of gnocchi with sauce still in her hand. Both ran towards her and kneeled on the cold tiles at a safe distance.

'Paulita,' tried Joaquín.

'Tía . . .' tried Sorolla. He only managed to make her relinquish the pasta.

She was inconsolable. She cried and cried in violent sobs. She got the hiccups. She had to divert her attention to fight the convulsions. She grew angered by them. She cried even more. Both men came closer until the three were one mass of limbs folded upon itself. She finally came to a halt.

They stayed like that, uncomfortably, for a long time.

'NOW,' WAS THE FIRST THING Paula said after she refused both of their help to get up, and she got up. She straightened out her green summer dress, cleaned the little mascara she dared to wear from under her eyelids, and firmly cleared her throat.

'You,' she started with Sorolla. 'You weren't even born when the events that you speak of so matter-of-factly took place.' *He was.* 'I've come to realize over the course of this evening that, indeed, you don't have the slightest idea – maybe just a vague notion – about what happened to your parents. And that's definitely our fault. But we can change that. From now on, you can ask, and we'll give you answers. *Proper* answers.' She motioned to Joaquín, who nodded. 'In the meantime, you must know that, even though he'll *never* tell you, your uncle loves you above all things.' Then she added: 'Except me, of course.'

Joaquín smiled.

'And you,' Paula turned to face her husband.

His smile vanished instantly.

'You . . .'

She needn't say more: he knew.

Paula folded the dish towel she had been using in six perfect squares. 'Fortunately for *both* of you,' she hung the cloth on the oven door and distributed her stern look evenly, judicious like an angry Argentinian King Solomon, 'you've got a head of the family who performs well under pressure.' Joaquín furrowed his brow but emitted no sound. 'So, you can trust that I'll make a good decision. First: Joaquín put on your jacket.'

'In this heat?'

'Fine. You can go without your jacket.'

'Oh, I'm not going,' Joaquín retorted.

'Yes, you are.' Her decision had been made.

Alzada started looking for his jacket. *Did I take it off in the living room when I came in?*

'Joaquín.'

'What now?' he replied from the hall.

'I mean the other Joaquín.' There was a perfectly good reason why they didn't call their nephew that. *This means she's furious.*

'Yes, tía.' Sorolla was slurping his coffee, surely cold by now.

'Apologize to your uncle.'

The inspector reappeared in the kitchen. His jacket was meticulously folded on the cabinet on which he had been leaning. Sorolla must have removed it from the chair when he set the table. 'Ah, there it is.'

Sorolla waited for his uncle to put it back on. 'Tío, I'm sorry for what I said. I didn't mean to—'

'That's enough. Thank you,' Paula cut him off and rubbed her hands together. 'We've wasted enough time as it is. The gnocchi are probably cold—'

Joaquín looked down at the bowl: steam still emanated from them.

'I didn't knead them from scratch for you not to eat them. We're going to have dinner. Then the two of you can go to that cacerolazo downtown.'

'And you?' they asked in unison.

'Ah, no,' Paula dismissed the idea with an exaggerated wave, as if that were the silliest idea she had ever heard. *Is that a smile?* 'You boys have fun.'

25

(2001)

Wednesday, December 19th; 21:55

They travelled in exquisite silence.

Joaquín had always hated driving at night. Now that his optometrist had recommended prescription glasses, there was that too. 'They make me look old,' he'd complained when he first put them on.

The swish of the very few other cars that had dared defy the curfew provided an ominous soundtrack. Joaquín ignored them and insisted on staying under the speed limit. An idiotic logic, for sure: he was being most prudent while taking Sorolla to the most imprudent of places. Twenty minutes after leaving the house, with a silent, reluctant nephew in the passenger's seat, Joaquín still believed that a cacerolazo wouldn't solve anything. Not even one of the magnitude announced on the airwaves. If the government had ignored all previous demonstrations, they would find a way to disregard this one, too. Originating as a symbol of the people's desperation – housewives brandishing the pots and pans they couldn't fill to feed their families – it had evolved into a reliable instrument for people to show dissent. It was cheap, it was instant, it was loud. It needed no organization. *Their spontaneity is precisely their problem.* Cacerolazos were known to turn from peaceful marches to violent rallies in a matter of minutes.

What *was* organized were the optics. The architects of the phenomenon had managed to shift the discourse on poverty from the usual – the shanty towns, whose existence was almost required of a Third World country – to the novel: Argentina's middle class. An endangered species. No, the optics weren't just well thought out, they were phenomenally effective: even people in suits attended the protests now, people with whom the television viewers could easily identify. *That* was what had caught the attention of international audiences, hypocritical as it might be. In all their flawed glory, these relatable images had made Westerners shift uncomfortably in their seats at the thought that the same could happen to them. Less than fifty years ago, Argentina had symbolized the promised land for many a European immigrant anxious to leave misery behind and never look back. Nowadays, the tables had turned, and anyone who could prove a connection – a long-lost Galician great-uncle, in the case of the Alzadas – applied for a visa and fled. *At least I have that to say for myself: I stayed.* Out of the corner of his eye, the inspector reassessed his nephew: what he'd initially interpreted as pouting was more probably sleepiness. *Look at this little revolutionary.* As they drove off the Panamericana highway, Joaquín had to nudge his arm to change down gears. Sorolla came back to life.

'Where are we going?'

'To the cacerolazo. I thought that's what you wanted?'

Sorolla snorted. 'I mean, where *exactly*? I know you're not parking this beauty just *anywhere* . . .' he said sarcastically, stroking the car's worn dashboard as if it were a pet.

'Yes, no.' Joaquín shook his head. 'I was thinking around Vukić's.'

'Your old boss?'

'Yes.'

'I don't know him.'

'Really?' Joaquín could think of at least one instance in which they had met. 'Well, you're in luck. You were saying earlier that you wanted to know about the past, no? He's an important part of ours, and I thought you might want to meet him. Not only meet him: you can ask him anything you want.'

'Will he be awake?' Sorolla seemed suddenly uneasy, as if he wished they would find Vukić asleep.

'I hope so. I'm counting on him needing only a few hours per night. And it's not that late yet.'

'Where does he live?'

'In Chacarita.'

'That's good. We can walk from there to Parque Centenario.'

'Is that where people are gathering?'

'Among many other spots,' Sorolla said. 'Or perhaps you'd prefer to go to the Plaza de Mayo instead?'

The location of every single massacre in Argentinian history? 'Parque Centenario sounds perfect.'

'That's what I thought,' Sorolla smirked.

On any other day, if Joaquín had chosen this snail's pace to take Calle Estomba, a handful of impatient drivers would have formed a line behind him, pouncing at the opportunity to overtake the moment the solid white line broke. Now, they were alone. In a couple of blocks they would arrive at Vukić's. When they reached the last light before the corner of Roseti and Lacroze, Joaquín found the perfect spot, right in front of a little café that looked familiar. As they approached, he remembered the place: it was where they made those delicious sandwichitos he brought up whenever he'd visit his boss. Or should he say, *when* he used to visit. Joaquín pointed up across the street to the only building on the block with more than two stories. 'Es allá.'

'No one in their right mind is going to touch a car parked under the ex-police commissioner's house.' *Great minds.* Then, as Sorolla discovered precisely where his uncle had planned on parking: 'It's a little tight, no?'

'I'll manage.'

It was more than a little tight. The spot was snug for a car ten centimeters shorter. Joaquín would have to work for it. After the third maneuver, his sweaty hands smacked on the leather as he turned the wheel.

'Do you want me to do it?' offered Sorolla.

'I don't know,' replied Joaquín. 'Did you bring your inhaler?'

Sorolla rolled his eyes at his uncle's childishness, but then admitted: 'Yes.'

The inspector pulled up one last time until he heard a soft thud, then turned the wheel in the opposite direction. Ya está.

THE BUZZER.

'Fernando?' Alzada inquired into the shiny metallic intercom.

In response, a persistent white noise.

Vukić couldn't possibly be scared of allowing them in. If he hadn't lost his magic touch, he'd seen them coming from a distance: Alzada knew he was one of those policemen who retire but never cease to be a cop. He had probably scoped them out the moment they had pulled up on the block, then observed them park and approach the building. *Why is he taking so long?*

Alzada wasn't a fan of standing around. Especially when they were the only two people on the street, only accompanied by the glow of the streetlights. Hadn't Sorolla said there'd be crowds everywhere? The revolution had apparently not made it to this neighborhood yet.

Should he try the buzzer again? *It'll make me seem impatient.* More importantly, Vukić might read it as an insult, and to offend 'the Wolf' was never a good idea. *No.* They'd have to wait.

This gave his shirt a chance to dry before he put his jacket back on. Joaquín looked at the Clio and admired his work. *Thank God. Otherwise I'd have to listen to Sorolla for a week.* He eyed his nephew. Young and tall and dreamy. *Innocuous.* And his back turned on the outside world. *Clueless.* Why was he facing the building?

'Your attention should be on the street.'

Sorolla protested: 'There's no one there.' Yet, he obeyed.

'Precisely.' Alzada instinctively reached for his belt, even though he had decided against carrying tonight. 'A little too quiet for my taste.'

An artificial dawn provoked by the multitude of flares in the distance only accentuated the quiet. *The calm before the storm.*

A SHADOW ON THE OTHER side of the gate.

'What are you doing here?' asked a hoarse voice. *Why has he come downstairs instead of buzzing us in?*

'Nice to see you, too, Fernando,' answered Alzada.

'What are you doing here?' Vukić repeated. He stressed every word.

'Come on.' Alzada observed the panic rise in Sorolla's eyes as the boy caught up and discovered the gun pointed at them. The inspector calmly put on his jacket. 'Lower your weapon, will you? It's just us.'

'Who's "us"?'

'Me and my nephew,' Alzada said. 'Sorolla, remember?'

A grunt came from the other side of the metal-paneled fence. Finally, a hand emerged from between two thinner bars. Sorolla rushed to shake it. *Good boy.* The expression on his face revealed he didn't often have physical contact with old people. The common misconception – people did the same with reptiles – is to expect their skin to be chapped, when in reality an old hand feels more like it belongs to someone who's been swimming in a pool for a long time: pruned and soft.

'You *do* know there's a curfew, right?'

'Will you let us come in already?'

'Look who's getting nervous now.' Another grunt, this time with a smile.

The fence slowly opened.

26
(2001)

In the darkness of Vukić's living room, Alzada and Sorolla waited while the former commissioner made coffee in the kitchen. He had insisted. A solitary Tiffany lamp with a dragonfly motif was the only source of light. The inspector immediately recognized mindfulness in the way it had been positioned: close enough to the couch where they were both sitting, and at the same time, a safe distance from the window, probably to prevent a passerby on the street knowing if someone was home. *Has someone become paranoid with age?* After a couple of minutes, Sorolla made a motion to stand up and investigate. Alzada abruptly grabbed him by the arm and made him sink back into the couch. Vukić would have heard the footsteps from the kitchen, and he would certainly not approve of someone sniffing around his lair. Because that's what it was: a lair.

Sorolla would have to content himself with studying the room from a distance.

It was only after Vukić's wife's death that Alzada had first stepped into the apartment. The neighbors had gossiped about how he was losing his mind. The inspector had worried Vukić might shoot himself; Paula had worried he would starve to death. Not knowing how else to cancel their debt, they had decided to at least take on the task of caring for him. Alzada had left the owner of the corner shop in charge of delivering weekly groceries; he himself visited regularly with Tupperwares of home-cooked food. Slowly, his visits had grown shorter and sparser; eventually, they had stopped altogether.

In the shadows, Alzada realized not a lot of changes had been made since. Every wall was covered with light pine shelves, conveying to the visitor the impression of being in quite the modern, neat study. This was reinforced by an abundant collection of books, organized in immaculate rows. He almost certainly had done it all himself; the commissioner was too suspicious to have anyone enter his apartment without a thorough background check. Alzada knew the subject of the library to be almost exclusively war: from on-the-ground fighting technique to global strategy, from historical accounts to fictional depictions, from the Crusades to the Boer War. He drew Sorolla's attention to the darker side of the dining table, on which had been set up a complete model plane workshop. From there, once finished, Vukić seemed to have paired the models he built with the tomes corresponding to the conflicts in which the planes had served. There were some famous ones too. Alzada recognized the Spitfire, the pride of Britain during the Second

World War, next to a book on Malta; the German Messerschmitt was sitting with a biography on Rommel; the P-47 Thunderbolt with its checkered snout bookended what could be a flight manual. Apparently, Vukić had taken to retirement well.

'Sugar? Milk?' Vukić called from the kitchen.

Like two children caught planning mischief, both composed themselves and sat up straight.

'No, thank you,' Alzada yelled back.

'REALLY, FERNANDO,' ALZADA SAID WHEN the former commissioner brought in a shaking tray. 'We only wanted to say hello.'

'The Wolf.' Vukić had been nicknamed that not so much for his last name's Balkan etymology, but for his lupine appearance: grey and smart and ruthless. Now, his thin white hair and freckles had softened his frame, and although his posture remained impeccable, his voice vibrated with the weariness of a long life. *If I'm sixty-five, he must be at least eighty, eighty-five years old.*

'You shouldn't have gone to all this trouble,' Alzada tried again.

'I'm happy to see you.' Vukić ignored his comment by handing him a cup of coffee. 'Do you remember this set?'

'Yes, I do,' the inspector lied. Trying to win time, he tilted his head, as if the new angle could make him recall where he had seen the cream-colored porcelain with golden edges before.

'It was your gift, when Marisa and I got married.'

'Of course,' Alzada confirmed, hoping he had sounded convincing. *If only Vukić weren't a human polygraph.*

But the commissioner had already turned to Sorolla: 'You see, I've been married twice. And twice I've been widowed. The second one was your age. Still no luck: she also died before me. Are you sure you don't want any milk?'

'Fernando,' Alzada interjected.

Vukić understood. 'Has the war started already?'

'That's why we came into the city,' Alzada replied.

'You always had these delirious ideas . . .' the commissioner smirked. 'I'm glad to see some things never change.'

Holding his coffee cup in one hand, the saucer resting on the lower fold of his dark blue vest, he was no longer the man who had made Buenos Aires tremble for more than a decade.

Alzada grinned: 'Don't make me blush, Fernando.'

'So, are you still an inspector?'

'Yes,' Alzada answered, resigned. He was beginning to think there was a general conspiracy to raise every single thorny issue in his life. *Vukić is just trying to be friendly.* After all, they had barely seen each other since the commissioner had finally retired from the force.

'I thought I had told you to leave as soon as you could.'

'You did. Several times in fact.'

'And you *did* have the perfect excuse.'

Alzada furrowed his brows.

'I'm sorry. You're still an enemy of the word "perfect", yes?'

Alzada smiled. 'Especially when it's not applicable.'

'How is Galante managing the station?'

As soon as democracy had set in, the old guard had been immediately sacked; Galante became the main beneficiary of that operation: he was dirty enough to get the job done, and clean enough for the public relations department. Alzada had long resented Galante for how he had dealt with their former superior, but in retrospect maybe Vukić had been the smartest of them all. *He got out just in time for his name to be forgotten when the trials started.*

'I mean. I was assigned to robbery but guess who is dealing with a missing person . . .'

Vukić shrugged his shoulders: 'Well. At least you know something about *that.*'

Alzada opened his eyes wide and nodded towards his nephew.

'Very subtle, tío,' Sorolla said. Until then he had remained a fly on the wall.

Didn't you want his attention? You have it now.

'And what is it that *you* do, you little bird?' Vukić accompanied his question with a beckoning head tilt. *Standard procedure to lure him in, to take his measure.*

'I . . . I . . .' Sorolla stammered, all his previous resolve gone.

'You're not police.' An affirmation, not a question.

'No, I . . .'

More difficult than it looks, isn't it?

'He's a revolutionary.' Alzada attempted to fill the uncomfortable silence. He knew that to Vukić, anyone who believed the country could change, and especially through amateur violence, was highly gullible at best.

'He looks just like him, too,' Vukić said.

What the fuck?

'You knew my father?'

Vukić swallowed. Could it be? Was the big bad wolf getting emotional? The commissioner cleared his throat and shifted in his seat; immediately he became himself again. *That's more like it.* With a mixture of amusement and disdain, he said: 'A revolutionary, I see . . .'

'On that note.' Alzada gulped down the remaining coffee. 'Fernando, it's getting late.'

The inspector stood up and approached the window. Although the blinds had been tightly wound down, a small vertical shaft on the side between them and the wall allowed whoever stood in this position to catch a glimpse of what was happening on the street without being seen. *Not accidental.* He adjusted his eyes to the distance and saw his car. He smiled. Vukić had indeed seen them coming long before they rang the buzzer. *He might have gotten old, but he hasn't lost it.* How would *he* have handled the Echegaray situation? He wouldn't have given a fuck about any of the 'inconveniences of democracy': the due process, the search warrant, the parliamentary immunity, the succession of reports. 'It takes a wolf to catch a wolf,' the former commissioner liked to say. Alzada knew that had they taken Vukić's approach, the case would already be solved.

'Please tell Paula I said hello.' The sound of Vukić's voice made Alzada return his attention to the room. Sorolla was standing by the door.

'But of course,' Alzada said deferentially. He had some time to decide whether he was going to mention the visit to her. *The only thing she'll want to know is if he finally asked for something in return.* 'About that—'

'Now is not the moment.' Vukić gave him the same dismissive wave he had got every time he had brought up the subject. Petacchi had received a succulent envelope – two months of Alzada's salary. Why had Vukić never cashed in the favor? 'Come visit more often, you bastard. It feels like I haven't seen you since . . .' Vukić went quiet. 'And don't worry about the missing people. Retire already. You've done enough. You *did* enough.'

The inspector lowered his head.

'I'm serious,' the commissioner went on. 'Just because you would do things differently if you had the chance, doesn't mean you were wrong the first time. When you ask the old man for the check,' he pointed to the ceiling, 'you can be sure that he'll agree with me. Now get out before it's over. Enjoy yourselves.'

'Our plan exactly,' Sorolla jumped in.

'I must say, I'm surprised, Joaco,' Vukić said nonchalantly. It sounded like a thought he could have had after they were gone. 'I would have never imagined you to be the politically conscious type. I figured you'd be home reading.'

'That was the original plan, indeed. But what can I say?' Alzada affectionately grabbed Sorolla by the back of the neck. 'This one.'

As soon as they stepped onto the landing, Sorolla reached for the elevator button. Alzada had to slap his hand to prevent it. The whirr of the elevator would inform the neighbors that Vukić had visitors. Another thing he wouldn't miss when he retired: the strenuous hikes to high floors when they paid people surprise visits. Apparently Sorolla understood immediately. And yet, to Alzada's surprise, he proceeded to trot down the stairs, regardless.

'You know we're taking the stairs to avoid the noise of the elevator, right?'

'Yes,' Sorolla said. *He doesn't.* His nephew started to descend more mindfully of his sneakers on the stone.

When Alzada arrived downstairs, Sorolla was holding the door, contrition on his face. 'Tío, thank you for coming tonight. And bringing me here.'

'It's fine.' Alzada pressed his lips together, almost making them disappear. 'Just . . . well. Don't mention any of this to your aunt, yes?'

'Does she not like Vukić?'

'I think she actually does.'

'I understand.' Sorolla nodded. *No, you don't. And that's okay.*

While Sorolla opened the door to the street, Alzada took advantage of standing in his blind spot, and crossed himself. Then he stepped past his nephew. 'Here we go.'

27

(2001)

Alzada and Sorolla hurried down the avenue. *We've wasted enough time already, and now this detour.* The detour itself wasn't the problem. On the contrary, if Sorolla had started walking in the direction of Chacarita, Alzada would certainly have intervened and suggested a different route. No conversation had been necessary: they had tacitly agreed on avoiding Jorge Newbery, the street that left only a wall to separate them from the biggest cemetery in the country. Who knew? Perhaps his nephew held his same respect for the dead. Not that Alzada was superstitious. And, for the most part, one couldn't even tell from the outside. The perimeter was strictly surrounded by a five-meter-high concrete wall, of which only the bottom quarter was periodically repainted white. At this time of night, they would have found it illuminated by languid streetlights, like every other street in the city. Only the main entrance made Chacarita stand out from what could otherwise very well be a prison: two lion statues, zealously guarding the remains of half of Buenos Aires. The remains of the founding fathers. The remains of Carlos Gardel. The remains of Jorge Rodolfo – if he had been given the chance. Instead: many thousands of pesos to a compliant undertaker, a furtive trip to a remote cemetery, an unmarked grave. *Yes. Better to take Dorrego.*

On both sides of the street, Alzada observed people leaving their apartments and joining them in walking towards the Parque Centenario. The demographics of the protest had changed considerably in the past couple of days. These weren't the initial hungry mobs from the provinces anymore, nor the delinquents who had used the opportunity to turn the city into a pitched battle and had ended up cornering De la Rúa into declaring the state of siege. *These are families like ours.* Men in shirts with rolled-up sleeves, women waving their fans, children everywhere. A lot of Diego Maradona T-shirts, who in Argentina had ousted Saint Jude as patron saint of lost causes.

The rhythm of the march picked up, as if an invisible force had instilled in them a sudden urgency, a fear of missing out. Sorolla, with his usual insouciance, was almost jogging, helped by his triple-striped training shorts, and his youth. Alzada remained a couple of steps behind him to catch his breath. But no more than that: he knew how fast one could lose someone in a crowd. People around them chatted in a spirit of victory. The inspector found himself fighting the contagious cheerfulness he read on his nephew's face, the temptation to lose track of the situation and 'go with the flow', as he was sure Sorolla called it. No, he needed to stay alert.

When they turned right on Juan B. Justo, Alzada made a note of two midnight-blue police vans, bars covering their windows, strategically parked on either side of the avenue. Behind the one on their left, a water cannon. Ready for a two-pronged maneuver. Ten riot police on foot, ten tear gas guns in their holsters, ten short-sleeved shirts. *Heat, like violence, is democratic.* The inspector was sure they would encounter more along the way. *So this is what it feels like to be on the other side.* A sense of unease much like what people described experiencing when stopped by the police for speeding. *I'm nervous even thought I haven't done anything wrong.* A lack of control. Around them, the crowd was getting thicker.

The pace of the demonstration adjusted to accommodate the many people who had joined in the last few minutes, the avenue now a sclerotic artery clogged with the discontent of a deceived nation. At least Alzada could comfort himself with the idea there were nowhere enough officers in the city – or even the province – of Buenos Aires to constitute a serious threat: many would be dedicated to securing the Plaza de Mayo in front of the presidential Casa Rosada, the most coveted destination for protesters. If they kept their distance – and now that was almost six kilometers – they would be safe.

Every time Alzada found himself relaxing his stance, he started scanning for possible trouble stirrers again. He couldn't help himself. One angry boy throwing a garbage can against a police car was all it took to provoke a massacre. And there were more than just innocent citizens in this crowd. Alzada didn't need to take a second look to distinguish the indignant paterfamilias from those trained in street gymnastics, even though tonight they were making a special effort to blend in with the group. The scarves and handkerchiefs that normally covered their faces had fallen off. Still, the choice not to wear shirts – *it's close to impossible to get a hold of the exposed ribs of a running teenager* – and their conscientiously tied sneakers – *they know they can outsprint any armor-wearing officer without breaking a sweat* – were more than enough to tell them apart. Their only jewelry: whistles around their necks – *the only effective armor against a mounted police charge.* Plus, they didn't give into the natural urge to walk in the middle of the street because today one had permission. These people were familiar with police tactics, they knew the handbook inside and out. The most effective dispersal method is to attack the center of a crowd and chop the enemy into smaller, more manageable groups. Precisely what Napoleon III had in mind when he built the first avenues in Paris: room for frontal cavalry charges, room for crowd control. *That's the reason these clowns keep on the pavements.* Exactly what Alzada was doing. Like Sorolla would do, if he were to pay attention.

Claps. And whistles. And shouts. The clatters and clunks of pots and pans and skillets banged on with skimmers and spoons. A nation finding its rhythm. Alzada was mesmerized by the force of the crowd. The tide had turned. The hunger had given. Now it was rage. Syncopated spasms of revolt. Flip-flops thudding on the asphalt. Hands clenched tightly around the Argentinian flags in which so many were wrapped in spite of the heat. To Alzada's surprise, it was in the thick of this cacophony that he finally felt safe: he stopped scanning the faces around them for suspicious behavior. He ceased strategizing an escape route and instead let the crowd simply guide his next steps. He even allowed himself to get caught up in the anticipation when they turned left into Avenida Dr. Honorio Pueyrredón; they were almost at the end of their pilgrimage.

Alzada shouted a nervous '¡Hijos de puta!' and was startled by the sound of his own voice. He pointed out the Christmas tree to Sorolla as soon as it appeared, towering over the horizon of sweaty foreheads. He smiled. This year they wouldn't be celebrating the nativity of Jesus, but the forceps-assisted birth of a new Argentina. *Jorge would have loved this.*

Next to them, Alzada recognized a reporter from Cadena Nueve. She was in no hurry to get ready to be on camera: TV stations couldn't transmit for the moment. Whatever they shot tonight would have to be packaged and stored until martial law was revoked. He heard her mumbling about 'the last dictatorship' and had to chuckle. *Half accurate description, half wishful thinking.* Past her, a couple of international news reporters struggled to shove people aside in an attempt to open a path wide enough for them to capture solid footage of the demonstration to present to their bosses and justify their overseas expense accounts. Without giving them a second look, Alzada knew they would fail. *Fortunately for the police – and for the majority of world leaders – demonstrations just don't photograph well.*

It was the most anti-democratic paradox: the more success the organizers achieve, the more complicated it becomes to make the size of their protest come across, be it through words, still pictures, or even film. From the ground, the images systematically fail to capture the magnitude of the crowd, since no lens is wide enough to include rivers of people. That's the reason photographers tend to stick with emotional shots – one furious protester, one crying mother, one significant banner – against a blurred background. Those pictures are the equivalent of the tale of the blind men who reached out to touch different parts of an elephant, each giving a completely divergent description of the animal as a whole. Conversely, from the air individuals are barely discernible, and the footage can't possibly transmit the energy of the protest on the ground. The indignation. The feeling of being in such a crowd, of *being* the crowd, is irrevocably lost on the spectator. Not that this government was particularly worried about being the subject of embarrassing international news coverage – on account of not possessing that difficult-to-shake inhibition that comes from being watched. These were the heirs of the same leaders who had not only hosted but also won a World Cup while carrying out the Dirty War. They hadn't blinked then; they wouldn't do so now. If they considered it necessary, there would be tear gas and rubber bullets. And worse.

'¡Las manos arriba! ¡Esto es un asalto!' a voice rallied through a megaphone. Hands in the air, this is a robbery! Alzada found it a quite ingenuous slogan against corruption. It was contagious, too.

'¡Las manos arriba!' he yelled out somewhat half-heartedly, afraid he would sound ridiculous.

A woman who had been walking next to him for a while turned to him, surprised by his unexpected contribution, and smiled in approval.

'¡Las manos arriba!' Alzada tried again, this time with conviction. After a couple of times, he lifted both arms to match the rest of the crowd, palms facing the Argentinian political Mecca. Under the spell of the phrase, which like a mantra gained momentum through repetition, Alzada raised his voice. He felt strangely relieved. He felt the pain of every person around him. He felt an anger he had never experienced. He suddenly needed to cry for no reason – or every reason, he couldn't decide. He felt good.

'¡Las manos arriba!' Alzada finally caved under the weight of his arms, his heart thankful it could stop pumping against gravity. As he lowered them, he put one hand on Sorolla's shoulder. His nephew had been quiet for a while. Alzada felt him shrink. He looked at Sorolla and Sorolla looked pale. *This isn't good.*

'Breathe, gordo, breathe,' Alzada reminded Sorolla. *Why the hell did I let myself get carried away by this fucking nonsense? I should've been paying attention, that's what I should've been doing. Not singing along like an idiot.* He stopped in his tracks. *We don't have time for that now.* He had to rapidly compose an escape route from the crowd and, more urgently, find a landing spot for when his nephew collapsed. *How much time do we have?* Because Alzada had seen that face before: if twenty years of bringing him up had taught him anything, it was to know the question was not if Sorolla was going to collapse, but *when.* Alzada linked his arm with Sorolla's. *I'm not going to lose you now.* He scoped out his surroundings. Left, and right, then left again. Alzada swirled around, desperately scanning the area for somewhere quiet. People everywhere around them. They were trapped.

There, yes! Twenty meters away, a bakery had a recess entry. Pastelería Jerónimo was the name Alzada managed to discern on the green-and-white-striped awning. He felt Sorolla's weight on his arm grow heavier. *Twenty meters in this crowd, and in his condition, we better start now.* Alzada looked down one last time. His nephew's face was blank. It wouldn't be long before he fainted. Terrified, Alzada considered the possibility he wouldn't be able to carry Sorolla.

'Disculpe. Permiso. Permiso.' Alzada pushed his way through the throng. Firmly but softly. The last thing they needed was to create panic and prompt a stampede. He had wrapped one arm around Sorolla's shoulders; his free hand held his nephew's chest trying to keep him upright. Alzada's shirt was already drenched in sweat. People hardly moved to let them by, reluctant to give up their front-row seats to the revolution. The few faces that did showed worry. Sorolla was barely dragging his feet now, his arm limp around Alzada's neck. They were still at least ten meters away. Every step they took came with a thud: Alzada's increasingly impatient shoulders against somebody else's. He staggered beneath his nephew's weight. *I can't do this. I have to do this.*

Alzada looked up at the sky, not to implore divine intervention, but to clear his head and think of alternatives. The flares lit up in excitement had turned the night a cloudy red. *We'll stop here.* He would have to lower Sorolla to the ground and stand watch over him while the panic attack passed. *There's nothing else I can do.* After that, they'd reassess the situation.

'Lo siento, gordo,' he apologized to his nephew as he set him down.

In that moment, a stranger lifted up Sorolla from the other side. He was sinewy, the same age as the inspector. He didn't say a word. He held Sorolla up as if he didn't weigh at all. He surveyed his surroundings like Alzada had done before him, and also deemed the bakery to be the most suitable shelter. Without looking at either of them, the stranger pulled Sorolla quite efficiently in that direction. Alzada rallied his last energies and helped him maneuver his nephew into the little nook created by the store's front door. *Is that dry blood on the ground?* When he looked up to thank him, the stranger was gone.

'Okay, we're here,' Alzada announced, hoping to sound reassuring. He turned his back to Sorolla, who leaned against the iron bars that protected the inside of the shop. *We're in the middle of fucking nowhere.*

'Sorolla?' Alzada's voice was mixed with the progressively agitated shouts behind them. '¡Ladrones!'

No answer.

He squatted down next to his nephew, his eyes on the crowd, and tried again: 'Are you okay?' *What kind of question is that?*

Alzada knelt closer and placed two fingers on Sorolla's fluttering carotid artery. There was too much commotion around them for him to be able to discern a pulse. He realized he himself had also started to hyperventilate, which didn't help. *Just remember, Joaquín: no one ever died from a panic attack.*

Eventually, Alzada managed to find a beat. He carefully pulled up his other hand and cross-checked it with his wristwatch. One fifty. The bad news: at that speed, panic was hitting its peak. The good news: at that speed, it wasn't going to last much longer.

'Did you bring your pills?' Alzada asked a barely responsive Sorolla. 'Where's your inhaler?'

Sorolla opened his eyes, staring into the distance as if he couldn't see. Still he answered: 'The inhaler is only for the asthma.'

Why the fuck didn't he bring the pills? 'Okay, okay. Listen to me,' Alzada said, and held Sorolla's face with both his hands. 'You just have to breathe. I know, easy for me to say. But if you focus on the breathing, you'll be fine.'

'Tío?'

'Yes? What do you need?'

'I need you to let go of my face.'

'Of course, of course,' Alzada obliged, embarrassed. He was no Paula.

What would *she* have done if she had come to the demonstration instead of him? *She'd probably have had some extra pills in her bag.* He half smiled. *If only she could see us right now. She would turn to me and say, 'You've reacted rapidly. He's safe. Now think about what's next.'* Or so he needed to believe. Alzada deliberately planted his feet wide so as not to be swayed by the moving crowd and stood tall, both to tower over Sorolla, and to breathe.

How in the world am *I* going to get him out of here? Without moving his feet, Alzada leaned out of the nook and considered his options. They were four blocks north of the Christmas tree. If this had been a government-approved demonstration, the mayor would have chosen that spot to station at least one ambulance. They couldn't count on that being the case tonight. And he couldn't possibly risk the physical effort of advancing through the crowd with Sorolla in tow just to arrive there and find there was nothing waiting for them. *The tree is not an option.* They could try the opposite direction: reverse course and retrace their steps to the car. Then again, it had taken them almost an hour to get there – and that had been following the current. If they went against it, that meant at least doubling that time. *Is Sorolla even going to be able to walk?* Alzada wouldn't be able to carry him, that much had been proven. On top of that, both alternatives depended on Sorolla standing on his own and not having another panic attack in the midst of their expedition. He could always undertake the trip on his own, and come back with help, but that meant leaving him alone, unaware of what the demonstration had in store. If he weren't standing there, the crowd would already have trampled over Sorolla. He was stuck. He was more than stuck. *We're royally— wait.*

Alzada fished his phone out of the pocket of his pants. *Thank God. Let's see.* He couldn't try to reach Paula, who was always his first call. She wouldn't be able to do anything from home, and she would certainly not be able to come into the city. *Why worry her?* No. It was better to leave her in the dark, at the very least until he had figured out a plan. *I need . . .* He needed someone young and fit and politically engaged enough to be out this evening. Or bored enough. There was no one in Alzada's contacts matching that description: most of his friends and acquaintances were either retired, or on the brink like him, and he could bet his left kidney all of them were at home sipping on their mates, unimpressed with the news. Then, it dawned on him: Estrático.

Unintelligible shouts in the distance. A couple of steps from Alzada, a man held his radio high above their heads for everyone to hear.

'Listen to this,' he proclaimed, turning up the volume. Was *he* the stranger who had helped them? The inspector couldn't be sure. Reports of demonstrations in other parts of the city. In Palermo, Belgrano, Almagro, Caballito, even in Boedo and Villa Crespo, citizens everywhere had decided to defy the martial law. Alzada leaned further into the neighboring circle when they announced riots in front of the Casa Rosada. *Of course.* The police had received the order to clear the Plaza de Mayo – perhaps the last of this government's bad decisions – and encountered ardent resistance. The crowd roared as they heard the news of dozens of wounded. *Let's hope the unrest doesn't spread. On either side.* He could go the rest of his life without hearing the thud of baton on body ever again. Estrático sounded like a better option by the minute.

True, he might not be the most appropriate choice. Calling a subordinate this late at night for a personal favor? At the very least, Alzada would owe him. Then again, what was the worst the deputy could ever ask of him? The inspector had survived the considerably more harrowing threat of Vukić asking him to return the favor hanging over his head like a guillotine for over twenty years. No, what held Alzada back was that it would mean opening up about his personal life to Estrático. He took a deep breath. Estrático would know to be quiet. *What other option do I have?* He looked down at his right hand. When he focused, even after all those years, he could still feel the prickle on his palm from when he had hit Galante. Alzada caught himself gloating, and immediately shook off the exuberance that had flooded him. Estrático didn't look like the stay-at-home type. With any luck, he'd be downtown. Or even nearby. *Let's see where he is.*

'WHOM DID YOU CALL?' SOROLLA wanted to know, attempting to stand.

'Stay there, yes?' More an order than a question.

'Not tía Paula, I hope,' his nephew ventured from the ground.

'How do you think I'm stillmarried to her after forty-two years?' Alzada paused. 'I called Estrático.'

'Who?'

'Someone from the station.'

'Is he in the neighborhood?'

'Not really. He says he'll be here in twenty minutes. Let's see how long it really takes him.' Suddenly aware that anxious Sorolla might need some reassurance, he added: 'Don't worry. If he says he's coming, he's coming. Everything's going to be fine.'

Alzada turned his back on his nephew. Like the solicitous watchdog his job had shaped him to be, he devoted his full attention to reading the crowd. Only a couple of minutes ago people had still been shifting in the direction of the square; now the mass had become completely stagnant.

'Everything's going to be fine,' Alzada repeated, this time more to himself than for Sorolla. Still, he turned to make sure Sorolla had heard him, and in the process, he met his nephew's gaze. The exact look he had given him twenty years ago on the morning he had come to live with them. The exact look of complete mistrust. Alzada turned again, embarrassed.

Everything *was* going to be fine, except that Sorolla had 'episodes'. That was what his therapist had recommended they call his panic attacks, which, like clockwork, appeared every week. Alzada had opposed the idea: 'I think we should call them what they really are. What kind of service is it to him if we lie about this? He has to take medication and everything. It's not like he's not going to know what's happening.' Paula had barely lifted her head when she'd replied: 'Are you sure *you* of all people want to play the radical honesty game?' They had returned to calling them 'episodes'.

Everything would be fine if Sorolla weren't desperately afraid of darkness. Sure, his night light was of help when Alzada shuffled to the bathroom in the small hours, but also a perpetual reminder of the things they had lost in the dark. Everything would be fine if only Sorolla could face the neighbor's cat without breaking into screams. If he could accompany Alzada on his weekly Saturday trip to watch a war movie. Everything would be fine if only the boy hadn't been ripped from his home to begin with. If he still had parents. If they hadn't been disappeared. Why *did* they insist on using that term? It wasn't like there remained a secret hope they would return some day. 'Murdered' was more accurate. And not only murdered but wiped permanently from public memory. As if they had never been. When were they going to start calling things by their proper name? But Paula was right: that wasn't a game he could play, and win. Alzada felt faint.

'¡El pueblo unido, jamás sera vencido!' the crowd chanted. Was it just another contagious slogan or an accurate aphorism? Could citizens' actions actually yield political change? Alzada hated to think that idea might be true. Mostly for what it meant for his generation: could *they* have overthrown the dictatorship if they had taken to the streets in 1976 like the people were doing now? Why hadn't they protested then? Of course, there had been the Madres. Then the Madres had stopped being a novelty and become another Argentinian idiosyncrasy, a pale testament to the nation's permanent stain.

Why had there been only *them*? Could Alzada have attended those meetings? Certainly not if he had wanted to keep his family safe. Was there something he could have done differently, before the disappearance? Could he have warned Jorge Rodolfo? But he had, he reminded himself every time a nightmare woke him. Could he have warned him *more*? *But I did.* Alzada almost said the words out loud. No matter how many times he repeated them, they didn't wash off his guilt. His only relief was thinking that Jorge, stubborn as a mule, would never have stopped, regardless of anything Joaquín might have said or done.

And yet, Alzada knew, watching the crowd, he could have done more. He pressed against the part of the shop window that wasn't protected by metal, Sorolla at his feet, and welcomed the cool of the glass on his soaked back.

28
(2001)

Someone stepped on his foot. A neon-green sneaker. *Who the fuck are you?* Alzada rose instantly, angry at the stranger for his carelessness, angry at himself for having let his guard down. But when he looked into the friendly face that met him, he hesitated. Before he could decide on what course of action to take with the stranger, Estrático jumped out from behind the man: 'The cavalry is here, Inspector!'

On any other day – under any other circumstance – Alzada would have rolled his eyes, annoyed with his deputy – why did he always have to be so ridiculously cheerful all the time? But at this moment, he couldn't be happier to see him. Alzada looked at his watch. Almost midnight. *How long have I been on the ground?*

'This is Mati.' Estrático interrupted his train of thought, introducing the man with the green shoes.

Alzada stretched out his hand to meet a solid grip.

'I'm sorry I stepped on you, sir,' Mati said.

Did he just call me 'sir'? Alzada liked Mati already. Mati with the luscious long hair gathered in a beautifully drawn bun on top of his head. Alzada reassessed their surroundings. The masses were encroaching on the nook; there was now barely any place to stand. No wonder the boy had stepped on him.

'Don't worry about it. And please, call me Joaquín.'

'If I may, sir, I would never have thought of you as someone who attends a cacerolazo,' Estrático tried to lighten the mood. In his eyes, the inspector read the same worry that filled his. 'And much less without a jacket.'

'I'm only here tonight because of him,' Alzada smiled, moving to the side to reveal a human bundle in fetal position on the ground. He motioned for Sorolla to rise, but his nephew didn't move. 'This is Sorolla.'

'Has he been conscious the whole time?' Estrático asked.

'Barely,' Alzada said.

The deputy crouched next to Sorolla and pulled out a tissue to expose a couple of pills. *Does he just carry them around with him?* Alzada followed Estrático's lead, not before checking that Mati had turned towards the demonstration to momentarily relieve him from his lookout duties. He squatted to the ground only to realize that, to hold that position, he would have to keep his balance with at least one hand on the ground. *I'm much too old for this.*

'What's that?' Alzada inquired.

'Something to soften the blow,' Estrático offered, holding a pill out for Sorolla to take. 'It's a panic attack, isn't it?'

Alzada confirmed with a nod. The insouciance with which young people talked about those things always left him feeling half relieved, half uncomfortable.

'Sorolla?' Estrático tried.

Sorolla remained unresponsive. *Even now, he looks just like him.* The last time he had seen his brother, Jorge had been agonizing in the back of Vukić's car, in a race against time that couldn't be won. *Not now, Joaquín.*

Sorolla brought himself to look at the deputy. Without skipping a beat, Estrático fed him one of the pills like a bird mother would its baby chick. Sorolla immediately retreated to his original stance, head between his shoulders.

Estrático turned to Alzada. 'Does he have them often?'

This is too much for my knees. Alzada stood up, then mumbled: 'From time to time.'

Estrático rose too, eyeing the crowd. 'You drove here, no? Where did you park?' Apparently he had understood the need to change the subject.

'Under Vukić's place.'

'Commissioner Vukić? He's a little before my time . . .' the deputy acknowledged cautiously.

'On the other side of Chacarita.'

'Do you want us to carry him there?' Mati volunteered, turning around. *Someone's been paying attention.* In his sleeveless Nirvana T-shirt, he had the air of a Greek statue, chiseled in seasonal bronze.

'I mean . . .' Alzada hesitated. Then, as if apologizing for having had to ask for their assistance, he added: 'It's quite far.'

'It is,' Estrático said. 'And with this amount of people, it's going to be hell.'

'Okay,' Mati conceded, 'but we need to move now.'

'Definitely,' Estrático assented. 'The only question is where . . .'

Alzada had already gone through his contacts when he had tried to find someone who might be nearby, and the deputy was all he had been able to come up with.

'Wait,' Estrático grinned at his own idea. 'Now that I think of it. You know who lives two, maybe three blocks from here?'

Alzada was puzzled.

'Dolores, sir.'

'*Dolores* Dolores?'

'Yes, sir.'

Joaquín had known la Dolores for almost twenty years, and only now realized he barely knew anything about her. Had she stopped coming to the station, he would have had no means of contacting her. 'She's not far from here. The only thing is . . .' Estrático hesitated. 'What if she's working?'

'Today?' Alzada couldn't hide his surprise.

'You never know . . .' the deputy said, 'Let me call her and check if she's home.'

'Who's Dolores?' Sorolla asked from the ground. *Oh*, now *you're awake.*

'She's a . . . she's a . . .' Alzada struggled to find the right word.

Estrático covered the mouthpiece of his phone and lent him a hand: 'She's a friend of your uncle's,' he whispered, 'from the station.'

'You'll explain later why you have her phone number,' Alzada quipped.

'Easy,' Estrático volunteered. 'You told me to do her paperwork this morning. And I have an eidetic memory, sir. That's when—'

'I know what "eidetic" means, Estrático.' *It's when you only need to read something only once to memorize it. What I* don't *know is how she can be so reckless to give out her number and address.* What had all his precautions been for?

The deputy was on the phone, one hand pressed on his left ear: 'Yes. Dolores? It's Orestes. From the precinct?' *How many Orestes can there be, we're not in a Greek play.* 'Yes. Are you home? Listen. I need to ask you a favor.' Orestes cackled. 'Don't flatter yourself! It's not that kind of favor . . .'

Alzada snickered and saw Mati do the same. *Why does* he *find it funny?*

'Can we come by?' Estrático continued. 'Come on . . . It's Inspector Alzada and— Yes? Okay, okay. Yes. Got it. We'll be there in a couple of minutes. Thanks. Bye.'

Mati squatted next to Sorolla. 'Okay, young Alzada. I think that was our signal.'

Alzada thought about objecting. After all, it was *his* nephew. He could do it himself. But he saw the tenderness with which Mati secured his grip under Sorolla's legs and around his back, the skill with which he brought him up in one swift motion. Alzada was disarmed.

'Let's do this, then,' Mati announced in a cheerful tone that reminded Alzada of Estrático.

29

(2001)

Thursday, December 20th; 00.05

'Good evening, Inspector.'

La Dolores didn't open the door to her apartment in a negligee, as Alzada had half feared, half hoped. She escaped the cliché of temptress with considerable decorum, he found: blue striped men's pajama bottoms and a grey T-shirt that read 'UBA'. Universidad de Buenos Aires. Alzada's alma mater.

'Good evening, Dolores,' Alzada felt relief in the little routines that never changed.

Mati bowed in greeting, and gently pushed past them. He had carried Sorolla single-handedly for what had ended up being five blocks, and had done so without any apparent effort, and without saying a word. He set Alzada's nephew down on the long white geometrical couch that presided over the living room and used the blanket on one of its corners to cover him. Sorolla didn't spend a second settling into his new surroundings: within a moment he was sound asleep. *When the gypsies come, they will find you on the anvil with your eyes closed.* Alzada shook off the memory of the Lorca poem; it didn't end well for the sleeping boy.

'Come in, Inspector. Come in,' Dolores said to Estrático and Alzada, who had stayed at the door. She leaned out into the hallway as if she were worried someone had seen them.

'Good evening, Dolores,' Estrático kissed her on the cheek as he walked in, and promptly joined Mati on the edge of the couch, where they started going through a stack of glossy magazines.

'Thank you,' Alzada said when it was his turn to cross the threshold, using excessive ceremony to mask his discomfort.

So this is where the enemy sleeps . . . Dolores' living room was unlike anything he could have imagined. Then again, what exactly had he imagined? Something more romantic, for sure. This looked like the inside of a fridge: white, sleek, all design. Alzada could tell because every piece of furniture seemed uncomfortable. Except one in the corner, a lounge chair with an ottoman. On it, a book. Open Veins of Latin America. Alzada smiled.

'I don't bring them here, Inspector,' Dolores said, interrupting his train of thought.

'Excuse me?' Alzada answered absent-mindedly.

'You know what I mean, Inspector.'

'I didn't . . . I wasn't—' Alzada protested, embarrassed to have been caught.

'Of course you didn't, Inspector,' Dolores said amused. 'Does anyone want some red wine?'

Both Estrático and Mati nodded. Alzada shuffled by the entrance, hesitant about whether to sit. Before he could answer, Dolores disappeared into the kitchen. He decided to follow.

DOLORES WALKED PAST THE FRIDGE, sink, stove and microwave to reach the window. Every piece of equipment had been aligned against one of the walls of the small, immaculate space. *More an operating room than a kitchen.* She picked up a half-smoked cigarette from the edge of an ashtray and leaned on the windowsill.

Alzada approached. 'I didn't know you smoked,' he said. He tried to remember whether he'd ever seen her with a cigarette at the station. Among the countless hours she had spent in his vicinity over the years, no instance of her smoking came to mind.

'Oh, I don't,' la Dolores answered nonchalantly, two pillars of smoke coming out of her nostrils. 'I quit years ago.'

Alzada smiled.

'For me, it's always only this one, while I wait for my nails to dry,' she explained, waving her hands at him. Cobalt green.

Alzada reached for the pack. 'May I?'

Dolores nodded. 'And you?'

'I quit, too,' Alzada said once his cigarette was lit. 'You won't tell Paula, no?'

'I'm not *that* bad at my job, Inspector. Did the tip help?'

'I'm not bad at mine either,' Alzada said with a smile.

He was suddenly aware of how close they were standing to each other. Dolores must have sensed it too. She put her cigarette back down, and dexterously grabbed a bottle of red wine and four glasses.

'Besides. You've never introduced me,' she added without a hint of malice, and walked towards the door. 'Come join us when you're done, Inspector.'

OUTSIDE, THE NOISE HAD STARTED to fade. Alzada leaned out the window. On the street, a row of ambulances. *That's why she can afford rent in this neighborhood.* It had been at least a decade since Alzada had been in a hospital. The advantages of raising a boy whose whole idea of fun was a one-hour-drive to the Buenos Aires Zoo because 'the lemurs, tío, the lemurs', then a walk from exhibit to exhibit memorizing every little animal fact off the signs they encountered until they got to his favorites. Alzada knew the hospital visit had taken place around the time Sorolla had started with the questions.

JOAQUÍN HAD BEEN HELPING PAULA out with preparations for the asado. Cuts of meat lounged on every horizontal surface of their kitchen. The inspector peeled potatoes under the watchful eye of his wife, who was simultaneously chopping vegetables in julienne. Both were silent, both had a lot on their minds, both were thinking about what had happened the night before.

Sorolla had sat down for dinner next to Joaquín as Paula made the final touches to the gnocchi. 'Does the Full Stop Law mean the judiciary isn't going to prosecute the military anymore?'

Here we go. How did he know what it meant to 'prosecute' someone? *He's ten!* And 'the judiciary'? Gone were the days when Argentina's Supreme Court had sentenced no-longer-General Jorge Rafael Videla to life imprisonment for crimes against humanity.

Sorolla had laughed for days at the images of the señor con el bigotito. That's what he had decided to name him, 'the man with the little moustache'. Otherwise known as the most fearsome henchman of the dictatorship. For a very long time, they had been able to dodge their nephew's questions without major complications. 'We're going to have to talk about it eventually, you know?' Eventually had seemed very far in the future. First, he'd been young and susceptible to being easily distracted from the issue. Then, his attention span had increased, but evasive answers had still sufficed. Now nine or ten, Sorolla's doubts were slowly shaping up to be less haphazard, and he himself more persistent. Whenever he arrived at the kitchen table, his questions obviously rehearsed, Joaquín felt as if Sorolla thought he was on to something. And he was.

'Yes.' Paula had armed herself with patience. 'It's because they already put the bad guys in prison.'

'So, there's no more bad guys,' Sorolla had wanted to confirm. Joaquín had been hopeful at his nephew's comment: maybe it was about knowing he could sleep soundly.

'No, mijo.' Paula set the serving spoon into the bowl and sat down. 'Eat.'

Unconvinced, Sorolla had chewed on his first gnocchi, then asked: 'What about the ones who took mami and papi?'

Paula had looked at Joaquín in a panic. Joaquín had suggested they walk over to Chungo after dinner. Sorolla had eaten his whole bowl of pasta without further questions. *Ice cream is not always going to work.*

Now Joaquín's focus was split between finishing up the potatoes and finding a solid excuse to leave the kitchen. Their guests would arrive in an hour. It was perfectly possible for him not to get into an argument with Paula about how they had barely gotten away with it the night before.

'I've been thinking all morning,' Paula said. *Too late.* 'We need to present a common front, Joaquín.'

'We don't need to "present" anything, Paula. We *are* a common front,' he'd replied somewhat bitterly, hurt at the thought of being considered disloyal.

Alzada looked up at the kitchen clock. Fifty-five minutes. Fifty-five minutes to figure out how to explain to Sorolla the things even *they* found inexplicable. The Full Stop Law wasn't exactly quantum physics: it put an end to the prosecution of people involved in crimes against humanity during the last dictatorship. Their freshly democratic government had chosen to move on from their collective past in a revolutionary manner, the first people to try their own former heads of state. Argentinian courts, Argentinian judges, Argentinian laws. Only one hiccup: they had tried the junta leadership but spared its subordinates. As a gesture, to show that the country as a whole was committed to the idea of a clean slate. It meant that they were ready to begin restoring a long eroded social peace. It meant Vukić would never go on trial. It meant the Alzadas would never see justice done. All for the sake of a new Argentina. How does one explain the concept of a 'loose end' to a ten-year-old?

'You're taking half of the potato away with the skin,' Paula had said, the only thing still under her control. In that split second, she'd averted her eyes from her own knife. Forty-five minutes for the guests to arrive. Seven stitches on the left index finger of Mrs. Alzada.

'INSPECTOR?' ESTRÁTICO LEANED INTO THE kitchen. 'Cavallo has resigned.'

'Oh,' Alzada answered, distracted. If the Minister of Economy had faltered under the pressure, did that mean De la Rúa could eventually also hand in his resignation? It would certainly put them at the mercy of the incompetent amateur next in his line of succession. It would also mean they had won. We *have won*.

'Sir . . .' Estrático hesitated. 'It's quite late.'

'Yes.' Alzada took the last drag of his cigarette.

'Now that Sorolla is safe, I think we're going to leave.'

'Of course, of course,' Alzada said, crushing his cigarette next to Dolores' unfinished one. 'I understand.'

'Do you need anything else?'

'No, I'm fine. Thank you.' Alzada was still not completely present.

Estrático turned to leave.

A thought tugged at Alzada: 'Wait . . .'

'Yes, sir?' Estrático reappeared. *Always solicitous. Always pleasant.* When he retired, Estrático would do it better.

'Tell me in all honesty. Is the beard that bad?'

'Well, sir . . .' Estrático said, making his way to the door. 'Dolores is in the living room.'

'One more thing.' Alzada cleared his throat, finally collecting himself. 'I don't know how to thank you, Estrático. Por todo.'

'You're welcome, Inspector,' the deputy waved it off with a smile. 'Nothing a good night's sleep can't solve. I'll see you on Friday.'

'You're not working tomorrow?'

'No, sir. The new rotation.'

'That's a shame.'

Estrático was interested.

'All of this got me thinking… I want to pay a courtesy visit to a certain congressman…' Alzada hesitated. 'And I would need a partner for that…'

'I'll go with you.'

'You will?'

'I'm here, aren't I?'

Alzada nodded in acknowledgement. 'You take care, Orestes. Do you hear?'

Estrático gave half a smile. 'Yes, sir.'

ALZADA RETURNED TO THE LIVING room. On the couch, Sorolla as comfortable as if in his own bed; la Dolores reading on the ottoman. When she heard him come in, she lifted her eyes from her book.

'I have to finish this for class tomorrow—'

'I don't think you're going to have class tomorrow.'

Alzada realized that he hadn't found a moment to think about the consequences of what had happened today. *Am I going to walk into the station tomorrow as if nothing has happened?* What would his day even look like? He would probably come in late, watch a cleaning crew scrub the debris from the Molotov cocktail off the façade, have his cafecito, reopen the Echegaray case. *We can start from scratch.*

'You can stay as long as you want.' Dolores motioned to the one empty glass on the coffee table. 'Have some wine, Inspector.'

Alzada sat on the corner of the couch by Sorolla's feet. What a little pleasure, to watch the boy sleep. At least he had done *that* right.

He grabbed the bottle, refilled Dolores' glass and poured himself one. 'I didn't know you went to university,' he said, awkwardly pointing at the letters on her T-shirt.

'There's a lot of things you don't know about me, Inspector.'

'Yes.' He sipped on his wine.

Tomorrow— today is Thursday. In the afternoon, like every Thursday for the last twenty years, he would drive to the San Isidro cemetery to tell Jorge about his week. Maybe this time he would bring the boy along, and Paula.

Paula. Alzada pulled out his cell phone and dialed home. *How am I going to explain what happened to Sorolla? And that I'm in this woman's apartment?*

One ring. He doubted the call would wake her up, with them both gone.

Two rings. *Did she actually go to bed?*

Three rings. *Okay.* Even if she had been asleep, she would have gotten to the phone by now.

Four rings.

¿Paulita?

On the other end of the phone, a crisp '¿Dígame?'

ACKNOWLEDGMENTS

Infinite gratitude to the village it took to accompany and guide and nurture me through the making of my first novel:

The wonderful people at Pontas, and most especially María Cardona, for their enthusiasm, their tireless efforts, and for holding my hand throughout.

Federico, for his editorial wisdom, and for making me sweat: you saw the novel *Repentance* could be and were willing to walk there with me.

The team at W&N.

My readers, through all stages of it, at Columbia University and outside of it, and especially: Natasha Naayem, Satoshi, Kara, Javi, María Aguirre, and Amelia.

Ben Metcalf, for the Fanta, the laughs, and the perspicacity.

Clare, the best reader I ever met, for your insight with Alzada and your patience with me.

Karen, for making the vital introductions that set this all in motion.

Olga, for convincing me to send out the manuscript.

Everyone I ever bored talking about that book I was writing.

For very particular reasons and in no particular order: Basak, Chris Yeung, Vicky, Esther, tía Car, Satoshi, Ron Wong, Irina,

Natalia, Maricarmen, María Boada, Rosalie, Elena Pastor and María Fernanda Estrático.

Juan Andrés Requena, for introducing me to Antonio Machado and for telling seventeen-year-old Eloísa to work on her craft.

María, for reading the novel "in order" and for reminding me I have agency.

Nina, through all the time zones.

Tía Chipi, for the late night phone calls.

Miriam, for calling me hermana.

Pablo, for finding me on my first day of high school and for everything since.

Javi, por todo. For setting a beautiful example of how to be in the world, and, especially, for showing me what love can look like.

Tía Blanca, for teaching me the hard stuff.

Écol, whose tender courage is an inspiration, for holding space for me.

Mamá, for teaching me how to read.

ABOUT THE AUTHOR

Eloísa Díaz (1986) is a writer and lawyer from Madrid, Spain. She completed her MFA in Creative Writing from Columbia University in 2013. *Repentance* is her debut novel.